HOW DARK THE VOID

HOW DARK THE VOID

❖

JASON SALLEE

ISBN-13: 978-1-7353906-0-4 (*ebook*)
ISBN-13: 978-1-7353906-1-1 (*hardback*)
ISBN-13: 978-1-7353906-2-8 (*paperback*)

PROLOGUE

The Void. That is what we call her. She is cold and without emotion and does not care if you live or die.

She is the space between systems, without life and without a sun to warm her.

She is dangerous, but we accept the dangers in exchange for the freedom and independence she offers. The Void was free of Corporate involvement for the most part. But that was changing. We felt it closing in on us.

Twenty years had passed since the fall of the great experiment called the Galactic Federation. Some say we were better off under the GF, but it was all a dream, and dreams of galactic freedom and prosperity are *haachee*.

The one real thing is the Void. She is cold and cruel, but honest, and sometimes she dealt you a fair hand and sometimes not. We all knew the rules of the Void and that she held no promise for anything, but we were free.

At least, that is what we told ourselves.

ONE

N ATHARA STATION WAS my home. At first glance, it looked like any other asteroid drifting in the Void, but as you drew closer, large hangars dug into one side became visible. The hangars led to hallways carved deep inside the rock making a pathway to a small city of bars, cafés, stores, apartments, havens, and centers for almost every form of entertainment. The walls and ceilings were bare rock and the floor was white, textured brinite. Like other Stations in the Void, just about everything came from refurbished or repurposed material.

There were far nicer Stations in the Void, but Nathara was farther from Corporate territories than many of the other Stations. But most importantly, my closest friend, Challa, called Nathara home, and that was important to me. Home was too strong a word for him or for me; nothing was permanent in the Void, but it was good to have friends around and to have a base of operation, even if we all knew it was temporary.

Our real homes were our ships. The *Asron Sun* had been mine for over twenty years, which was not that long in the Void. There were ships still flying that were built fifty years before the Fall of the Galactic Federation. Mine had been updated, rebuilt and modified so much that it did not look much like the original, but the bones were the same. She was still the *Sun*. The modifications made her faster, stronger and better equipped to get me out of the *chee* when it came. She was not large, just a class two cargo vessel, but anything larger would make her less maneuverable and bring more attention than I wanted. Plus, a bigger ship required a crew and I liked to work alone.

I set the *Sun's* system to manual and angled her in toward Nathara's hangar doors and sent in the code.

A female voice came through, "Code confirmed. Stand by for bioscan."

Belith had a husky, melodic voice with just a trace of accent from one of the backwater planets in the Jikeara sector. She had guided me in hundreds of times, but the bioscan was new.

"Bioscan?"

"'Nother Station got hit."

A cold fist hit my stomach, but I still gave her *chee* for the scans. "I doubt a request for a bioscan would make a Corp fleet light out and leave the Station alone."

I palmed my bio scanner and then flipped on the vid system and stared into the screen, saying, "Captain Jlaeal of the Independent Trade Ship *Asron Sun*, requesting entrance into Nathara's delightful facilities."

"You *mata*," she said.

I smiled and gave her a wink. After they scanned the ship, the coordinates for my assigned docking bay and specific pad popped onto the screen. I shut the vid down and steered the ship toward the port entry.

The ride into the docking bay seemed long, as I worried over which Station was hit and which of my friends had bought it. News of Stations getting *chaffed* by Corporations used to be a rare occurrence, but it was happening more often.

I let the auto guidance take the *Sun* in, so I could take a look around and look for other changes and see whose ships were already docked. It was a medium-sized bay, but still enough room for more than a hundred ships the size of the *Sun*.

I smiled at the sight of Challa's ship. It was good to see he and his crew were still alive. I looked forward to spending some time with them.

The *Sun* guided itself over the rows of ships and into my

assigned pad. Once landed, I shut her down, stood up, stretched and strapped on my blasters. I had double holsters that hung down a little below the hips. We all had our different opinions of weapons but I preferred the simple use of hand-guns with one on each leg. I was not the quickest draw in the Void, but I could give a good account of myself. I was still alive and that said something.

I walked through the ship to the main hatch, released the seal and stepped out onto the dock. Some Stations required a meeting with a dock manager every time you landed, but since I was a permanent resident at Nathara, they did not require it of me. I closed the ship and programmed the dock's security protocols. Normally I would go straight to my apartment to clean up and stow my gear, but after hearing about the Station that got *chaffed* I needed a drink.

I marched through the dock past the rows of ships. Some of them looked familiar, but the bulk of them I had never seen before. I called Nathara home, but others in the Void lived as transients, traveling from Station to Station with no plans or direction other than profit.

I took a deep breath and took in the familiar smell. Every Station had its own smell, its unique mixture of metals and oils and electro burns. Nathara smelled like the rock it was carved out of, mixed with ionized atmosphere and synthmetals and various lubricants and gases. Stepping out of the *Sun* and into Nathara felt like stepping into the mouth of a giant creature and feeling its hot warm breath wash over you.

Stations are like living, breathing beings. Smoke and gas expel into the atmosphere like great breaths. People from across the galaxy rush through its hallways like blood pumping through veins. The command center acts as its brain, setting rules and commands for the entire Station and keeping things in order.

The heart of Nathara is the Cavern. The rest of the Station had textured brinite covering the floors, but when they built the Cavern, they ground down the asteroid rock and smoothed it over. It looked like it was worn down by millions of footsteps pressing down on it over millennia. The tables were carved out of the same rock and made to look like stalagmites growing out of the floor, with the tops polished down to a shine. The seats were made of the same material, but hovered over the ground, like small meteorites sculpted into chairs and placed in orbit around the tables.

The Cavern was busy when I got there, with all sections and races of the galaxy represented. It was always dark, but with just enough warm light to see what you were eating or drinking, but not enough to make you suffer if you had too much drink the night before. It smelled of sweat and food and krem and jak fumes. I scanned the crowd for familiar faces and spotted Aesal and Challa and his crew.

Challa spotted me and shouted out at me, "Jlaeal! My old friend! Join us!"

Challa was an oddity in the galaxy — half Drakkaran and half human. Most Drakkarans thought humans were too tall and found their lack of hair repulsive, while humans found Drakkarans equally unattractive with their short stocky build and hair from head to toe.

Challa had the full beard of a Drakkaran and hair exploding from every other surface of his body. He was tall for a Drakkaran, with the top of his head almost reaching my chin. He had the dense body of a Drakkaran, as if he was formed out of stone. Another oddity was his thick black hair, a rarity for a Drakkaran, and sparkling dark-blue eyes that seemed to pierce through into your soul and see all your hidden things.

"Slide over," Challa commanded his crew. "Make way."

The crew slid over and opened a space for me next to Aesal, across from Challa.

"Vhell!" Challa yelled at the server, waving her over.

The Cavern was an old-fashioned type of joint, with no auto servers or food dispensers. Male and female servers, wearing very little clothing, took orders from the tables and walked them over to an actual bartender, who put in their food orders and made the drinks by hand. Other bars on Nathara were modern and automated, but after weeks of dealing with nothing but the ship's systems, we liked the personal interaction, especially if they were attractive and scantily dressed.

Vhell was stunning, even for a Diviian. I had a thing for Diviians and Challa knew it. He gave me a knowing smile as she approached. She was just a touch taller than I was. I was tall for a human, but Diviians were usually several daparlons taller than we were. Vhell had firm alabaster legs that climbed forever, and emerald-green eyes that drew you in and made you forget who and where you were. Her hair was white, almost clear and cut short to her pointed ears. She wore a very short green skirt that complemented her eyes, with matching oversize suspenders that covered only a thin line of flesh.

She approached the table with the grace and fluidic motions of a dancer.

"Jlaeal." Her voice had an echo of two separate voices blending to a sound like a running brook. She gave me her smile, the one that always melted me down to my basic elements.

"Vhell. You look radiant."

Her smile broadened and she gave me a wink that said she knew.

"Gru, my love," Challa said. "Two rounds for the entire table and another round of krem."

"That all?" she asked with a smile.

"Just make sure we do not run out."

"Of course," she said and threw one last smile my way before sauntering over to the bar.

When I turned from watching her, I saw that the rest of the table was watching her as well. Except for Aesal, who had his eyes on the male server.

"One can see why it is argued that Diviians are the most beautiful creatures in the galaxy," Challa said. He leaned into me like a conspirator. "You do not plan on doing something foolish, do you?"

"Me?" I flashed him a grin as he frowned at me. "We both

know how that would end. I like it here at Nathara and I like this place and I like being with my good friends. I like it too much to make *chaff* of things for a *gaihini*."

Challa let out one of his great big laughs and Aesal gave a laughing snort. Vhell was very beautiful, but I was here far too often for it to end any way but bad. Pleasure in the Void was a beautiful thing when enjoyed with a real woman who was looking for the same thing you were, but if you were not sure of her intentions, things could go bad.

If she and I enjoyed each other and it turned out she wanted more than just pleasure, it would sour things and end our enjoyment of the Cavern. If she did not work there, I would have taken the risk, but I did not think it was worth it, despite her great beauty.

Vhell returned with the drinks. Gru is one of the best drinks in the Void. After every swallow, your eyes and all other senses shut down and you go into a momentary euphoria, forgetting all your problems for a delightful moment.

It was not found anywhere but in the Void, and some parts of GalactiCorp territory. The other Corporations, TriKarre Industries and Nallimar Inc., outlawed the drink because its temporary side effects made it too easy for people to get robbed or killed. People were robbed and killed in the Void while under as well, but not in the safer Stations. Very few people in the Void tried to rob or kill someone under the influence of gru, knowing that others in the bar would not allow it. There were codes for living in the Void. Some of them were just tradition, but others carried penalty, to be meted out by other travelers.

I once saw a pirate try to take out a competitor while he was under the influence of gru and the pirate's own men took him down. Of course, there were less civilized Stations, and you had to know not to risk gru on those places, but Nathara was one of the safer ones.

We all saluted one another with the gru and shot them down and everything faded to black. I forgot about the *chaffed* Station and forgot about the Corporations and forgot about everything. For a short time, it all disappeared and my mind was dark and peaceful.

TWO

MY VISION EASED from black to dark gray and then all the way back in, along with all the stressful thoughts I had before taking the shot. But the stress was muted and did not bother me as much as it had before. The others were already several shots in and it took longer for them to come out of it.

I took a sip of krem and waited. It was a solid brew, dark amber and real Drakkaran, where krem originated and was always the best. In fact, some krem was called krem, but wasn't true krem. It was not real krem unless it was made on Drakkara.

Challa came out of it first. I waited for him to take a sip of krem before speaking.

"I heard another Station got hit," I said to Challa.

He nodded. "Pintoc."

"*Benetchos*. Filthy lizar' *benetchos*," Bentook said.

Bentook had a cute face, with light-blue skin and short, dark-blue hair. She was full of passion and anger and was often the first in a fight or argument. Bentook was from a small planet called Otcha on the edge of GalactiCorp space where all humans ranged from light blue to dark blue.

There were many types of humans in the galaxy, with dozens of variations depending on their planet of origin, or their ancestors' planet of origin. The spectrum ranged from almost translucent white skin to stark black skin, blue skin, red skin, green skin or even bright orange. There were more skin colors and tones than there were planets from which humans originated. These humans originated from multiple planets in nearly a dozen different systems, which doesn't make sense in terms of science or biology. It was argued for centuries that humans from each planet were a different species altogether, but after countless studies and research it was firmly proved that they were all different races, but of the same species.

I have never understood the science behind it or how it was possible that different humans so similar could come from different planets, but they did. There are thousands of people throughout the galaxy whose sole job was to argue and research the issue and they could never agree on it either. Most of the rest of us think that humans must have had the ability to travel between planets long before our current period and something happened to throw them all back to the dark ages.

Challa grabbed Bentook's arm and looked at the corner where several Fillonians were drinking their krem. One of them was glaring at her. "Bentook," Challa said. "I agree with your sentiments, but I would rather not get into a fight in the Cavern and risk banishment."

Bentook took another swallow of krem and glared back at the Fillonians, daring them to make a move.

Aesal said, "Yes. It was Nallimar."

Nallimar was the worst of the Corporations. Run by Fillonians, who were without argument the cruelest of the peoples in the galaxy. They stripped everything from a Station when they attacked it, "confiscating" all ships and goods. The lucky ones on board were killed. The rest were made into slaves.

"Anyone we know on board?" I asked.

Aesal looked at Challa with a grim face. Aesal was a smuggler like me, but he was more of a romantic. He was often sucked into deals where he did not make much profit, but the deal helped certain groups with philosophies he supported. He wore his blonde hair long and tied it to the side. He also had a beard, trimmed close. He was always clean and well dressed, like he was not just a smuggler, but a gentleman smuggler. I gave him *chee* for it all the time.

"Rich got it," Challa said.

"Rich Lalla?"

Challa nodded.

"Fuck," I said and stared down into my krem.

Rich was an old-time smuggler, who had shipped contraband throughout the GF long before the Fall. He was good, professional, and honest and was the first to jump into a fight to protect a friend.

Challa raised a fresh shot of gru. "To Rich."

"To Rich," I said with the rest of the table. We downed our shots and disappeared into the darkness, forgetting about Pintoc and Rich and everyone else we knew who died because of fucking Nallimar and the other fucking Corporations. I slipped out of the darkness first and took a long draught of the krem. Fucking Nallimar. They would not be satisfied until all of us were dead or slaves.

The rest of the table came out of it at different times and each took a sip of krem. Aesal was the first to speak.

"We need the Federation back," he said.

We all groaned or glared at him for bringing it up. Leave it to Aesal to take a good moment and turn it into foul talk of the GF. He was a die-hard defender of the Galactic Federation and never passed up the chance to convert someone to his cause. He was one of the smaller humans at the table, but he was tough and fearless and could handle himself in a fight. He was too serious though, and had dedicated his life to the GF, in spite of the fact that it had dissolved over two decades ago.

Challa let out a chuckle and I knew he would save the night. One of Challa's great joys was to badger Aesal on his political views. Most would learn their lesson and not bring politics up around him, but Aesal could not help himself.

"And just how would the situation be different if the glorious GF were here to help us, Aesal?" Challa asked.

"We would not be slaves for one thing."

"No? Well, that is nice," Challa said.

Aesal nodded, but looked at Challa with suspicion. He was

very passionate about the GF, which made him an easy target, and based on previous experience, he knew more was coming.

"Would I pay taxes?" Challa asked him.

Aesal hesitated. "Of course."

"Yes, of course. It stands to reason. And would I have a say in how much and when I pay these taxes?"

"You would have a representative in the Senate who would have a vote to determine your taxes."

"And if I do not like when the fat-assed *haachee* senator decides to make me pay half of everything I earn to pay for his big fancy ship and big fancy house on two planets, can I refuse to pay?"

"Wait," Aesal said. "It will n—"

"So then, fifty percent of the time I work for the GF, giving all of my money to the glorious fat-assed senator, and the glorious, fat-assed GF."

Aesal was turning red, trying to keep his calm. "It is n—"

Challa interrupted, "So what you are saying, is that I am a slave to the GF for merely half of the time and all the rest of the time I am free?"

"That is not—" Aesal stopped himself, realizing there was no point. We were laughing too hard to hear anything he said. None of us cared for the GF or wanted any part of it and he knew it. His emotions got the better of him, but he was smart enough to know when his talk of the GF was falling on deaf ears.

There was always risk of death or capture in the Void, but we paid no taxes, we followed no laws, other than the unspoken rules between travelers and the rules set on a Station. And we could go wherever we pleased, whenever we wanted.

"I think Aesal was a politician before the Fall, no?" Challa said.

We all laughed harder as Aesal yelled out, "Fuck you, Challa. *Benetcho* pirate."

This made us laugh harder.

I slowed my laughter enough to take another sip of krem and

noticed a beautiful dark-skinned human enter the Cavern. She wore skintight pants and a matching shirt made of Meek, a flexible material designed to withstand the bulk of what you would encounter in the Void. She had the look of a smuggler or pirate. She had long dark hair flowing down her back and the most beautiful face I had seen on a human in a very long time. It had a chiseled hardness to it, showing her to be both fit and hard.

She strode to the bar with the cool confidence of someone who had spent time in the Void and knew how to handle herself. She spoke to the bartender and he slid over a shot of gru and a glass of krem.

"You sniff out trouble like a craundack sniffs out prey."

I did not even look back at Challa as I said, "If she is trouble, I want to swim in it."

Challa chuckled. The rest of the table had split off into their own conversations.

"Why not go to the Havens," Challa asked. I looked at him and shrugged in slight distaste. "You get the same results, but without the *haachee*."

"We have been over this," I said. "I like real women."

"Haven women are as real as any other. They are as real as her," he said as he nodded at the woman.

"I mean real women. Someone who does not live their life waiting for a man to pay them for pleasure. I want the challenge of a real woman and I want her to want me just as I want her."

Challa always took this too serious; always afraid for me going after real women. He put his hand on my shoulder. I glanced back and could see the seriousness on his face as he leaned into me.

"Jlaeal, listen. I know we have fun and jest, but listen to your old friend. The Void is no place for love. It leads to pain and heartache and disappointment."

I chuckled, "Who said anything about love?"

Aesal laughed with me, but Challa stayed serious.

"You listen to me," he said. "Pleasure with real women with

real hearts leads to love and it will break you. Leave the real women. Let us go to a haven."

I could not help but laugh. Poor Challa. He preached the havens like Aesal preached the GF — both true devotees. Travel to the farthest corner of the galaxy and Challa could recommend the best haven and tell you which girl to ask for. I did not fault him for pushing them though. He was a good man who cared for his friends and wanted what was best for them.

I patted his knee and looked him in the eyes. "I do not want a haven girl. I want her."

I looked back over to the woman at the bar. The gru was gone and she had already come out of the darkness. She was leaning against the bar sipping her krem and assessing the crowd. Challa was not wrong about love in the Void. But I was not looking for love. I was looking for pleasure. And with luck, this woman was looking for the same thing.

"Want to meet her?" Aesal asked.

I did not agree with Aesal on his politics, but he was a good man and looked out after his friends when he could. Loyalty was very important in the Void, and these friends at the table had proven themselves to be loyal and good friends.

"You know her?" I asked.

"Do not encourage him, Aesal," Challa said. "Go find a GF conspirator somewhere and pleasure yourselves in the ass."

Bentook overheard the jibe and laughed. I could not help laughing myself. Even Aesal smirked, but he was not dissuaded.

"Fuck you, Challa," he shot back. "You want to meet her?" he asked me.

"Of course."

"Djana!" Aesal called out to her and waved her over. She did not seem thrilled by the idea, having seen us staring, but in spite of this, she picked up her krem and a fresh gru and strolled over to the table.

"Djana," he said as she approached the table.

"Aesal. How is business?" she asked while scanning over the rest of us.

"Profitable. And you?"

"Business is fine."

Aesal moved to the next seat over, leaving an empty seat between us. "Join us."

She sat down with cool fluid movements that showed confidence and a preparedness for any difficulty.

"This is Djana," Aesal said to the table. "Djana, these are unscrupulous, devious *benetcho* pirates," indicating Challa and his crew.

"Do not forget conniving and opportunistic," smiled Challa.

His crew gave a chuckle.

"My kind of people." Djana smiled.

"And this *mata* is Jlaeal. He is a smuggler."

"I prefer *mata* trader," I said with a smile.

She returned the smile and raised a fresh glass of gru to all of us.

"To Pintoc."

We raised our grus to her and said, "To Pintoc."

She was also a smuggler. We spent the next couple of rotations drinking gru and krem, comparing stories and strategies and various deviancies.

Much later, Aesal stood up and almost fell to the floor as he stepped back from the table.

"Enjoy th'res' of th'night," he said with a slur. "I've a me'ing in the morning. Alrea'y too much gru."

"There a gathering of GF enthusiasts tomorrow?" Challa asked. Aesal sent him a rude gesture.

"Rest well, Aesal," I said.

"Res' well. And the res' of you, in spite of your jokes, you're all my frien's."

"But'chou—" Bentook began to say, and started to rise from the table, but then collapsed.

Challa laughed the loudest of the group with his great booming laugh and then stumbled from his seat.

"Come, Aesal," Challa said. "Help me get her to the ship."

They held Bentook between them as they swayed back and forth, somehow staying upright as they stumbled out of the bar. The three almost toppled near the entrance and the rest of the crew stumbled over to help. As I watched them go, I took it as a good sign that Djana had not left.

"When do you ship out?" I asked her.

She looked me in the eyes and smiled with meaning. "Tomorrow." She grabbed me by the back of the head and kissed me long and hard. She broke off and said, "Late."

She stood up, took my hand, pulled me out of the Cavern and led me down the hallways to the dock and then onto her ship. As with most nights in the Void, we knew we might never see each other again, so we made the most of it. For that night, each of us was everything for each other, and nothing. It was a beautiful night of passion and we would never see each other again.

THREE

DRAKKARA WAS A close call. I never had any real issues there before, but TriKarre was cracking down on the krem distilleries and forcing them to increase security. Although the krem distilleries had different names, they all fell under the TriKarre umbrella. It was just a trick of marketing.

I had a good relationship with Menmassa Brewery. In fact, I considered the owner a good friend and often stayed overnight just to have dinner with him. I could tell he felt bad pushing the rings into me, but I knew had no choice. They were requiring additional authentication of my distribution license and the transport license for *The Sun*. They all cleared the test, but just barely. As close as I was with Jakorra, I knew he would turn me in without any guilt if I did not pass the test. Given the option of losing his business or turning me in, there was no choice.

I was relieved to get off the planet safely, but knew I would have to update the licenses to match the new restrictions. That would cost creds in bribes and smuggling fees I did not want to spend, but it was the cost of doing business in Corporate territories.

During the trip from Drakkara to Dellinar I reviewed my GalactiCorp ID and trading licenses. Although, you never really knew if your licenses were updated until you were in system and being checked through their security.

I lit into the Dellinar system and set standard approach speed toward planet Dellinar and the com system lit up.

"*Asron Sun*, this is GalactiCorp DSC Command. Please proceed to the in-system coordinates sent to your navigation. Prepare for boarding by system security."

Chee. It had been a long time since I was boarded in the Dellinar system. I paid good creds to several people to make sure it never happened. I contemplated making a run for it, but then I would be *chaf* in all GalactiCorp systems, unless I completely overhauled the ship and my licenses and that took more creds than I had to spend.

"Copy command. Locking in coordinates."

I locked in the coords they sent and set the ship to auto. I thought about my options, but none of them were good. Run for it and spend most of my creds on a new ID for me and my ship, or risk being boarded. I was fully licensed, but the licenses were not authentic and based on the Drakkara experience, I was nervous about them passing.

It was a risk to stay for the boarding, but for some reason my gut told me to ride it out. I learned to trust my gut and do what it told me. The times I ignored it rarely ended well.

The nav system was taking me to a station at a moon circling the fourth planet. It was a small station, but a full cruiser fleet was stationed there, plenty of firepower to take me out. I took a deep breath and hoped that my gut was right.

As I approached the station, the same voice came over the com.

"*Asron Sun,* just anchor where you are, shut down your engines, shields and weapons systems. The boarding team is en route."

"Copy Command."

My gut was having second thoughts, but it was too late. I locked the *Sun* into place, shut everything down and waited. It did not take long before the scanners showed a frigate and two small patrols approaching. I was tempted to pull out my guns, but I knew better. At this point, that would lose any chance of making a deal with whoever came on board.

Whether in the Void, or in civilized systems, guns were always a last resort. I was *pada* good with a gun, but there was always a long line of consequences if they were used. Guns were strictly outlawed in all corporate systems. Owning one guaranteed prison time or worse. Using one could save your *mata*, but at the risk of prison time, or losing the ability to trade in that corporation's market.

The frigate approached and the com lit up again.

"*Asron Sun*, prepare for docking procedures."

"Docking hatch ready."

I watched as the frigate slid alongside the *Sun*. As our docking hatches locked onto each other, I left the cockpit and made my way to the hatch. The system showed the hatch was sealed, so I took a deep breath and opened my own hatch doors, prepared for the worst on the other end. The doors opened, revealing the short hatch tube coming from the other ship.

The hatch doors on the other ship slid open and a short human with a *facha* grin on his face walked down the tube. He didn't hold a gun, but the two drones hovering over his head had plenty of firepower. He approached my hatch doors and stepped aboard without asking permission.

"Jlaeal?" he asked as the two drones flew into the ship.

"Yes," I said and reached out my left hand palm out in greeting. He looked down at it, smirked and placed his right palm down onto it.

"Jlaeal, I'm glad we finally meet."

This caught me off guard. It was not the type of greeting you get from a sec officer. In fact, there should have been more soldiers with him. It was all unusual and put me on edge.

"Do I know you?" I asked.

He laughed.

"You will."

He was an arrogant *mata* and it took a great effort not to punch him right in his teeth.

"I hope it turns out to be a good relationship then," I said.

"Oh, I'm sure it will be," he said, that smile still on his face. The two drones came back and hovered over his shoulder.

"Command Chi-Alpha," he said. The drones remained in place without any sign of doing anything.

"What is Chi-Alpha?" I asked, trying to stay friendly.

"Chi-Alpha is a command I created that stops them from recording or broadcasting our conversation, and also prevents any other ship in system from recording us. We're completely alone here."

The hair on my neck stood up, thinking of what that could mean. It was either a good sign that he was prepared to deal, or it was a sign that he was going to have fun with me and did not want proof of the damage he planned to create.

"You wanted to speak alone?" I asked.

"Yes," he said. "We have a mutual friend. I was told it would work out to my benefit if we were to meet."

"Who is this friend?"

"Naden. Naden Helahi, in Port security."

I tried to keep my Setrak face on, as I had just entered a field of *Conjas*. I had dealt with Naden for years and considered her a friend. An expensive friend, but still a friend. I had paid her a personal fee every time I docked on Dellinar, in exchange for a relaxation of security toward the *Sun*. She had found out who and what I was through someone I traded with and I had convinced her to take a steady flow of creds instead of a one-time reward from GC. But I had to be cautious. I knew it could be a trap. He could have found out about the arrangement and was looking for evidence against me.

"Yes, I have known Naden for years. She is a good friend, but can be harsh on protocol."

He laughed again. He had such a snide laugh. I almost hoped he was GC security so I would have an excuse to lay into him.

"She is as harsh on protocol as you are a licensed krem dealer."

"You are welcome to check my licenses."

He smiled. "I'm sure they'd all pass the test."

"They are legal."

"Tell you what. Why don't I call the drones back in, call in the guards and confiscate the ship. We can sift through the paperwork and once my boss and her boss and her boss's boss all go through the paperwork and we're all satisfied that things are in order, we'll let you continue on your way. Shouldn't take long. Maybe six galactic months?"

I did not respond right away. He gave me that arrogant smile and waited. The next words I spoke could have sent me to a prison ship. I felt a trickle of sweat roll down the spine of my back.

"I would rather we were friends," I said. "That does not sound like friend behavior."

"No. No. You are right. I would rather be friends too."

"Like Naden?"

He nodded. He wanted a bribe. Or, at least, he was playing as if he did. Did he really want a cut? Or was he security?"

"Well, friend. First of all, as a friend, I would ask you to remove the drones from the ship and then I would ask you in for a glass of krem to discuss the new friendship."

He smiled. Somehow the smile was even worse than before, full of condescension and greed.

"I enjoy a good krem, even the stuff you drink out in the uncivilized parts of the galaxy." He turned and said to the drones, "Chi-Alpha Two. Exit ship. Wait on the *Selandra*."

He turned back to me with a smile as the drones flew off. I took him deeper into the ship to the small lounge area. It was small for a ship the size of the *Sun*, but I preferred to use as much space as possible for cargo. I poured two krems from my personal stash and handed him one.

He took a long sip of it.

"Not bad. I prefer something tasty from GalactiCorp space, but this will do."

I ignored the jibe at the krem. Most GC residents had no taste in krem and I did not take it personally.

"How do you know Naden?"

He took another sip of the krem and considered, looked at me with a smile.

"She is my sister by marriage."

I kept my Setrak face on, but felt better about the situation. Although I did pay Naden, we were very friendly and talked enough that she told me about her brother-in-law. She had little to say about him that was good. She did say he was part of the Dellinar security force and warned me about crossing him if he ever stopped me. She always swore to keep our arrangement secret, but he must have got to her somehow.

"You are Kranten then?"

His smile faded for an instant, but then he forced it back on. It was less arrogant though, as if he lost a chink in his armor.

"She spoke of me?"

"She mentioned you."

"I hope she was not disparaging."

"On the contrary," I lied. "She said you were very smart, but that you were serious and meant business."

The *facha* smile returned to his face and he took another drink. I did not show the smile I was feeling. I had lied to him. She did not like him at all, and said he was dangerous.

"What did she tell you of our friendship?"

He paused. "She told me enough. Told me she gets paid for your friendship. I like that kind of friendship."

"She did? I have lent her money from time to time, but I do not pay for her friendship. She is a good friend and I like to help out friends when they need help."

"Is that so?"

I nodded and took a sip of my own krem. It was real krem and had the right buttery taste, but it did little to wash the sour taste he brought to my mouth. Kranten looked at me, considering. I was not sure that he had ever done this before, which made him more dangerous.

"Perhaps you could loan me money from time to time," he said.

It was my turn to smile. I had him now. If he turned me in, I would help them find the vid files the lounge system was logging. I was sure the drones had scanned for that type of equipment, but I knew they did not find anything. They were too well hidden. He still had me by the *cojos* but now I had his in my hand as well.

"I am always happy to help a friend," I said. "Especially when they help with my struggling business. Times are hard lately, no?"

"Yes, times are always hard." He thought a moment, looking down into his krem. He was new and it showed. Sweat was forming on his brow. "My boy - he's had medical problems. Galacti-Corp has so many expenses with defending her territories that our pay can't be increased. You see?"

I nodded, wondering how much the expense would cost me, or if he even had a son. I did not remember Naden mentioning a nephew, but none of that mattered.

"Maybe I could help," I said.

"I was hoping you would," he said with a smile.

"How much do these medical issues cost?"

He gave me a number and I nearly choked on my krem. It was more than the value of my entire cargo and I told him so.

"Well, perhaps you could help a little then," he said.

"Did Naden tell you what I loan her?" I asked.

"Yes," he said, although I could tell he was lying.

"Perhaps I could match it," I said. His eyes lit up. "As I said, times are tough and additional expenses pop in all the time. But I may be able to loan you what I have loaned her and still have enough left for a krem from time to time."

He nodded. "That would be appreciated, friend." He smiled.

The rest of the "friendship" we worked out over another krem. It was all distasteful, but part of the job. It could have gone badly, but once I figured out what he was about, it was an easy deal to close. I paid Naden five hundred creds per trip, which was too high, but she really was a friend and other benefits came with that relationship. I convinced Kranten that I only loaned her two hundred fifty creds. I planned on visiting Naden when I returned to tell her of the arrangement and warn her about telling him what I really paid her. If he found out, he might throw us both in prison for the insult and then she would get nothing.

After giving him his payoff, I walked him back to the hatchway. Before he went back aboard his ship I made a point of showing him the vid I had of the transaction. It terrified him, as I had hoped, but I reassured him, "This is just insurance. I do not know you yet. I am a man of my word. I will loan you money when I can, when I am in system, but this assures me you that you do not turn me in for a larger reward and that you do not ask for a larger loan. Do we understand each other?"

"Yes, I understand."

"Good. I am glad to know you."

He still tried to hold onto his smile, but it was weak and forced. I opened my hatch doors and he stepped out into the docking tube.

"Oh, and Kranten."

He stopped and turned.

"There is probably no need to remind you, but if I get boarded, or the ship gets confiscated – well, I always try to fry the system files, but you know how quickly security retrieves them."

I said this with a genuine smile as his evaporated. He walked through the tube to his own hatch and disappeared. He had made a windfall for himself, but at a cost. Now I had the upper hand. It was still a mutual relationship, but I would call the shots. He could threaten to turn me in, but I knew it was an empty threat. He had too much to lose. I would get into the system without problems and would ask him for information from time to time. I would have to thank Naden when I saw her.

FOUR

I DELIVERED THE krem to Dellinar, making a point of having a meeting with Naden. She was surprised about Kranten and swore she never told him, but it was a good warning for her to be more cautious. I convinced her to keep an eye on him and even offered her an additional one hundred per trip for the trouble. Afterwards I took her to dinner and drinks and then we spent the night in a room I rented in the city. She was beautiful and fun and made the trip worth the trouble, almost as much as the profit from the krem.

I made the trip to Drakkara and back to Dellinar a couple of times before going back to Nathara. More cautious traders avoided smuggling into corporate home planets, but it was not a problem if you knew what you were doing. Core planets had more security, but those running the security were more relaxed, thinking that no one was crazy enough to smuggle into a Corporate home planet. And I found it easier to bribe people on home planets and make long-term friends, especially in the GalactiCorp territory, where people loved money and things more than anything else.

I landed the *Sun* in Nathara's docking bay, took her through the shutdown sequence, then strapped on my weapons. I pulled each gun out and did a quick check to make sure it was loaded and charged. I tried to keep to the more civilized Stations, but it was still the Void and they were filled with pirates and smugglers and thieves. Like everything else in the galaxy, there were good smugglers and bad ones, good pirates and bad. Some of them were unstable or just enjoyed violence. There was always the chance that those types could move against you, regardless of backlash from travelers or Station authorities. A good traveler was always prepared for the worst.

Having checked both weapons, I grabbed my pack, locked the ship down, and walked toward the exit.

"Jlaeal!"

I looked to my left and saw Challa waving me over from the front of his main ship *Sh'kurah Nuilla*. He wiped his hands with a towel as I walked over to him.

Nuilla was a modified 2B frigate, designed for battle and troop transport by the GF, but converted by Challa years ago for his specialized line of work. He'd updated the weaponry and shielding, then removed the troop bays to make more room for cargo. The armor, shielding and weaponry were all modernized two years ago, meaning it was solid and did the job, but it was not top of the line. As with other pirate vessels, she was black with white flecks that adjusted to its background while in flight. She was covered in scorching and dents, but she was a good ship and had kept his crew alive through years of battles.

Challa wore a big smile as he grabbed my shoulders in greeting. I returned the gesture.

"Good to see you alive," he said and gave me a final pat on the shoulder.

"You as well, Challa. Heading out or coming in?"

"Out. As soon as we finish the inspection. Come. Talk while I work."

I followed him around the ship as he looked at the under carriage, inspecting every crevice. Challa was very thorough and never flew a mission without giving his ship a full inspection.

"I got a lead on an unsecured cruise ship. Easy pickings."

"Tip is solid?"

"Yes. Very."

"Any other news?" I asked. Challa always seemed to be one

step ahead of me on any important information. I had a decent network going, but his was very good and very reliable.

"More Stations have been hit. I am sure you heard."

"I heard of Sintin and Bento."

Challa nodded. "And Chim."

"Chim? *Pudak*." Chim was deep inside the Void, far away from the Corporate borders. It was surprising to hear of an attack that far in.

"We are making changes. We are always on standby. No more overnights off ship. We will be prepared to leave fast and hard from now on."

I nodded. I did not like to argue with Challa about security measures, but I did not think his precautions would matter that much. If a Corporate fleet lit in, there was little chance of getting out alive.

"Enough of that," he said. "Tell me of your trip."

"I did very well."

"I was not speaking of business."

"Neither was I."

Challa laughed. He had a big thunderous laugh that made you feel as if nothing was wrong in the galaxy.

"I want to hear everything," he said. "Where? Drakkara? Dellinar?"

"Yes."

Challa let out more thunderous laughter. As much as he preached the havens, he delighted in my stories of women.

"What of Drakkara?"

He was looking over the engines as I went into detail about my trips and the pleasures I had planetside. Challa never went planetside and always had questions about my trips there. I did not discuss the close call I had on Dellinar or the incident off Drakkara. I know those were not the stories he wanted to hear.

When I finished, he pulled me aside, looked around to see where his crew was and said, "I have a new crew member." He had a mischievous grin on his face, the one he reserved for his more outrageous stories. "I think you will appreciate her."

"Her?"

"Jlaeal, my friend, it will be very difficult for me to obey my own rules of keeping pleasure in the havens and not having relations with members of my crew."

"She must be something."

"She is beyond imagining. Your type — tall, beautiful, Divian. And very tough. She walks and talks with complete confidence of herself and her surroundings. I doubt there is a gun she could not shoot or a ship she could not fly."

"Former Companion?"

"I believe so, but she has said nothing. You know how they are."

"True."

I slapped his shoulder with a smirk. "Well, I am glad I do not share your views on free women, Challa."

"Well, in spite of her great beauty, you will stay away from her if you are smart. I have told you this to prepare you, but this one will bring you nothing but pain. Trust me."

"You always say that, but I always have the opposite experience," I said.

Challa barked out a sharp laugh. "Good advice is wasted on you. At least promise me, whatever you do, you will not cause her to leave my crew. I would hate to lose her."

"When have I ever chased a woman away?"

Challa gave me a dirty look, then shook his head and chuckled. "I do not know why I bother saying anything."

Bentook walked over, wiping her hands on a towel. "Jlaeal. Gla' to see you alive."

"Bentook, I am glad to see you alive," I said as we grabbed each other's shoulders.

She turned to Challa. "Ship clear. All ready."

"Good. Round up the crew. We launch as soon as they arrive."

As Bentook walked off Challa grabbed my shoulders again. "Until next time."

"Fly safe, Challa."

He climbed the steps to his hatch and I turned and walked away. This was always the way of the Void. Friends come and go, with little time to talk or catch up or spend any amount of time together, other than the occasional night of drinking.

I could base my operations out of any Station in the Void and have similar results, maybe better, but I operated out of Nathara because Challa was there and he was my closest friend. If either of us worked out of another Station, we might never see each other again, and if we did, it could be years or even decades.

I decided I would stay away from his new crew member, if nothing else to keep from losing a friend. But also, if she was a Companion, they were trouble. Companions were raised from birth to serve the Diviian home planet, regardless of cost to themselves. They were trained in the art of love, fighting, flying and weaponry. Some of the most famous Diviian wives of famous leaders turned out to be Companions, although it was never admitted to. A Companion never admitted to what they were and never admitted to any of their training. Their secret went with them to the grave. This also meant their loyalty was always to Diviia first. I was surprised Challa had brought her onto the team.

I walked to my apartment, stowed my gear, cleaned up and headed to the Cavern. Walking the cave-like hallways of the Station, I noticed subtle differences from the last time I was there. The hallways and empty spaces of the Station were filled with more refugees, traders, transport pilots and pirates. They had a more harried look, like they were one trip away from meeting a corporate fleet.

When I arrived at the Cavern I scanned the room for someone I knew and spotted Aesal. He was sitting alone at a table off to the side, drinking krem and reading his com. He spotted me, smiled and shut off the com.

"When did you get back?" he asked.

"Just did," I said and sat down across from him.

I locked eyes with Vhell as she approached the table. She looked stunning, wearing a tiny blue sundress so short that it covered just the top half of her ass, and cut so low in the front you could see most of her tight belly. She walked with a confident swing to the hips and the strut of a woman who knew the power she had over a man and what she could do to build him up or destroy him. She wore a big smile with sparkling eyes I could not look away from.

"Jlaeal. I am happy to see you alive."

"Vhell," I said, returning her smile, "Somehow, you look better every time I see you."

"Is that your best line?"

I laughed. "A large part of my brain shuts down whenever you approach. I am proud I can speak at all."

"One day, you will catch me when I have had as much gru as you and these lines will work," she said with a wink.

"Maybe I should work on some better lines."

"Maybe," she said with a smile. "Are you eating today, or just drinks?"

"Eating. What should I have? Anything fresh?"

"Grilled picti bird. Just came in."

"Sold. With ochols and greens."

"Gru and krem?"

"Always."

"Another krem, Aesal?" she asked.

"Yes. And a gru."

I enjoyed the show she put on as she walked away from the table. She knew all the buttons to push on me, and pushed them hard, in a way that held little mystery.

"How was Dellinar?" Aesal asked.

"Successful," I said.

"Did you meet up with my friends?"

"No. I got distracted." I gave him a smirk and he understood.

"I see. I wish you would meet with them."

"Listen, I have no interest in getting involved."

"But they need help."

"I am not a charity."

"They can pay."

"Not enough."

"You already take risks bringing contro into the heart of GalactiCorp. What difference would it make?"

"The difference is that I bring non-lethal items like krem or jak or exotic goods from Drakkara, not weapons for a revolution. For what I smuggle in, they would send me to a work camp and confiscate my ship. They do not waste work camp space on weapons smugglers."

Vhell arrived just in time with the drinks. When Aesal got started on GF *haachee* I got a strong urge to drink or leave.

"You have saved me, Vhell. Things were getting political." I smiled at her and winked at Aesal. I gave Aesal a hard time, but I was much nicer about it than Challa or his crew. Aesal was a good man, he just had odd political leanings for someone who lived in the Void.

"Always happy to come to your rescue, Jlaeal," she said.

"Good to know. I might need further rescuing later."

"I will keep my eyes on you then."

"That would be a nice reversal," I told her. "My eyes cannot tear themselves away from you."

"I would hope so," she said with a smile and walked away with an extra swing to her hips. She looked very good tonight and her flirting mode was on full power.

I continued to watch her serve other tables and said to Aesal, "I do not know if I can stop myself tonight."

"You will ruin this bar for yourself."

"Some things are worth the chance of ruin."

FIVE

I WOKE UP with that special kind of hangover brought on by too much gru and krem. I had spent the last week at Nathara, waiting for a trader with a shipment of a very rare Drakkaran krem. I did not like to stay at the Station so long, but the opportunity was worthy of the wait.

"System on," I croaked while hiding in the warm safety of the bed. "Lights, level one." The lights came on at the lowest level, but it still felt like daggers stabbing into my eyes.

"Glephash," I said. The liquid dispenser popped a small clear cup out and a thick dark-brown liquid poured into it. It looked awful, and tasted even worse, but it was the best formula in the galaxy for quick relief.

I eased myself to the edge of the bed, fighting the sour feeling in my stomach. I sat there a moment and took a few breaths to stabilize, then stood up and waited to make sure I would not be sick. I lumbered over to the dispenser and sipped the drink a little at a time until I felt confident enough to chug the rest in two big swallows, then I fell back into a seat. In spite of the abysmal taste, I felt better right away; the sick stomach and pounding head and blurry vision had all disappeared. The next step was a nice hot cup of caf.

After drinking two cups of steaming caf while scanning through my messages and news feeds, I took a quick cleanse and made a trip down to the main merchant hall. It was rare for me to spend any time there. The vendors in the temporary stalls were too desperate and their products too cheap, but once in a while I found a hidden gem.

I passed by a worn-looking Shiltian selling homemade weapon mods, a Drakkaran man selling religious artifacts from several of the popular religions and a human woman selling handmade blankets. Nothing caught my interest.

I walked by the two havens. Holos of its residents teased their naked bodies and flirted with everyone passing by, trying to convince each of us to join them in an hour or a night of pleasure. The women of the havens were the first tempting thing I had seen all morning, but havens were never as good as what they appeared. As much as Challa liked them, paying a woman for pleasure was always disappointing and never as rewarding as sharing pleasure with a real woman.

I had enough of the crowds and noise of the merchant hall and made my way back to the dock. I had a Station mechanic running a full diagnostic on the *Sun* and making a couple of mods. She was an old Drakkaran who was not that impressive by appearance, but she was one of those engineering genius types, who could tweak any type of engine and make it better than new. I had wanted her to work on the *Sun* for a while, but had not had the time. When I arrived at the ship, she demonstrated improvements in speed and efficiency of the engines by point three percent, as well as upgraded weapon systems and targeting software.

After going over all of her improvements and paying her for the work, I still had a full hour before the meeting with the Drakkaran trader, so I went over some of my own ship mods and did some minor repairs.

When the trader showed up, he tried to jab me with higher prices. I knew what the product was and its value and we had agreed on a price already. He could have found some trader to pay the higher price, but we had agreed on terms before the meeting. I told him I had waited a week for him and threatened to spread word that he was dishonest and made some other physical threats. In the end, he stuck to the original deal.

I was tempted to hop into the ship and light out right away, but Challa and his crew were scheduled to arrive. I finished stowing the krem into the hold and went to the Cavern.

I took a seat at the bar and ordered a krem. I was sipping on it when Vhell walked up to the bar with an order from one of the tables.

"Two minshis, dry and clean," she said. "Two purple drins."

"Vhell," I said and gave her one of my best smiles.

"Jlaeal," she said with an empty smile. She did not say anything else as she waited on the drinks. She was still friendly to me, but the friendliness was for the job and had no real warmth to it. I had succumbed to my urges with her, but it did not end well. We had a beautiful night of pleasure, but afterward she insisted on a conversation about what it meant and about a future. If she was on any other Station it would not have been necessary to have that talk, but this was home for both of us and it was important to her. She knew who I was before that night. I made no pretensions of wanting anything other than pleasure, so it was a surprise.

Our philosophies on the Void were very different. I saw life in the Void as tumultuous, and the risk of separation too high for any type of emotional attachment. I did not see any problems with pleasure with no attachment, but she wanted more. She thought the risks of the Void meant we should embrace connections and love as much as possible and enjoy them in the brief moments we had. I told her love made no sense in the Void. She was fine about it, but the flirtation was gone and I could tell she held some resentment.

I should have known better, or maybe I did and decided to forget about it that night. Those of us who travel and deal with the cold realities of the Corporations and the Void know the futility of love and what it leads to. Those who work and live on Stations sometimes buy into the fantasy that living on a Station can be just the same as living on a planet, as if they are insulated from the risks of the Void. But the rest of us knew it was *haachee*.

I took another drink of krem as she walked away. Her sweet

fragrance lingered and I watched her sashay to the table to serve the drinks. If the Void was anything but the Void, I would consider something more with her, but it *was* the Void and there was no place for that kind of nonsense.

I grilled the bartender on news of the Station. He had no important news to share. He kept going on with nonsense about a big crime lord coming to Nathara. He had no information on who the crime lord was or what he was doing on the Station, so I knew it was a false rumor.

There were "crime lords" throughout the Void and they came and went all the time. They were syndicate leaders, who used their accumulated power and resources to make bigger deals and strike bigger targets, but unless you borrowed from them or made some kind of deal with them, they did not bother the independent traders. It was still good to know when they were around though and stay out of their way.

I had a few incidents with crime lords and syndicates over the years, including a long-term relationship with a man who controlled the syndicates like a puppet master. I learned the hard way that it was better not to deal with them at all. In any deal, they held all the power cards and you held none. It was the same as dealing with Corporations — you were a *chonn* in a big game of Empires.

The puppet master was a man named Trask, the ultimate crime lord. He had the outward appearance of someone respectable and trustworthy, but it was just a façade. They were good times, filled with rich rewards and unlimited resources, but in the end, I watched too many friends die at his hands and I left him. He did not like the fact that I left and tried to have me killed. But that was a long time ago and there were no signs that he had any interest in me anymore. Although, it still kept me looking over my shoulder.

"Gru," I told the bartender.

He slid one in front of me and I downed it and everything faded to black.

Challa and his crew arrived just as I came out of it. They moved to an open table and Challa waved me over. They were all dressed in their flight uniforms, having come straight from their ships. Other pirates did not care what their crews wore, but Challa imagined that by dressing in similar outfits they would bond together as a unit and perform better. I gave him *chee* about it all the time. The uniforms were made of the flexible Meek stuff, which was meant to prevent just about anything from puncturing through and it was safe for a limited amount of time in the cold vacuum of space.

I wore Meek myself, but mine was not styled as a uniform. They were essential for space travel and were also *puda* good in a bar scrap. They all wore black pants and black shirts and kalachi flight vest flaunting Challa's logo on their chest. I thought it was ridiculous for a pirate crew to wear a uniform, but Challa liked it.

I took my krem to their table. "Good to see you all alive," I told them as I approached.

"You as well," Challa said. After I set my drink down, he stood up and grabbed both of my shoulders with a smile. I returned the gesture. We sat down and Vhell came over.

"Vhell! Good to see you! A round of gru and krem for the table," Challa told her. "And we have one more coming."

"Good to see you, Challa. Be right back."

"The new crew member?" I asked.

"Yes. Renlii," Challa told me as Vhell walked away. "She is locking down the ship."

"How is she?"

"She is as skilled in battle as she is at turning heads."

"The raid went well?"

"Very. We caught a GC supply ship with light security."

"It was rich," Bentook whispered at me with glee.

"Yes." Challa smiled. "Very rich for so little security. We will be comfortable for a while."

His crew were all smiles and winks my direction.

Vhell arrived with the drinks and walked away without comment and without the sway to the hips.

"She has lost her enthusiasm," Challa said to me with meaning behind it. He could tell what had happened. He had seen it before. I just gave him a shrug and he chuckled.

"To your rich conquest," I said to Challa and his crew and raised my cup of gru to them.

"And to yours," Challa said to laughter as we all threw the gru down our throats and fell into the darkness.

SIX

W HEN I CAME out of it, an angelic Diviian woman wearing Challa's uniform was sitting next to me. It was Renlii. The tight Meek uniform looked far from ridiculous on her. No outfit in the galaxy could make her look anything less than glorious.

She caught me staring and looked me in the eye with a smirk, not quite laughing at me, but an acknowledgement. She had the look of someone who had seen and dealt with just about everything in the Void and would not be troubled by someone staring at her. As soon we locked eyes I knew I was in deep. My stomach tightened and my throat swelled and my heart raced as if I had run a parsec to meet her.

"This is Renlii," Challa said. "Renlii, this is my good friend Jlaeal."

"Renlii." I nodded to her, playing it cool.

"Jlaeal."

She picked up her shot of gru and said, "Looks like I need to catch up." She drank it and set the cup down. As Renlii stared straight ahead with vacant gru eyes, Challa ordered more drinks from Vhell.

Renlii was a bit shorter than Vhell, but had a better form and a better face, which I did not think was possible. She had short black hair with light-blue streaks. Her eyes were exquisite, with bright-blue irises broken by tendrils of black shooting out from her pupils. It was common for Diviians to have natural multicolored hair and sometimes matching eyes. It was just one of the traits that give them an exotic look.

She came out of it, took a sip of krem and told Challa that the ship was secure. Her voice was strong and melodious, blending a firm undertone with varying higher pitches. It had the melodic sense of strength and beauty.

"Challa says you are a hell of a good fighter," I told her.

"I can hold my own."

"Have you done salvage work before?"

"Is that what Challa calls it?" she asked with a smile.

"He thinks salvage sounds better than pirating."

"I am sure that makes our quarry feel better. That and the uniforms."

I laughed.

She had an easy way about her that put you off guard, but the practiced eye could see that she was on constant guard. While she seemed at ease, she was appraising those around her and planning several moves ahead.

"Jlaeal," Bentook asked, "where have you been to?"

"Here. For the last week. Just closed a deal on some very special krem that will make it worth it."

"Then why are we drinking this swill?" Challa asked to laughter at the table.

We traded stories of our recent trips, which led to stories of the past. We drank more and told jokes and laughed. Renlii showed a talent for adding the right phrase to any story or joke to add the extra laugh. She was fun and delightful and the crew was at ease with her already. We continued with shots of gru and cups of krem and the stories continued to flow.

Challa told of a time he was stuck in a ship with a dead engine, miles from any Station. He was stranded a solid month before a Fillonian trader picked him up. They thought they would sell his ship and sell him into slavery, but he turned the tables on them, killed them and stole their ship instead.

Bentook told of a time she joined in the riots in the capital of Lenux the day of the Fall and celebrated for three days straight. We had heard the story countless times, but it was a good story and brought on the inevitable round of tales of where we were during the Fall.

It had been twenty years since the Galactic Federation had fallen, but it was still fresh in all of our minds. Twenty years was nothing in the Void. I was only in my fifties. If by some miracle I did not catch it early by blaster fire or a *paga* missile, I had a couple of centuries to go. If I reached that age, the GF would be ancient history, but it still seemed new and the wounds were still healing.

Challa told his story and we took a shot of gru. Then the rest of his crew, Ree, Da'd, Pell and Khiltala all told theirs. We had heard them before, but it always made for entertaining conversation as the tales grew larger and more dangerous with each telling.

Khiltala finished his story and we all drank a shot of gru. When we came out of it, we all had fresh shots of gru waiting and it was my turn. I had sculpted my story for years and was able to tell it without hesitation or worry of saying too much.

"I was trading on Belarioos. I just closed a deal and was drinking at a local bar when it hit. It began as a run on a bank. You know how that goes."

"Credit chips?" exclaimed Challa in shock. "We do not hold actual credit chips here in the bank!"

We all laughed at his performance.

"Exactly. The crowd tore the bank to pieces and burned the building down. When GF security arrived, the crowd turned on them, but when some of the security forces heard that the bank had no creds, they joined in the riot. It was chaos.

"I should have gone to the ship as soon as it started, but I stayed and watched instead. When the crowd began attacking anyone who was not joining in, I decided to make a run for it. On the way to the ship, it fell into madness; everyone accused everyone else of being a spy and they all turned against each other. It was friend against friend, brother against brother, children against parents."

I took a long drink of krem before going on.

"I do not like to go into details, but getting back to the ship was the longest and toughest battle of my life. They fought with guns and knives and pipes and with their bare hands. By the time I got to my ship I was scratched and bruised and covered in blood. I still have nightmares of that day."

Everyone took a shot of gru and went into the blackness as we did after every story of the Fall. I never told the whole story of what happened. I never mention that I was on a mission for Trask, or why I stayed to watch the bank, or why it *did* matter to me that the Federation fell or how much my life changed as a result. It was enough for the story that I was there and made it out alive. The rest of the story involved working for a man I hoped I would never see again.

I came out of it, took a long drink of krem and heard Renlii's dulcet voice.

"The day of the Fall was the day I won my freedom."

For the first time since she arrived, she did not make eye contact with any of us. She was serious and stared into her gru as if staring into the Void, looking for help or answers.

"I was a Companion to a Federation senator from the Jipthaa system."

We looked at each other in shock as she continued her story. We had suspicions she was a Companion, but it was never admitted to. They were secretive about their organization, even upon retirement. No Companion ever discussed what they did. Ever. I watched her tell her story in newfound respect, wondering what kind of a woman admitted to being a Companion.

"He was cruel," she continued, "and tormented me for pleasure. I could not leave him or deny him his pleasure, because it would shame my people. That mattered to me at the time, so I submitted to his abuses for several years. We were planetside on Soo, in the center of the Capitol when the riots began."

A few of the crew mumbled exclamations. Bentook whistled appreciation. The capital of the GF was the worst place in the galaxy during the Fall, no matter which side you were on.

"He had an apartment right next to the Capitol building. I watched from the window as the crowds gathered and the riots began. The news feeds played runs on banks throughout the galaxy. They showed everywhere, destruction and chaos. Outside my window was forming the largest crowd I had ever seen. Millions of angry citizens wanted blood in exchange for their loss of creds. Thousands and thousands of troops, backed by battle tanks, stood in front of the shielded Capitol buildings. The crowd grew larger and larger and their chants grew louder and louder."

We hung on her every word. I could not break my eyes away from her. She was fierce and full of life. She was far different than any woman I had ever encountered.

"The senator came into the apartment frantic. He began to pack his things and told me that we were leaving. Then the attack began.

"We watched out the window as millions of people rushed onto the soldiers. It was like waves of an ocean breaking onto a wall of rocks. Thousands and thousands were shot down. Maybe a million. They must have had friends inside the capitol building, because the shielding came down. The defenders were brave warriors, but the crowd was too large and they were overrun.

"The crowd killed everyone — troops, workers, servants — everyone. They hauled the Senators out from the Capitol building to the front steps, stripped them naked and humiliated them. They took turns doing foul things to them and torturing them as the crowd cheered.

"We watched it all from the window. The senator was frozen in fear. We knew there was no way to escape the building and get to his ship. The crowd began to break into the surrounding buildings and we knew they were on their way toward us."

She paused and finished her krem in one long pull. She stared at the empty glass and said, "There was only one thing I could do."

She paused again as Vhell arrived with more drinks.

She took another long draught from her fresh krem and continued, "I tied up the senator using devices he used on me for his pleasure. He tried to fight, but I was trained in combat. He did not know that until that moment. I took him to the window and shouted down to the crowd to get their attention. I announced his name to them and tore off all of his clothes, calling him a thief and a traitor. They cheered me and shouted to bring him down.

"I took him to the lift. He begged mercy of me, but I placed a gag in his mouth. I remember the miserable sounds he made and how he cried and shivered. I remember the smell in the lift as he soiled himself.

"They were waiting for us in the lobby. They patted me on the back and called me a patriot as they led him to the capitol steps and rushed into other apartments to find more souls to sacrifice."

She paused and stared down into her gru.

"After I handed him off, I snuck away through the crowd. I found a trader who still had a ship and left the planet that night.

"I heard later that more than any other senator, he was blamed for the fraud and failure of the bank. He spent several days naked in the capitol courtyard being worked on by the crowd. They took turns on him until he was almost dead, then they tore him apart with their bare hands."

She was very solemn as she lifted her glass of gru to us. "But I was free."

She shot down her gru.

The rest of us sat in shocked silence at the horror of the tale, but raised our glass to her and drank our gru.

We had all experienced horror. We pass through life acting as if everything was fine and hid these dark evil things deep down, but they were always there, waiting. And then, sometimes, as the gru and krem flowed, the stories came out and they disturbed the person telling the story as much as those who heard it. It drew us all closer, because we had all been there, and had all seen and done things that we did not like to believe or talk about. We knew we lived through the worst of times, and sometimes surviving the memories of the past was harder than surviving the troubles of the present.

When we came out of it, the mood was serious and somber. I was worried that Renlii's story was too dark and would ruin the night for us, but it was brave of her to share. My mind reeled thinking of her past and her willingness to walk away from the life of a Companion and to do it openly. I had never even heard of such a thing.

Challa began a story which fit our mood, but at the very end the story turned and became very raunchy and funny. This broke us out of the seriousness and we all laughed until we cried. Then we took turns trying to top each other with outrageous and raunchy jokes. Renlii took a turn and hers was one of my favorites, with the perfect blend of surprise and raunch and ridiculousness. She had won our respect with the first story, but she won our friendship with the joke.

That was life in the Void. There were times of great darkness, when we were serious and dwelt on dark pasts and the dark present and the dark future, but when gru and other drinks or drugs kicked in, we laughed our way to oblivion. We could forget everything wrong in the Void and enjoy the good things for a while.

The night continued like that until the crew started leaving for the havens or for their own beds. Before long, it was just me and Challa and Renlii at the table. Challa stood up.

"Jlaeal, my friend, when do you return?" he asked with a slur.

I shrugged. "Week?"

"I wish you safe travels and steep profits."

"You as well, Challa. Fly safe."

He patted me on the shoulder and stumbled out the door of the Cavern.

"How long have you known one another?" Renlii asked.

I paused to do some drunken math. "Fifteen years."

"How did you come to be friends?"

"We were on a small Station too close to Nallimar territory. Nallimar sent in a small fleet, but they were new at it then and did not know how hard we would fight. Me and Challa and another pirate fought our way through the Station to our ships and then blasted our way out. It was a hard and bloody battle, but we made it and we found out who each of us was during the fighting. We have been friends ever since."

Renlii nodded, "Battle does that. You find out the best or worst in people. Friendships made in battle last for always." She raised her krem to me. "To good friends."

We drank the last of our krem and set the glasses down.

"I think I am ready," Renlii said as she stood up. I left enough creds to pay for whatever Challa did not cover and stood up with her. I walked out behind her. In spite of my drunkenness, I was still in my head enough to know that I was in trouble.

We walked out of the Cavern and down the hallway and continued talking. I was curious about her childhood and training as a Companion on Diviia and had question after question. She was patient and had a good sense of humor about the matter, and even the questions that should have had boring answers were exciting.

My performance in the conversation was stilted and awkward. I was distracted by how good she smelled. She was not wearing perfume, but Diviians had a natural scent better than any perfume. Her scent reminded me of a time I visited the forest planet of Zendo and parked my ship in a meadow clearing. When I opened the ship hatch, I was overwhelmed with the smell of flowers and trees and nature unlike anything I had seen before.

I realized I missed the hallway leading to my apartment, but I did not care. I kept walking with her, without thinking of where we were going. She did not seem to be anxious to get rid of me either and we continued talking. When we passed by the hallway leading to the docks, I asked her if she slept on the ships with the rest of the crew.

"No. We sleep in racks enough while we are out. I sleep in a real bed when the opportunity presents itself."

"I do the same."

We walked a few more steps and stopped at the hatch to her room. It was one of the small overnight rooms with a simple bed and cleansing unit; cheap but clean. She put her palm on the panel and the hatch slid open. If she was any other woman, I would have made a move, but I thought of Challa and the situation and I hesitated.

I could not help but think of the consequences of what I wanted to do. It was a true battle of forces within myself as we paused at the hatch. I stared into her blue and black eyes and looked down at her inviting lips. She saw my hesitation and made the move herself.

We were in each other's arms and kissing with a fierce passion and stumbled into her room. She stopped just long enough to seal the door, saying, "This is the Void. Fuck consequences. This might be our only chance."

SEVEN

I LEFT EARLY the next morning while she was still sleeping. Things were better that way. No *haachee* discussion or awkwardness. If we needed to talk about it, we could talk later, not right after, when passions were still high.

I stepped out of her hatch and walked the hallways to my own apartment. Everything was different that morning, as if I had crossed an invisible line. I was worried about Challa and his reaction to it, but it was done and she seemed fine and did not seem the type to make things difficult. When I got to my apartment, I made a cup of caf, packed my bags and headed out.

During the walk to the ship I thought of Renlii and our night together. With other women, I could walk away without a second thought, but there was something different about her and about last night. I tried to wipe her out of my mind and focus on the trip. I knew I should not think about a woman the way I was starting to think of her. It was a dangerous wormhole and I needed to reverse course and jump out of it.

Challa's ship sat dark and silent as I walked up to the *Asron Sun*. I shut down the security, unsealed the hatch and stepped inside. After a long stay on Station or planetside, it felt good to step inside the *Sun*. She was an older ship, and she was showing her age, but she was mine and she was home. She had a similar smell as the Station, a mix of Sethorian synthsteel, lubricants and a slight undertone of aging Vgerian leather.

I announced myself to the *Sun* and told her to begin the startup sequence as I walked to my room and stowed my gear.

When I got to the cockpit, I called into the Command Center and requested clearance to leave. It came in fast and I raised the *Sun* off the deck and took her through the dock toward the exit.

The entrance into the bay was not smoothed out, but made to look like a natural hole in the asteroid, and maybe it was. I had never asked anyone, but it was possible the asteroid had a natural cavern when they found it, and they just dug deeper to make room for the Station. There were no bay doors to open and close. The Station had an enviro shield built around the entrance to keep the Station pressurized, but still allowed ships to come and go.

I flew the *Sun* into the endless sea of stars and took a deep breath as I flew her under a small asteroid and veered around another medium-size one. I flew her on manual to help relax my nerves. I could feel the muscles in my neck and back loosen up.

I had not realized how tense I was, but as soon as I hit open space I felt at ease, weaving in and out of the sea of asteroids. I flew past the last of them and blasted into the wide open space of the Void. I locked in the coords for the Aritham Station and set the system to light out once the ship was far enough away from the gravity pull of the asteroid field.

I eased back in the seat and watched Nathara disappear behind me and thought of her sleeping in her rack. The computer counted down the last ten seconds and the wormhole opened and the *Sun* leaped inside. I was still thinking of her as I looked ahead into the swirling inky blackness of the hole and all I could see was trouble.

By the time I reached Aritham, I felt better about Renlii. The trip was a quick two days, but it was long enough for me to calm my nerves and get her out of my head. I decided I was just caught up in the moment and was nervous about how Challa would react. I knew Challa well enough to know he would give me a hard time about it, but he would be fine.

I lit in from the wormhole and the Station was dead ahead, far in the distance. It looked like a rusted out, derelict ship, floating inert, light-years away from anything. But, as you drew closer to it, there were signs of life.

It was once a proud battle cruiser in the GF fleet, but the ship was abandoned after a large hole was punched into the engine during a tense battle years ago. Soon after, a group of raiders took the ship for themselves and turned it into an operational Station. It was not pretty, but it did the job, and in spite of its looks, it was a fine Station and well maintained.

I sent a request for docking.

"Wait for full ship scan and identification procedures," came back the response.

"What?" I sent back.

"New regulations."

"Fuck new regulations."

"You want on board, then we do a full ship and ID scan."

I wanted to tell them to pleasure themselves, but I had a buyer waiting on the Station. A ship scan and ID scan were *puda* intrusive, giving them every piece of info about the *Sun*, what she was carrying, where she had been and every other piece of information I did not want spreading across the Void. On top of that *haachee*, they were going to scan me, which did not give them any new information, but I found the process *puda* invasive.

"Fine. Run your *puda* scans."

They ran a full scan of the *Sun*, confirming my identity and everything about the ship, including her contents and whether I had a tracking device attached. I expected these kind of scans while flying in corporate territories, but not at a Station in the Void. With a few exceptions, Stations knew that we would not put up with it and did not try it. My ship was none of their *puda* business.

I knew the captain well and decided I would have a talk with her.

"All clear, Jlaeal. Docking bay two. Space fourteen."

"Copy."

I angled the ship toward bay two, which was now lit up with a nav targeting light on my system. I flew the *Sun* through the bay doors and guided her into the designated spot. As I started the power down sequence, Noolie, the Shiltian docking coordinator approached the ship with five security drones.

My first instincts were to power the ship back up and blast him and his droids to hells, but I took a few deep breaths and calmed myself down. They were treating this Station as if it were a dock on a central corp planet and treating me as if I were a suspected criminal. I stood up and loosened the binding straps on my gun holsters and triggered the safeties off. I stood little chance against five drones, but the hells with them if they thought I would not fight.

I walked back to the entry hatch with my right hand on a holster. I took a deep breath before telling the system to open the hatch. When it slid open, Noolie stood waiting at the bottom of the ramp. A single drone was poised on each side of him, three others hovered above him with guns aimed and ready.

Noolie himself was no threat, but the drones were hovering death. He was average height for a Shiltian, with his head topping out at my knees. He was bald, with pink eyes and was missing one of his ears. The line of scars on that side of his face made it look like he was leering. I had dealt with Noolie many times before, but it was always cordial and friendly, with no strike drones.

"Captain Jlaeal."

"What is this, Noolie? Why the special greeting?"

I stood at the hatch with my hand ready to pull, waiting to see how things rounded out. If things went bad I would dive back in and seal the hatch.

"Standard protocol. Nothing personal. Every ship scan and search."

"I was scanned on approach."

"Yes. Drones scan ship interior. With permission."

"And, if I say no?"

"You leave."

"*Haachee.*"

"Protocol. No exception."

He was not going to budge and my buyer was already on the Station.

"Fine," I said. "Do what you have to."

He nodded to me as the drones flew up into the hatch. I stepped aside and watched them scan and inspect the interior. The other drones waited outside, waiting to see if they needed to blast me. I stepped out of the ship and stood next to Noolie, waiting for the drones to do their work.

"Tell the captain I want a word with her," I said.

"Captain in meeting."

"She can cancel it."

Noolie sat unmoving as if he was ignoring me, but I knew he was sending word. Noolie looked normal enough, but his head was filled with biocybertronic enhancements, giving him improved memory, vision and hearing. Plus, he was cerebrally connected to the Station's communications and security network, including the drones.

"Meet after inspection."

"How long will this take?"

"Done."

The two drones flew out of the hatch and came over to float next to Noolie. The other drones flew off to harass the next pilot.

"Where is she?" I asked.

"Command Center."

I walked up to the hatch and put in the lockup and security sequence.

"Special instruction for ship?"

"No, you did enough already."

As Noolie walked away with his drones in tow, I finished the lockdown procedure and took a few deep breaths. Although I had a relationship with the captain, any captain held absolute power over their ship or Station. As much as I wanted to give her an earful, I had to play it just right or I would find myself floating naked in space.

But hells with it. Things were getting worse in the Void and *pada* if I would go down without a fight. I checked my guns again, took a deep breath and stepped away from the ship.

EIGHT

THE BASIC LAYOUT of Aritham Station was the same as when it was a battle cruiser. They converted the crew quarters to apartments, overnights and havens, and the mess halls were converted into bars and food areas. She was built at the height of GF power and was once a proud ship, made from the best synthsteel available at the time, which was advertised as rust-proof for centuries. But there were signs of rust and decay throughout the dock; the captain was in a constant battle with corrosion and corrupted systems.

I walked straight past the line of ships to one of the lifts and told the system to take me to the Command Center. I placed my hand on the command console and the doors sealed. I felt the lift move sideways a bit, lock in place and travel up.

The lift smelled of aging metal and mildew and looked like it was in bad need of maintenance or maybe even replacement. Several screws were missing and some panels had rusted all the way through. The rest of the Station had a similar appearance and smell to it, as if the whole thing was breaking down. But in spite of appearances, the captain spent great efforts on improvements. There was too much to fix on a budget of a station that size, but she was wise enough to spend her creds on operations and effectiveness rather than aesthetics. It looked like a floating *haachee* bomb, but everything worked fine.

The lift doors opened onto the Command Deck. I stepped out to find two very large armed and uniformed humans barring me from going any further. As they stared me down I gave them the smile I used on women I was chasing, but they did not see the charm behind it.

"Leave them alone, Jlaeal."

Behind the huge men, Captain Finael was bent over a holo screen, reviewing a screen with a tech. I was tempted to make a retort, but held off. I knew the captain well enough to know when to push her buttons and when to play along. In private, I could speak my mind and push her a little, but she did not allow that in front of her crew. Cross her in front of her crew and she would show you why she was in charge.

Also, she was giving me a nice and distracting view as she bent over the console. The captain was not young, in fact she had several decades on me, but she was beautiful and worked hard to keep in fighting shape and could still stop a man in his tracks just by looking at him. Her looks were just a distraction though. First and foremost, she was a captain. A *puda* good one. She was intelligent, fair and serious.

I forced myself to look away from her figure to inspect the Command Deck. Like the rest of the Station, it had patches of rust, a few missing bolts and a distinct metallic smell, but the working equipment was shiny and new, and if not the latest technology, it was new enough to get the job done.

She gave her tech one last instruction, stood up from the holo screen, and walked to a side room without giving me a glance.

"Let him through."

The two guards stood aside. I knew I was pushing my luck, but I gave the larger of them a fuck you wink as I walked by. I caught a hint of perfume or delicate soap from the captain as I followed behind her, which took me off guard. I had never known Finael to wear any type of scent. Perfumes were reserved for soft people on civilized planets or haven workers.

Some women were able to give themselves an edge in the Void by mixing a hard-ass demeanor with pleasure appeal. The perfume the captain wore gave her that edge, but the perfume was out of character. Then again, the combination of perfume with the tight pants was working. It was a struggle to force thoughts of pleasure out of my mind and focus on what I came to discuss.

She sat in a shiny metallic hover seat at a matching desk, put her hands behind her head and leaned back, crossing her legs on the desk in one fluid motion. Like the rest of the office, the desk was spotless and organized.

"What is the problem?" she asked, as she shifted her hips in the seat and stretched a little.

"What the hells is going on with the new protocols."

"Do not take it personal. Every ship coming into my Station goes through the same process now."

"Why?"

"You know why."

"The Corps? How the hells will a ship and cargo inspection prevent one of the Corps from finding you?"

"We are not inspecting cargo. I do not care about cargo."

"Trackers?"

She nodded. "Trackers, bugs or even signs of frequent communication with any of the Corporations."

"Wait. How would -," but the last word trailed off as it hit me. I tried to keep cool, but I was overheating fast, and this time it was not her legs or ass or perfume.

"She said she was scanning the ship, not getting into my system. What the hells right do you have to scan my system?"

She kicked her feet off the desk and sat forward, "Sit."

"I want an answer *pudak*!"

"Then sit down!" The captain glared with growing impatience. "Don't try me. Not on my Station. Sit down!"

I had a sharp response on the tip of my tongue, but I held it back and sat in the nearest hover chair and returned her glare. This was her Station; she owned it and made all the rules for it. She could shoot me or launch me into the Void without a second thought, and keep my ship and cargo for herself with no repercussions. If she did this too often, she would lose customers and find herself captain of an empty Station, but it was still her prerogative. I was not about to find out where her line was.

The captain eased back into her seat with a sigh. "Jlaeal, things are changing. Corporations are taking out Stations every week, regardless of protocols. So far, there seems to be one guarantee for survival."

I laughed. "Death is the only guarantee in the Void. We just put it off as long as we can."

She shrugged. "I have found another."

"What are you talking about?"

She considered a moment, then stood up and walked to a alidnum cabinet near the hatch. She opened one of the doors and pulled out a canister of blue drin and poured two crystals. It was very thick and viscous, showing its value.

She handed one of the crystals to me and we gave each other grim salutes before taking a sip. It was dense, nearly gelatinous, and it was dry and delicious. I did not have drin often, but I did enjoy it when given the opportunity. I was not an expert on the various drins and could not identify its planet of origin or location on the planet. I was lucky if I could determine which race cultivated the lontch; but even I knew it was of good quality.

"Have you heard of a man named Trask?" she asked, nearly causing me to choke on the drin. I forced myself to swallow and kept my face clear. I did not know if she was talking of the Trask I knew, but it would take more time than either of us had to explain his importance and everything we had experienced together and why I did not want to see or work for him again. But that life was far in the past and I never spoke of it with anyone.

"I know several Trasks," I lied.

Her face smiled, but her eyes were serious. "Trask is Trask. The only one of that name. If you knew him, you would know this."

"Why is this one so important?" I asked.

"He is going to save the Void."

I laughed so hard I had to set my drink down on her desk so I would not spill it. It was the same Trask all right. Always trying to control the galaxy with claims he wanted to save it.

"That is some man," I said.

"He is," she said.

"This one man is going to take on all three Corporations and save us all like the Jtarran Savior?"

"Yes," she said, taking another drink and staring me in the eyes as if she had told me a basic truth of the galaxy.

I had a sudden urge for gru, but we were drinking drin and it would have to do. I took the drin back off the desk and drained the crystal. Finael was not a person to fall for superstitions or false rumors. She believed in cold hard facts. I knew she believed what she was saying and that she had researched the matter with the thoroughness with which she did everything. I set the crystal back down on the table.

"Go on."

"He was once head of GF Intelligence. Heard of him now?"

A chill ran down my spine. "Yes."

"He disappeared as soon as the first protest began. No one knows where he went and no one cared. He was not a politician and not a soldier, so he did not matter as far as the public was concerned."

I nodded. I knew where he went and what he did. Everything about the Fall was ugly, but what I found about him during that time turned my blood cold. I found out who he really was and what he was capable of.

"Somehow, he not only kept part of his spy network intact, he grew it."

I raised my eyebrows feigning surprise, but I was not surprised at all. I knew the story better than anyone.

"None of us heard anything about him since after the Fall, but he has grown to be a major player among the Corporations."

"What do you mean?" I asked. This was new intel. I had not heard from him in nearly twenty years.

"I don't know the specifics of how it works. He has his own

Corporation, but does not compete with the others. He has no product to sell. He calls his company 'Universal Intelligence.'"

I laughed. That sounded like Trask. Arrogant *mata*. "Sounds *pada* arrogant."

She noticed my empty crystal and offered to pour more. I lifted the crystal to her and she refilled it and then refilled her own.

"If a man can back his claims, is it arrogance or confidence?"

"What claims? What does he do?"

"He sells information to each of the Corporations about their competitors. This funds his enterprise and guarantees his safety."

"How does he pull that off? Is he in hiding somewhere?"

"In plain sight," she said.

"What do you mean?" I asked.

I swallowed more drin and tried to keep my cool. Trask's intelligence and skill were unmatched, but this was insane. I knew where things stood when I left him, and I knew part of his plans to rebuild, but this went far beyond what I knew.

"His operation is based on an old GF Star Base in the center of the Void. Any Corporation or Station captain who wants to deal with him goes there."

"Impossible. Even if it was operational, they would just blow the thing to the hells."

She grinned. "I have no doubt they want to, but I assume he has intel on them and a legitimate threat to release the information if something happens to him. So they play his game."

"Holy hells."

"This is where it gets really interesting. He claims he can protect a Station if they work with him and join his organization."

"What do you mean join his organization?" I asked. "Just what the hells is that supposed to mean?" I slammed my empty crystal onto her desk and leaned in.

She finished her drink and leaned forward. "We have known each other for a while, Jlaeal, and I trust you." She paused and smirked. "Scratch that. I trust you to keep your mouth shut. If he knows I told you he would kill both of us. That is the deal."

I nodded. That sounded like Trask. He was fair, but he was also deadly.

"You know me," I told her. "I do not talk. Especially, when my own ass is on the line."

I got the feeling she was telling me this less because she trusted me and wanted me to be well informed, and more because she could not trust anyone else on the ship and needed to tell someone to gauge their response. She leaned back in her seat and looked down at her empty crystal, turning it in her hands.

"Our entire system is now linked to UI. Everything we see or hear on this Station he sees and hears on his star base. Everything but this room. That was the deal. Plus, we pay him one percent of all revenue; kind of a tax."

I sat back in my seat, eyes wide, mouth open. "And what do you get in return?"

She looked me dead in the eye with no shame or reluctance. "Safety."

"From the Corporations?"

She nodded.

"How do you know he can pull it off?"

"How does he pull any of it off? I don't know. I know he can back his side of the deal though."

"How?"

I was trying to piece what I once knew of him with what I was learning now and it created a frightening scenario.

She sat up again, refilled her drin and then held the canister toward me. I took it and emptied it into my crystal.

"A GalactiCorp fleet lit in close to us last week, just after I made the deal with Trask."

"How close?"

"Close enough. They scanned over the Station and lit back out. Not a word was said. I have seen no sign of them since."

"What does that mean?"

It was impossible. The whole situation made no sense. To hold that kind of sway over a Corporation, he would have to have all of their balls in his hands with a threat to crush them. Even then, it seems they would call his bluff.

"It means the Void is changing."

"For good or bad?"

"What difference does it make? The Void changes and then we change. For now, we live. This Station lives."

"And the rest?"

"To the hells with the rest. This is my Station. My people. The rest can burn. I survive. My Station survives."

That was how it worked in the Void. She was pain and struggle and death. You did what you had to do to survive against her. Finael had made a deal with the *conja* and now she would either suffer for it or benefit. I was silent for several moments, staring down at her desk, thinking of what it all meant and what the future held. Then it hit me.

"Holy hells!"

She looked at me as if I had just claimed to be the heavenly god Trill himself. "What?"

"He is giving the Corporations the locations of all the other Stations. That is why they are all going down. Trask offers them protection and if they turn him down, he sends the coordinates to the Corps and they take down the Stations with his blessing."

She shrugged. "Maybe."

"What else?"

"How hard do you think it is for the Corporations to find us?"

I had not thought about the matter too much. The Stations did not move. Moving was bad for businesses. And if a Corporation got its hands on any traveler's system, which happened often, the Corporation would have access to the ship's entire history, including the location of all the Stations it had gone to. Standard protocol in the Void was an immediate system wipe if your ship was confiscated or damaged, but all it took was one ship captured before its system was wiped for the whole security system of all Stations to fail.

I stared at her with more compassion. As hard as it was being a smuggler, running a Station had greater challenges. She was under constant threat of Corporate attack.

"He did not give you much of a choice did he?"

She shook her head and looked down at her half-empty cup. She gave me a grin and raised her cup to me. "To the Void."

"And survival," I added and we both finished the rest of our drin.

"Did you get an overnight?" she asked as she stood up and walked around the desk. There was something different about her now, whether from the drink or something else. She had more sway in her hips.

"Not yet."

She had a look in her eyes as she approached and my heart beat faster and the room seemed to heat up.

"Good," she said.

I stood and she was there, kissing me hard and pulling me close. I felt her firm body and soft curves pressing against me. I smelled her sweet perfume and tasted the drin.

She pushed me back and we stumbled through the room to a hatch on the opposite side of where we came in. She palmed the security screen and the hatch slid open. We shuffled into her quarters and tore at each other's clothes without saying a word, going after each other like it was our last night in the Void.

NINE

I SOLD HALF of the krem for a nice profit and lit out for the Mmpar-Ra Station to sell the rest. It was a long three-day trip, as I thought about Renlii and then Trask and Universal Intelligence and what it meant for us all in the Void.

I thought back to my years working for him. He had seemed a fair man and loyal and of supreme intelligence, with the ability to remember anything he saw or heard. Whether that was due to natural ability or his cybertronic implants, no one knew, but even cybertronic implants had their limitations. His real talent was his ability to reason things out, predict his opponents' reactions and make plans ten, twenty, one hundred steps ahead.

When I first started working for Trask, I was young and idealistic and believed in him. The GF had captured me for smuggling back before I was out of my teens. I grew up an orphan on the streets of Kepta and one of the syndicates had me helping out with some of their smuggling operations. Trask and the Intelligence Division of the GF had a special program for guys like me. They took me off planet, trained me for special missions and espionage, then spit me back out into the Void to infiltrate the underground. But smuggling was different when backed by the GF. Instead of struggling for every cred and worrying about every deal, I had the latest toys and ships, made to look like they were old and worn out, and if things got bad, they would pad my account to get me out of trouble.

Trask seemed fair and gave things to me straight. I respected him at the time and thought we had a special relationship compared to other agents in the field. Of course, that is the way men like Trask ensure loyalty.

Turns out it was all a ruse, a shell game. I did not find out until too late how he manipulated the truth and used people and controlled them for power. It was terrifying when I found out the magnitude of the power he held.

In addition to running the intelligence division of the GF, Trask controlled all criminal syndicates in the galaxy, both in-system and out. If any syndicate plotted to leave his control, he sent other syndicates after them and carved out their territory between the other groups. These same syndicates and criminal groups killed dozens of my friends over the years. When I found out that Trask had sanctioned one of these deaths, I got out, but at a huge cost.

Trask was no saint. He once portrayed himself as GF's protector, but I knew better. I saw behind the mask into the darkness. The man was capable of calculation and manipulation beyond anything I had ever experienced, and it scared the hells out of me. I wanted nothing more to do with him.

What he had planned for the Void, I could not imagine. I could not think of his end game, or why the Corporations would allow it to go so far. They were benefiting from his services, but I did not think they had any idea of the scope of his power. They would be better off without Trask. He was not pro-Corporation and a partnership was not in their long-term interests. And no matter what things seemed on the short term, he always worked the long game.

I sold the rest of the krem on Mmpar-Ra and did not stay overnight. Instead, I lit out right away for Nathara. Under normal circumstances, I would have stayed at least a day and gathered local intel, but after hearing about Trask I was anxious to get home.

I was happy to find no added security measures at Nathara. This put me at ease, as I did not want to be part of a Trask Station, or Universal Intelligence or UI, whatever the hells he was calling it. On the other hand, I knew it put us all in greater danger. Going with Trask seemed like the safe bet, but I knew better. He offered safety from the Corporations, but there was always a price working with him, and the Station captain would never be told the real price.

Fuck Trask. If I wanted safety, I would live on a Corporate planet and let them watch over me. What was the difference? The Void was about freedom to do whatever the hells I wanted. Trask was just another Corporation with rules and restrictions on how to live and how to run my operation.

This line of thinking put me in a foul mood. After docking the ship, I packed my sack, locked up the ship and headed to my apartment. The familiar scene of the Station was comforting, with its dark stone corridors, and the cold damp feeling that came from the porous asteroid rock. You could only heat the place so much; the cold of space always found its way through. Somehow this put me at ease.

I pushed my way through the busy hallways, making my way past the entertainment section and into the merchant section. My breath caught in my throat when I saw her standing at a merchant table negotiating for some small item. She wore the tight Meek weave pants from her uniform, but instead of her uniform top, she wore a bright-orange patterned shirt that hung loose from her shoulders. It was open in the middle all the way down to her waist, giving more than a hint of what was underneath. The orange worked well with the blue streaks in her hair, producing a beauty that stood out in the merchant quarters. She looked *pada* good and I grew more excited with every step.

I tried to keep her out of my mind during the trip, but now a rush of exciting thoughts and feelings flooded back into me.

If I was thinking straight, I would have avoided her and headed straight to my apartment. Once was a risk, twice was asking for real trouble, but the game was lost as soon as I saw her.

I came up behind her with stealth, not wanting to interrupt the negotiations. As I approached, she turned and winked, as if she had been expecting me, then continued the negotiations without pause. I stood next to her, not willing to interrupt. It was not so much negotiations as it was a humiliation. Her flirting distracted him, and her logic and arguments left him stammering and trying to remember lines he used before.

As she wore the merchant down I began second guessing the situation and whether she was as excited to see me as I was to see her. I had not talked to her since the night before I left and it felt awkward standing there. I assumed she would be excited to see me, but I was having doubts. It was a rare thing for me. As I stood watching her, I felt like a kept man, waiting on his woman to call him.

The young merchant gave me a nervous glance, as if he were dying from exposure in the Void and looking for a lifeline. I imagined he was a competent enough negotiator, but he was overmatched.

She finished the deal with the merchant and faced me, ignoring the now-disgraced man who was willing to look anywhere but toward either one of us. She looked me over, glanced at my pack and then grabbed my shoulders in greeting and looked into my eyes.

"I am glad you are alive," she said.

I returned the gesture. "I am glad you are alive."

We both let our arms down and I looked into her bewitching eyes and looked for something to tell me she was excited to see me, but she looked at me with the same flirtatious look she gave the merchant. She wore her mask well and it was hard to see through it.

"You just arrive?" she asked.

"Yes. I was heading to my apartment to unload my gear."

"How was the trip?" she asked. "Profitable?"

She began walking toward the residence section and I walked alongside her.

"Very. Bought some high-grade krem and turned it around for a high profit."

"You do like your krem."

"I do. I also like creds, and krem and creds seem to like each other."

She gave me a smile and polite chuckle.

"How was your last mission?" I asked.

"Not easy. One of the fighters took heavy damage." She shrugged. "But none of us were injured."

"What happened? Challa said there would be no escort."

"He was misinformed. The cargo vessel was escorted by a 2D Fighter and two dozen drones."

I whistled. That was a lot of firepower. Challa had a 2D himself and a 1D, but depending on how advanced the escort and drones were, it could have gone bad, fast.

"How did it play out?"

"Challa sent his drones to battle theirs, while the rest of us engaged the fighter."

"Makes sense."

"Yes, but their drones were far more advanced. They took ours out quickly. *Sh'kurah Nuilla* destroyed the last of them, but it took too long. By the time Challa could focus on the fighter, Bentook's fighter took several hits."

"But you said she was fine?"

"Yes."

"Good."

We arrived at my apartment and I pressed my palm on the scanner and the hatch slid open.

"Drink?" I asked without thinking.

My breath held as I looked into her eyes. I had not intended to do anything more with her and this would put us to the test. Doing things once was risky, but we stayed on friendly terms.

Now I had opened the door to further danger. If she went into the room, I would fall deeper for her and she for me and things would be more complicated. But at that moment, I did not care about the bad things and wanted her to come into the room more than anything in the Void.

"Yes," she said, and I caught a flash in her eyes, just enough to betray the spark of passion she had been hiding. It was the first time I saw past the mask.

I could not help but smile as I stepped into the room. The lights came on and I set my bag down. I told the system to seal the door when she followed me in. I took one step to the drink dispenser, but before I got there, she flipped me around and pulled me against her, squeezed me tight and kissed me with a fierce passion.

Her soft lips pressed against mine and we held each other firmly, as if we were trying to meld our bodies together. I noticed everything about her at once — her firm muscles, her warm soft skin, her intoxicating smell and the softness of her curves pressed against me. She pushed so hard against me that I fell back into the hatch. She ran her hands over all of me and I ran mine over all of her, trying to touch every part of her at once. I kissed her check and her neck and took off her shirt.

"I could not stop thinking of you. Of this," she said.

"Neither could I."

"Liar," she laughed as I worked to undo her pants.

I thought about saying more, but stopped myself. I did think about her during the trip. I thought about her too much and it scared me. I backed up and looked into her blue and black eyes and wondered if she knew everything about me, but this did not last. She pulled me back in and kissed me harder, with more passion, but the mood was interrupted for me.

Pleasure in the Void was like a game. We both pretended that we loved each other and are only for each other, and this made the night better, more passionate. Sometimes this made it true, even if it was just for that one night. But she broke the rules of the game and broke the illusion, and it shook me to think that the feelings were real. I knew she meant what she said and she felt it more than I did.

She could sense this and stopped kissing me and looked at me. "I should not have said anything," she said. "It does not matter, Jlaeal. I did miss you and thought of you, but I do not care if you feel the same. I just want this. Now. I want this moment."

"I did think of you, Renlii."

I gave her an intense kiss and looked deep into her eyes, our lips not quite touching.

"The trip to Aritham was the longest I have ever had. I tried to think of something else during the trip, but I could not get you out of my mind. I thought of you and I thought of this."

And it was truth. I knew it was true and that scared me even more, but I gave into the passion. I convinced myself that it was one night. I could be in love for one night and the Void would not implode.

We were back into the original passion again and kissed each other hard as before and tore at each other's clothes again. We did not talk any more of anything but the moment's pleasure. We spent hours in passion as if we were long-lost lovers and had one night to make up for years of absence.

I lay on my back in the berth; she was face down, with her cheek on my chest and her legs entwined around mine. I ran my hand along her back and enjoyed the smoothness of her skin.

"Is this madness?" she asked.

"Yes."

"Should we stop?"

"Yes. But we are already too far in."

"Where will it go?"

"Truth?"

"Always truth," she said.

"Anything beyond pleasure leads to pain. You know this."

"I know this," she said.

"Challa will decide to move to another Station, I will have to find new trade routes, one or both of us will be captured and enslaved, or one or both of us will die."

She grew silent and I felt her chest moving in and out and I listened to her breathe and felt it warm on my chest. We both knew it was true. It was cruel to say it out loud, but that is what she wanted; to say what she was thinking in her head. She wanted truth.

"Still, I do not want to stop," she said.

She pressed herself harder into me and I felt the heat pulsating from her body and smelled the sweetness of her hair. I did not want it to end either. I knew that all of Challa's warning had come true. The biggest danger in the Void was not Trask, or Corporations or blaster fire. I was holding it in my arms.

"Neither do I," I told her in full truth. "But we should just do this and fight against the other."

"The other?"

"This is fine. But more than this will not end well."

"I know," she said. "But I already feel it."

"Me, too. But we can still fight against it."

She shifted around to rest her chin on my chest and look into my eyes and she ran her fingers through my hair. I smelled her warm breath as I looked back into her eyes. They were like the clear blue oceans of Tillian with islands of black and I could not look away. I wanted to dive in and swim into her mind and read what was there. She did not want to fight it. She wanted to submit to it, to feel it just once, whatever the cost; or maybe those thoughts were my own.

I could not figure why I was having these emotions for her. She was beautiful, but I had been with beauty hundreds of times. She was smart, but I had been with smart. She was charming, but I had been with charming women. It was something I could not put my finger on. Something indescribable and intangible but which had a complete hold on me and fighting it would be like fighting against all the powers of the Void.

I thought of this as we lay holding each other in silence, enjoying the warmth and feeling of each other's bodies and then we drifted off to sleep.

I awoke the next morning alone. I felt for her and she was gone and I realized I wanted her to be there and I knew I was in deep *chee*. I swung my legs around to the floor, lurched over to the dispenser and ordered up a hot cup of caf.

I drank the caf and read through the messages on my com and spotted one from Renlii. She had to light out with Challa for a last-minute mission. She said she knew the consequences of pleasure and the "other," but that she wanted to live, to truly live, in spite of the costs. True freedom was going after what you wanted regardless of risk or cost and she had come to the Void to be free. She closed saying that she loved me and wanted to love me and that it made her feel free and alive. She said one more time that she loved me and signed off.

A chill ran down my spine as I read her message again. Words like love were foreign in the Void and it brought a feeling of panic. She knew this and I was sure that saying the word brought her as much fear as I felt in hearing it. I wanted to feel it and might have actually loved her, but I knew it was still best to fight it. Or maybe it was just that she was brave and I was afraid.

I lay back down in the rack and thought about the future and tried to imagine that things could be bright, but I was never good at lying to myself.

TEN

W E OFTEN LIVE as if we are on a clear flight path and we
set our life on auto-pilot, unaware that we are about to
light into an uncharted asteroid field. By the time our proximity
alarms go off, we are out of time and all we can do is react using
our guts and instinct.

The next day I woke up to find that my main krem source from
Drakkara had been shut down by TriKarre. I traded in a variety of
products, from multiple sources, so I was not dependent on any
single route, but I had grown too reliant on this one source of
krem. It was some of the best in the galaxy, and I was able to buy
it cheap and sell it for a large markup. Because of this, I let more
and more contracts go in favor of this one. Now that the source
was gone. Over half of my income had disappeared and my next
deal was two months away.

I learned long ago to keep a stash of creds for down times, but
I was still worried. It could take a long time to build up my routes
again. I felt like a fool and a *mata*. I had taken too many chances
and it had caught up to me.

As soon as I heard the news I took a long walk through the
Station, ending up at my ship. I was feeling sorry for myself and
knew that I had to break out of it. I stared at the *Sun* and thought
about what I had in my hand. The *Sun* had just been run over
with a chemical bath and looked fresh and new. She was not new
by any stretch, but she was a beautiful ship, and she had a *pada*
fine engine with plenty of guts. Half of your hand in the Void was
having a good ship, and I had a great one. I had plenty of other

good chips in my hand as well; I had creds put away, contacts and resources throughout the galaxy, and a few tricks up my sleeve that other smugglers did not have access to.

I knew I would be all right. It would be a tough year, and the majority of my savings would be eaten up before it was over, but I would make it.

When I was through feeling sorry for myself, I walked down to the merchant quarters and spread word among those I trusted that I had a few slots available. One key to being successful in business was to act as if you were busy and successful. Merchants want to trade with someone who can get the job done, not someone who was desperate.

I let people know that something had opened up and I might be able to fit another route in, if it was a good one. I talked to all of the merchants I knew and even a few I did not, but none of them had a whisper of anything available. I played it cool and let them know to patch me in if something popped up.

I spoke to the captain to find out if they had any supply needs I might be able to help out with. I used to supply him with a few rare items on the Station, but I had eliminated those routes in favor of the krem. I still got along fine with the captain, but our relationship had chilled since breaking the business arrangement. Now he dealt with other traders and I was down on his list of contacts. He said he would keep me in mind, but that was Station double talk for "you lost your chance."

I walked down to the Cavern, trying to keep my head up and appear confident, but the day had got to me and I felt depressed and anxious about the future. I stepped into the dark and damp Cavern, happy to find that it was busy and loud. I felt like being alone and the best way to be alone was in a room full of people.

I weaved past tables full of traders and pirates and past a few entertainers and other travelers and made it to a small table in the corner. I sat down with my back against the wall and my face toward the door. More than usual, I noticed the strong smell of exotic drinks and foods mixed with stale sweat and alcohol. No matter how clean they kept a bar, some smells never went away, as if the fumes had seeped into the walls.

A beautiful human woman approached my table holding an order holo. Her head was shaved bald, except for short orange bangs hanging all the way down to her trimmed orange eyebrows. It matched well with her orange thigh-high boots and matching skirt that was so short it verged on non-existent. She had on a shirt that was too small to do anything but draw your attention to what it was hiding.

"Hey pilot. Whatcha have to drink?"

"Gru. Keep it full. And a side of krem."

She put my order on her pad, gave me a smile and turned to walk away, but I stopped her.

"Are you new?" I asked.

"Started yesterday."

"What happened to Vhell?"

She shrugged. "She left."

"The Cavern or the Station?"

"Not sure. Think the Station."

"Oh," I said. I had no idea she was leaving. "Well, welcome aboard." I tried to muster a smile, but it must have looked as rough as I felt and she gave me a bright smile in return.

"Thanks!" she said. "Edda."

"Jlaeal," I said.

"Be right back with your drinks," she said and walked away. As I waited for the drinks I wondered what happened to Vhell. The narcissist in me assumed it had something to do with what happened between us. She was disappointed when it did not lead to anything. She was a romantic. I was a realistic.

Then I smiled bitterly at the thought of Renlii. I had strict rules and precautions with Vhell and the others, but I was breaking all of them with Renlii and sliding deeper and deeper into the giant pile of *haachee* Challa always warned me about.

I could not say why I would break the rules for Renlii and not Vhell. Renlii was a hells of a woman. In truth she was parsecs ahead of Vhell. But that did not explain the feelings I was having. It was as if a wormhole opened up to my emotions and it was drawing me in.

Edda came back just in time with two shots of gru and an ice cold krem. She set them down with a smile and walked away with a noticeable sway to her hips. Challa's warnings flashed through my head as I enjoyed the show. And then Renlii flashed through my head. *Pudak.* I was in real *pada haachee* for sure.

I slammed the gru and dropped into the darkness. I came out too soon, but before I could phase back in all the way, I slammed the second one and dove back into it.

This time it lasted a longer. I eased out of it and looked down to see two fresh shots of gru waiting for me. I looked toward the bar and Edda gave me a smile and wave. She was very attractive, more cute than beautiful, with one of those adorable personalities that was good for surviving bars in the Void or one of the havens, but was not much help anywhere else.

We all had our stories, our histories. I sipped on my krem and wondered what hers was. Her accent pegged her as coming from one of the periphery systems in the Drakkaran territory. I would have liked to spend time learning about her and getting to know other things, but Renlii's image popped into my head again and the moment was ruined.

Pudak.

I took a long pull from the krem and tried to focus on finding new contracts. I would not find much on this Station, or any other Station for that matter. Stations had settled into a streamlined system of buying and selling that was seldom interrupted, unless the supplier got caught, or their supply disappeared like mine did. But if you had a good product, better and/or cheaper than the next person, finding buyers was easy. What I needed was more product.

The krem I lost was not replaceable. There was always krem out there, but not like the stuff I had sold. I would have to head planetside and look for another product. I thought through my contacts and speculated on where I could find another source of krem. I slammed another gru and slipped back into nothing.

I did not want to come out of the dark, but the gru wore off, as it always does, and I came out of it anyway. The world reappeared and molded itself into shapes and I could tell someone was sitting across from me. I concentrated on the face and the shape came into focus.

It was Aesal. He was smiling at me and sipping krem.

"You look like a man trying to find his way out of a shaha field."

I smiled back at him, "Glad to see you alive."

"You as well," he said and we both took a sip of krem.

"Here is to finding your way out of the shaha field," he said and raised his cup. We both laughed, but I made a point of grabbing my gru instead of the krem and we saluted each other and took our shots.

When I came out of it, he was looking at me with concern.

"How many have you had?"

"A few."

"The Void does not treat you well?"

I like to think I am a good setrak player with a good setrak face, but Aesal could always see straight through it. The day I could hide anything from him was the day I became the galaxy champion at Setrak.

"She struck a blow today," I admitted.

He pried more and I told him of the lost contract and what it would do to my year. Aesal was great at listening. No *haachee* advice like "things will get better" or "things are always darkest near the end of the wormhole." Sometimes life is just *haachee* and more *haachee*, and you work through it and maybe they get better or maybe they did not. But the survivors know not to live on platitudes or *haachee* quotes or hope for a better life. Every day you just keep going, keep walking, keep flying, keep working. Good, bad, neutral, it was all just life, nothing more, nothing less.

"What will you do?" he asked.

"Find more product." I shrugged. "Things got too easy and I got sloppy. So now I go back to work and build it back up."

"That is the Void," Aesal said and took a sip of krem.

I nodded and took one myself.

"I know you will not take one of my jobs so I will not offer," he said with a smirk.

I laughed.

"No, I am not that desperate yet."

Aesal looked down into his glass of krem and considered.

"Spit it out," I told him. "I know you too, Aesal. Let me hear it."

He smiled at me, hesitated and then picked up his second glass of gru.

"First this, then the question." He threw back his shot and I joined him.

It was long and dark this time; one of those long trips where you lose yourself in the euphoria. It took a while for the world to shift back into gray and then for mass to form and color to fade in. Aesal had plenty of time to sip his krem and collect his thoughts before asking me his big question.

I took a sip of the cold krem and noticed Edda had brought refills.

"I have a friend who would like to meet you."

"Meet *me*? Or someone like me to trade with?"

He hesitated.

"Both. He is not with the GF, but he does work with them, like me. He works with a variety of people and groups, buying and selling a large assortment of goods, including information."

"How does he know about me?"

"He says you have mutual friends. I suppose I am one of them. Maybe others? He does not say. He gives out less information than he takes in. He always has been that way. I have a feeling he works for someone else, but I have never been able to confirm who."

"And he asked to meet with me?"

"Yes. To be straight, he asked several weeks ago, but I did not think it would interest you."

"Why? Does it involve the GF?"

"He would not tell me what it was about. I do know he deals a great deal with the GF and I assumed it would switch you off."

"Is he exclusive to trading with GF groups?"

"No."

He took another sip of his krem and watched me over the cup.

"Do you trust him?" I asked.

He gave a slight shrug.

"I trust him to supply good product. I trust him to give me a fair deal. I trust his information. Beyond that?" He shrugged. "It is a business relationship. I trust him with business."

"What is his name? Who is he?"

"His name is Zhaji."

"I do not know a Zhaji."

"A human the size of a small starship. Once military of some type. If you had ever met him, you would remember."

"No. The name trips no alarms."

"If you have no interest, I will let him know. I do not know what the job is or the payout. I cannot vouch for it."

I took another sip of krem. It all sounded mysterious, and dangerous. This man knew me? But would not say how? It could be any number of things. I thought of Trask and wondered if this man worked for him. That was the worst-case scenario. But Trask had two decades and countless opportunities to seek me out and I had seen no sign of him. Regardless of the potential of a job though, or of the dangers of meeting this man, I was curious to meet him and find out why he was asking about me.

"What the hells," I said. "Set up a meet."

"Do not do this on my account. I brought it up because you are looking for something. I do not know if it is worth anything, and I do not vouch for what he is offering or even for your safety."

"If I get blasted, I will not hold it against you."

He laughed.

"To strange meetings then." He raised his gru up to me.
"To strange meetings and hidden fortunes."
We both drank our gru and slipped deeper into night.

ELEVEN

I WAS CAUTIOUS about the meeting with Aesal's contact. I was already on edge about dealing with a GF sympathizer. When the terms of the meeting came in, they set me on edge as well. There was no reason not to meet on a Station, but the contact insisted we meet out in the Void at specific coordinates, far away from any Station or Corporation. Aesal had reassured me this was how Zhaji did his business, but I did not like it. The kind of people that did business that way tended to be the worst kind of criminal elements; those for whom even Station rules were too restrictive.

It was a short one-day trip to the coordinates. Deep enough in the Void to avoid any Station trackers, but close enough to Nathara to make it somewhat convenient for me. I popped out of the wormhole a couple milipars outside the designated meeting place so I could get a read on things before jumping straight in. Scans showed a single ship at the correct spot, with no other ships showing on the system. I was early but Zhaji was already there.

I set the system to manual and headed toward the ship at a decent clip, giving myself just enough time to get a readout. It was a C2, same size as the *Sun*, with standard mods for a smuggler—hidden guns and improved defensive capabilities. It all seemed normal with nothing extravagant or suspicious.

I sent out the designated signal as I approached. That was another thing that set me on edge. Rather than just telling him who I was, he insisted that I send in a special code, like we were special agents on some secret mission. I did not like the situation.

Warning bells went off in the back of my mind, but I ignored them. I wanted to know who he was and why he was asking about me. If he had not been referred to me by Aesal I would not have gone. I shrugged off the concerns as I approached. If this man wanted me dead, there were easier ways.

I received his response to the code.

"All hyper-secret messages confirmed," I said. "Can we communicate like traders now?"

A deep and booming laugh came through the com system, "Yes. Apologies, Jlaeal. I have grown paranoid and use extravagant precautions. Docking specs coming to you now."

The specs arrived and I set the system to auto dock.

"I have not met outside of a Station in years," I told him.

"Yes. Again, apologies, but with all of the raids going on, I find it safer to do business outside of the Stations. I hope you understand."

"Sure," I responded, but I could not help rolling my eyes. This guy should be in a desk somewhere planetside, not making trades in the Void.

The *Sun* locked onto the other ship and our hatches sealed together. I loosened my gun in its holster and checked the primer before opening the hatch. I trusted Aesal and knew he would not send me into danger on purpose, but that did not mean I would go in naked.

The *Sun*'s hatch opened into the docking portal and the hatch to Zhaji's ship opened. Zhaji stood with arms out palm up in the sign of peace. I did the same. Zhaji was not the largest human I had ever seen, but he made the top three. He towered half a span over me and looked like he would barely fit through my hatchway. He was double my size and all muscle. I wondered if my gun could even punch through to hurt him.

"Come in. Welcome to *Shari's Fortune.*"

I stepped through his hatchway and locked wrists in greeting. My hand and arm looked like a child's grasped around his. His forearm felt like solid granite. We released our hold and he sealed the hatchway and led me deeper inside the ship.

"Aesal says good things about you," I said as he lumbered down a small hallway. He ducked through another hatchway into a large room.

"Aesal is a good man," he said.

He cleared the doorway so I could pass him and my breath caught. Trask was standing in the center of the lounging area.

My hand was on gun before I had time to think about it, tempted to pull, but I hesitated. Trask did not react. Zhaji walked past him as if nothing was going on and then dropped his bulk onto the couch to face me. Trask looked the same as he did twenty years ago. He was human, about my height, with thick white hair kept short, military style. He wore a crisp suit that looked like a mix between a military uniform and a business suit. He had the same *pada* black eye patch over his left eye he had twenty years ago.

No one knew how he lost the eye or why he never replaced it. The rumor I believed, was that he flew to a neighboring galaxy and disappeared for close to a decade. When he came back his hair had gone white, he'd lost an eye, and was inches away from death and insanity. He never discussed his past and his records were all gone. He was a mystery. But he was standing in front of me, unarmed.

"Good to see you alive, Jlaeal."

"Right."

Trask smiled. Any other person would have taken my lack of greeting as the insult it was intended, but Trask did not get emotional. I was of the opinion that he was a sociopath, without true emotion, but he had a disarming smile and charm you could not resist. I was frozen in place, undecided on whether to sit down and hear him out or blast him and run.

"You might as well stay and hear me out," he said, as if reading my mind.

He approached me with an arm outstretched. I did not take it.

I would not shoot him. I would hear him out. But I did not have to go through formalities with him either.

He let his arm fall and gave a wry smile. "It is good to see you," he said with a genuine-looking smile, and then turned away. "Sit down." He gestured to the other couch and sat down on a chair on the other side of the room.

I sat down and stared at him. I was tense from head to toe and could not take my hand from my weapon. He laughed. He and I both knew I would not pull on him. Part of his power was the mystery. I might get him. Or he might have someone else hiding with their gun trained on me or he might have a shield I could not detect. With Trask, you always assumed he was at least one step ahead, maybe three or four or a dozen.

"Jlaeal, you act like you have seen a ghost."

"Did Aesal know you were here?"

"No."

"Zhaji? That fly?"

"I doubt if Aesal even knows who Trask is."

"I apologize for surprising you like this," Trask said, "but I knew you would refuse to meet me otherwise. You have made your feelings about me clear."

"Yeah."

"I wanted to clear the air. I know there have been misunderstandings between us."

"Misunderstandings?!"

"Yes. I was disappointed in the termination of our relationship."

"Disappointed in the loss of the ship or that you lost a man trying to get it back?"

Trask cocked his head to the side. "He was not sent to get the ship."

"Like hells. He said you wanted the ship back and he was there to take it. I was fine giving him a simple no, until he went for his gun."

Trask blinked his one eye and looked down to the floor. This is as shocked as I had ever seen him. Trask had the best setrak face of anyone I had ever met. Not that he would ever play, but if he did, he would rule the market every time.

Trask was silent for a few beats.

"He was told to inform you that the ship was a gift for years of service and that I would like you to return."

Trask stared into my eyes with a fierce and hard determination. He was a lot of things, but he never lied to your face. He withheld information, he manipulated, he twisted, but he never outright lied.

"*Chee*," I said, shaking my head. How many years had gone by since that happened? How many years had I looked over my shoulder, worrying about the next hit?

"Zhaji. Can you give us a moment?"

"Sure, boss."

Zhaji struggled out of the couch and walked toward the cockpit. As soon as he was out of sight, I felt a buzzing and the hairs on my arms rose up.

"I just activated a sound disbursement device. Zhaji will not hear a thing."

"That comes in handy."

"Yes." He pulled out a very small device and looked at it. There were no buttons, no triggers. It was a simple ovoid piece of metal with no indication of being anything other than a keepsake. I assumed he triggered it with one of his internal biomechatronical systems. There were more biomechatronical parts in Trask's body than human parts. Those who knew him well speculated on how human he actually was. His advancements went way beyond biomechatronics and biosystem enhancements. He was a true cyborg, with a heart buried somewhere deep inside, and maybe a soul, but I was convinced he lost that years ago.

"Jlaeal, we had differences of opinion on a variety of matters, some of which were important, some of which were not, but you must know you were my favorite."

I laughed and shook my head in disbelief.

"When I found you, I was reminded so much of myself at that age; the fire, the tenacity, the intelligence."

"You were harder on me than any of your other recruits."

"True. I expected more."

"Listen, it is too late for any of this. I got a glimpse behind the hatchway. I saw you, Trask. I saw who you are - who you truly are. I spent the last twenty years looking over my shoulder, sure that another hit was on the way; or that some syndicate would get me, like they got Qodja and the others; maybe not for the ship, but at least to finish the job."

"I had no intentions of coming after you. Qodja was a different matter. I regret that you were involved in any of that. However, it was necessary."

"Sure. All part of the big purge, right?"

"There were elements inside the organization that were look-ing to take over. He was involved."

"*Haachee*! Qodja was a good man. He never betrayed anyone in his *pada* life! And you killed him! Him and Ctok and Rej and Klush and how many others, Trask? How many killed by syndicate thugs or pirates or smugglers? I have seen you, Trask. You play to our sympathies and claim to have our interests in heart, but I know your only interest is in helping yourself. You are greedy for power and manipulative and you are a killer. I want no part of you or any of your *haachee*!"

I did not intend to say it all, but it was bottled up for decades. I sat there spent, contemplating pulling the gun and taking a shot. He did not say anything. He looked at me and considered. Or maybe he was sifting through that cyber-brain of his and reading files or watching vids to see which of my friends he had killed.

We sat in silence for a while. I did not know whether to shoot him or try to get off the ship. If I thought I could get him, I would have gone for it, but it was Trask, and I doubted I could take him out without getting killed first.

"In spite of the past, I want you to consider working for me."

I meant to answer something, but it took me so off guard I just stared at him, unable to speak.

"I hear things have become difficult for you. I could cover the gap in income, in exchange for your services."

I stood up, enraged, taking a firm hold of my gun, no longer caring about the consequences.

"Did you hear anything I just said? You are lucky I do not clear this gun and blast you, much less work for you. The past is bad enough, with all of the friends you have killed, and now you want me to help you take over the Void and all the Stations? Should I help you kill more of my friends?"

Trask cocked his head again.

"Yeah. Word gets around. I know what you are up to with the Stations and the Void. Fuck you and fuck your plan."

"You do not know what you think you know."

"*Haachee*. Word is out."

"Jlaeal, I am doing what I am doing to protect the Stations from the Corporations."

I laughed. "Protecting the ones who pay you."

He shook his head. "I have not given the Corporations any information they did not already have. Those Stations I can protect, I do. The Corporations have spent a great deal of money and effort in creating spy networks within the Stations, with the intention of destroying them. I have spent as much time and effort convincing them that keeping the Stations under my protection, undamaged, is to their benefit. Keeping the Stations intact and independent fits with my long-range plans."

"Of course. More power. More control. More creds."

"It is necessary."

"You always said that. You make yourself out to be some altruistic hero, but you just want power. You are no different than the Corporations."

"Someone is always fighting for control. I do need control, but not for power's sake. I am trying to balance the scales."

"I did not come here to argue. In fact, I did not come here to talk to you at all."

I turned and began walking to the hatchway.

"If you ever change your mind, I will be waiting."

"Go to hells." I did not turn back.

"Safe travels, Jlaeal. Be careful."

I walked to the hatch and let myself out. I expected him to try to stop me, or Zhaji to come out and tackle me, but I reached the hatch and got back inside the *Sun* without a problem.

I released the coupling and eased the *Sun* away from Zhaji's ship – or maybe it was Trask's ship. Either way, light speed could not come quick enough. As soon as I was far enough away, I opened the wormhole and lit out.

I did not realize how tense I was until the hole opened up and I collapsed back in the seat and began to shake. I stumbled to the small galley and poured myself a shot of gru. I did not like to drink gru while in flight, but I needed it. I came out of it fast and poured another one and pounded it. When I came out of it, I felt relaxed enough and put the gru away.

I went to the rack and lay down and let my mind play out old memories and went through the conversation again and again. It was a very long trip back to Nathara.

TWELVE

I SENT A message to Aesal as soon as I lit in at Nathara. I did not give any details, but told him we needed to talk about the meeting when he returned to the Station. He was out on a run for another week or so, but I thought he should know who he was dealing with. I would not tell him everything about Trask, but certainly enough to warn him away.

I went through the security protocols with Nathara command, once again relieved that they had not been changed, and proceeded toward the dock. I guided the *Sun* through the cavernous opening and eased her to docking bay two. Traffic had increased since the last time I was there. Higher traffic could mean different things, but the more people who knew about a Station, the greater the risk of popping up on Corporate radar.

I landed the *Sun,* locked her up and headed straight to the Cavern. I did not even take my pack. I was spending a lot more time at the Cavern, but I had a lot to think about and that was always the place to do it. After the meeting with Trask, I had decided I should head planetside. Now was a bad time to do that, as the Corporations seemed to be cracking down more than usual, but I needed new product and that was the place to do it.

The Cavern had its familiar look and smell about it, but it was busier and louder. All the new and unfamiliar faces gave me guarded looks as I strode in, as if I was intruding on their turf rather than the reverse.

Edda was serving again and she treated me to a smile, which helped me forget the other grimaces. She wore tight black pants and a t-shirt with the sleeves cut off. The shirt was a bit large on her and the sleeve holes were cut out large enough to treat us to glimpses of the beauty inside. As she walked to the bar with a load of empties, I noticed her pants were near see-through and it made me like her even more.

There was a small table open near the back and Edda was there before I had even sat down.

"You look better today, friend."

"Do I?"

"Yep." She nodded.

"Maybe the shock has worn off," I said with a chuckle.

"Whatever it is, I like this Jlaeal better. Sad makes for ice but today you are *bacha*." In addition to being young, she was also planet city, using slang terms heard planetside in GC territory, but not in the Void.

"I was not handsome before?"

She laughed. It was a great laugh, natural and innocent.

"You'd always be *bacha*, but sad shines it away. A girl likes to see a man smile."

I laughed. She was delightful.

"Krem and gru? Or just krem tonight?"

"Both. I might eat too, but I need to take the edge off."

"I like your mod," she said with a wink while leaving the table. She kept the smile as she walked away. Some servers played it up and flirted at the table, but turned it off as soon as they left, melting the illusion. But she was either one of the good ones, who enjoyed her job and customers, or she enjoyed me as she claimed. She brought the drinks over right away and I decided to latch onto the fantasy that she enjoyed me.

"Icy cold and the good paya. Straight from Drakkara."

"Who brings it in for you?"

She shrugged. "That's Harvel's deal. I'm just here to be pleasurelike and bring drinks." She gave me one of her cheery smiles and winked.

"You do very well at both," I said and she giggled. I took a sip of the krem. It was *puda* cold and creamy. Every bar and tavern in the Void claimed to have real Drakkaran krem. Very few ever did, but the Cavern had the good stuff. I took another sip.

"*Puda* good," I told her.

"I know. I can only drink the Drakkaran paya."

I was about to invite her to join me for a drink when my old friend Sim approached behind her.

"Beware this man, young lady. He looks like a tasty aplom treat, but his bite is harsh and bitter."

I laughed and stood up. "Don't listen to this pirate."

We grasped wrists and he pulled me in for a hug. He was like Challa in that he liked to show his affection with touching and hugs. I did not prescribe to these social constraints, but if a friend insisted on them, I did not fight it.

Sim had dark-brown skin, black hair cut close to his head and a long beard. He always wore a big smile, like he had just heard some great joke. He was a pirate, but unlike Challa, he did not support a full-time crew. Challa went for multiple small-time plays, whereas Sim hired friends and people he trusted to partner with him on occasional big plays. He had a solid ship and a broad network of contacts he could partner with when a juicy target made an appearance.

"Gru and krem for your friend?" Edda asked me.

"Yes. Wait — you meeting someone or can you join me?"

"Of course I can join my good friend, Jlaeal."

She left to get the drinks, but turned around and said, "We can discuss the biting later." She turned around with a wink and walked back to the bar. I smiled and Sim laughed.

I was not sure why, but I had a tinge of guilt at flirting with Edda. I did not like the guilt and tried to push the feeling away along with thoughts of Renlii but it was no good. She was there and the guilt was there.

"I see your skills have not dissipated," he said.

I laughed, "How are you, Nyra? It has been a while."

I began calling him Nyra years ago as a dig. Nyra was an

infamous pirate that operated near Shilti centuries ago. He did fine for himself attacking Shiltian Royalty when they traveled off planet. The oppressed of the Shiltian populace did not care if a pirate robbed or even killed minor royalty, but one time, Nyra went too far and killed a very popular nephew of the King. The nephew was known for helping the poor and fighting for their cause. When Nyra killed him, the people demanded vengeance and the entire fleet hunted him down and killed him.

Like Nyra's attacks, Sim's jokes often went too far and pushed people into a fight. The second time I saw this happen I took to calling him Nyra. He loves a good joke and took it in stride.

"How is the salvage business?" I asked.

He gave me a sly grin. "Good. Always good. No matter how many times I take their ships, the Corporations send me more."

"I have not seen you for a while. Are you operating out of another section?"

"Off and on," he said. "I go where fortune goes."

"And fortune flies near Nathara now?"

"Some. I hear of a very nice Nallimar ship that they have tired of. It seems they are ready to gift it to me."

I chuckled. "Some day, I would like to know how you hear about these things."

"It is the Void. She loves me. She whispers sweet messages about this convoy or that convoy or a random ship separated from her fleet and tells me 'that one is yours, my love.'"

"She does, huh? You sure there are no contacts in some Corporate freight mapping center who loves you?"

He took on a sudden look as if I had insulted his family line. "Of course not. It is the Void. Bless her. She loves me."

"Fine. Fine," I said with a laugh.

Edda arrived at the table with cold krem for Sim, along with three more grus.

"This'll save me a trip," she said with a smile.

We laughed as she walked away. I picked up my gru and raised it to him. "To the blessed Void."

He smiled and raised his gru.

"May she never stop sending you gifts," I told him.

"Yes, my friend. To the lovely Void."

We saluted one another and drank it down, slipping into the dark and alluring abyss. The blackout was quick, but enjoyable. The first couple of grus set the stage for the rest and were always far too short, but the more you had, the longer the black numbness lasted, until the shots brought you into complete darkness and oblivion, where nothing ever bothered you or brought you harm.

I came out of it and took a sip of the cold krem. Sim looked at the next shot of gru and looked at me with a look and we both laughed. Without saying a word, we both grabbed our gru and slammed them down and slipped back into the nothing. It was nothing for a brief time and I enjoyed the peace of it and came out too soon and took a long pull of the krem.

"How are you, Jlaeal?" he asked. "I hear you are seeking whispers yourself, looking to build new routes."

"Who did you hear that from?"

"Friends. They said you had a couple of spots to fill."

I nodded and looked into the brew and then laughed.

"You could say that."

"Bad?"

I nodded. "Things happen that way. You know this. Things get bad, then we climb back up and they get good again."

"Are you in a tight spot?"

"No. Not tight. I have enough saved to get me through it."

"Well, I might have something for you. Something to add to your coffers? Extend the safety net?"

"Shipping?" I asked. "Or salvage? You know I do not do salvage."

"Sometimes you do what you have to do," he told me. "Would you like to hear of it before turning it down?"

I shrugged. "What the hells."

He explained the job to me over more krem. It was straightforward as far as pirating was concerned; a shipment of low-grade products from Fillonia to Sargenta with a stop between at a nearby mining operation on an isolated moon. The ship had some armaments and basic defenses, but no escort.

"If I did salvage work I might be interested, but you know that is not how I operate."

As a good salesman, he nodded and did not push, choosing to take another sip of krem instead. I could not help myself and asked another question of him.

"Where do you hit it?"

"As soon as it lights in. The actual mining operation sits deep inside an asteroid field. The field is large enough that wormholes are impossible anywhere close to the operation. The flight time from the mine to where ships light in is about thirty sets."

"Thirty sets — ?" That was more than enough time.

"Yes," he said with a smile and took a pull from his krem.

"What is the security situation? In-system Stations? Drones? Fighters? Gun placements?"

"They keep a couple of class three cruisers, a few fighters, dozen drones." I raised my eyebrows and took a slow sip. That was heavy security. No way I was going into that.

"But listen," he said. "The cruisers and fighters stay close to the mining operation, which is surrounded by millions of asteroids. The drones patrol the outer edge, but there are not enough to be any real threat. So we light in, take out any drones and wait at the edge of the field. When the ship arrives, we pounce."

"And make off with — what size did you say it was?"

"The cargo ship is a 3B, about ten thousand box capacity."

"That's a lot of low grade."

Sim smiled at me. "Listen, Jlaeal. The cargo makes no difference. We are after the ship."

"You have a buyer?"

"Yes. Always. I have a crew lined up to operate the ship and fly it to the buyer. I just need another fighter for escort."

I asked a few more details about the crew and the mission and he seemed to have all the angles covered.

"What would be my share?" I asked, not believing I was pursuing the conversation.

"Ten percent of the profit."

I looked him in the eye and tried not to scowl. With everything I would put on the line, ten sounded very low.

"Ten is a good number," he said. "I obtained the intel and it is not free. After, splitting with my source and then with you and the rest of the crew, I receive twenty."

"I thought the Void whispered in your ear."

He laughed. "Yes, but she speaks through friends who take a percentage."

"What about the *Sun*? Damage? Use? Supplies? That come out of the pot or my share?"

"You get ten percent of profits. We pay for all costs related to my ship and your ship first and then we split the rest according to prearranged percentages."

I paused to take a drink. I was no pirate. Smuggling was one thing, but piracy could go bad quick, even with a solid plan. I did not want to go down this path. But then again, one good haul could buy me extra time to rebuild everything.

"What about your normal people?"

He shook his head. "You know I do not have normal people. Things are very dangerous these days. I trust all of the people I use, but it is better to limit that trust, no?"

I shrugged. Everyone had their rules. I would have operated more like Challa, but Sim's method had worked for him a long time.

"Jlaeal, you need this and I need a good fighter with a good ship. Why do you hesitate?"

"Smuggling is one thing," I told him. "Piracy is another. If I have to fight or battle, then I am already in trouble. You are looking for a fight, seeking out trouble. They are two different things."

I had no problems with pirates or my friends that did the

work, but I did not want to be one. The risk was too high. Just thinking about it twisted me up inside.

"The Void has offered you a gift. Do not slap her hands away."

I let out a smirk.

"This is easy creds. A one shot. Enough to give you more creds and buy you time to build new routes the way you want to without pressure."

I knew he was right. In spite of the increased risk, Sim had a good history of taking the smart bets. He had worked the same way for as long as I have smuggled and he had never even had a close call. I thought of the creds and the time it would buy me. He was professional and good and did not take unnecessary risks, and he kept his word, which was of key importance. My gut told me no, but it was too good to pass up.

I let out a deep sigh. I knew I might regret it, but he was right. Sometimes you had to make the bold move to make the big *jecha*.

"To the Void," I said.

"And her many gifts," he said with a big smile.

We slammed our shots and dropped into a long and deep oblivion.

THIRTEEN

I MET UP with Sim and his crew down at the dock the next morning. Sim's ship, the *Arasmus*, was a very old ship which had gone through ages of updates and rebuilds. It was once a TriKarre pleasure cruiser, but was modified for combat and cargo storage. She was the perfect fit for Sim. It retained the look and feel of a pleasure craft on the outside, with sleek lines and multiple viewing ports for viewing the wide expanses of the Void, but hidden underneath the slick exterior were gun ports and heavy armor and powerful shielding. A cargo vessel would mistake the ship as a pleasure craft until it was scanned or until they were fired upon. Inside the *Arasmus*, the pleasurable elements were removed in favor of cargo space or rack space for combat crews.

We were in what was once a game room. Sim had left the gaming tables and kept its thick plush carpet and posters that replayed scenes from old holos and vid systems that replayed sporting games. But the room also had equipment for battle planning. We sat down around a large round holo table, while Sim shut down the games. A holo of the target asteroid field appeared over the table.

The crew he hired was a five-person Shiltian combat squad. They were average height and size for Shiltians, which was about half my height, but they had the look of hardened warriors. I knew from history and past experiences not to underestimate a Shiltian. They once ruled over a large section of the galaxy, and it was not through peaceful methods. They were known for their fierce intelligence and their incomparable knack for strategy in battle. This group had the look of Division H types from Shelarkers, Inc. Each of them wore a Meek skullcap and black flex body armor and lethal-looking weapons special built for their size.

Less than a decade ago, Shelarkers, Inc. was the largest Corporation in the galaxy. They were on course to take over the galaxy, but produced too many of their own creds in a last push for power. This created a massive devaluation of the creds and spiraling inflation and other internal problems. They had to stop their production of warships to focus on stopping the riots and unrest in their own territories. By the time they had everything settled, they found themselves outgunned and overmatched by the competition.

When Shelarkers, Inc. dissolved, the remnants of their forces scattered throughout the galaxy and became guns for hire. Shelarker combat troops were some of the toughest in the galaxy, known for their cold efficiency and lust for battle. Division H was their elite combat division, specializing in industrial espionage and black ops. I would have to ask Sim later how he ran into this bunch.

"Have you worked with Sim before?" I asked Jike, their leader.

"Yes."

"How many times? Sim?"

"Several times," said Sim. "They are the best."

Jike did not show any appreciation to Sim's compliment.

"Enough," Jike said. "We go over operation." Jike had a voice like gravel, deep and as rough as he was.

"Sure," I said.

Sim went over the plan twice. The first time, Jike listened all the way through without saying a word. The second time, he asked a deluge of questions about timing, placement and other specific details, showing a complete understanding of the entire operation. All I had to do was take out the cargo vessel's weapons and watch for Nallimar security. After we all felt that we knew the plan thoroughly, Jike left with his crew and Sim walked me to the main hatchway.

"You feel good about all this?" I asked Sim again.

He laughed. "Yes, my friend. You worry far too much. Everything will be great. You were the final piece to make this operation perfect."

"Fine. Fine. Are you coming to the Cavern?"

"Not tonight. I am superstitious and have always stayed in my ship the night before a mission."

"I was not inviting you out for a sleep over. Just dinner."

He laughed a big hearty laugh.

"Thank you, my friend. I will eat here and hit the rack early and will leave refreshed in the morning."

I patted him on the shoulder and stepped out of the hatchway, spotting the *Sh'kurah Nuilla* on the other side of the flight deck. It was not there when I arrived. Challa's team must have lit in while we were going over the plan. I crossed the deck to Challa's ship and noticed new scorch marks across the bow. Bentook was on the far side of the ship doing a final inspection.

"Bentook!"

She looked up from the panel she was inspecting and gave me a smile, "Jlaeal. You old coopli! How're tra'es?"

"Fine. When did you arrive?"

"Not long ago. They left me here to lock her up and give'r a quick lookover. They left for the Cavern for a 'rink. Much news, Jlaeal. Much news."

"See you there then."

I slapped her on her shoulder with a smile, then strode past the long line of ships, out of the main deck and into the main hallway. I pushed my way through the crowds of people in the hall and made my way to the Cavern. It was always a thrill to see my old friend Challa, but now I was just as excited to see Renlii.

I heard Challa's booming laugh before I even rounded the corner. Challa, and the rest of his crew, were sitting at a large table near the entrance, already a few drinks down. Challa stood up to wave me over with a beaming smile.

"Jlaeal, my good friend. Sit. Sit."

I walked over to the table and we clasped each other's shoulders in greeting and he pointed to a seat between him and Renlii. She had a smile for me as I sat down and she did not hide the hunger and fire in her eyes. Her smile was radiant and I could not contain my excitement either. I gave her a long kiss in greeting. Her lips were soft and moist and felt perfect and the rest of the room disappeared.

"Will you be leaving us for your rooms or will you stay for drink and food?" Challa asked.

Without breaking off from our kiss, Renlii and I both raised our hands up to Challa in a rude gesture. He and his crew laughed.

"Even better. I have not seen a live pleasure show in a long time. Let us clear the table for them."

Laughing, Renlii and I broke apart. The rest of the crew was laughing harder than we were.

"Alright, you pirates," I said.

Edda arrived at the table with more gru and krem for the table, including a set for me.

"Jlaeal. Food tonight? Or just drinks?" Her flirting was toned down, I assumed because of the long kiss. I was sure everyone in the bar had seen it. Edda looked damn good, but I only had eyes for Renlii.

"Are you eating?" Challa asked.

"Yes. We have ordered already."

"Good. Grontok steak then, bloody, with grilled finla stems. Thank you, Edda."

Edda walked away and I faced the group again, holding up my gru. "To being alive."

"To being alive," each of them said and we slammed the gru and entered the darkness. I came out of it before they did and took a sip of krem while waiting.

"How was the hunt?" I asked when they came out of it.

"The hunt grows more difficult," Challa said. "Fewer Corporate ships are unguarded. We have less intel. The web tightens."

His crew nodded in agreement.

"Have you heard the latest?" Challa asked.

"I have heard much."

"This is a rumor, but I have heard Captain Asa turned down an offer from Trask."

After hearing about Trask, I had brought him up to Challa and he had heard similar stories. I did not break the trust with Finael and kept my source private, but I did share the details with him. It seemed unnecessary though, as the stories were widespread and travelers across the Void spoke in the open about working with Trask or buying or selling intel to his company.

Challa and I both felt it best to stay away from Trask and the *pada* Universal Intelligence. We did not like the way things were heading, but that had nothing to do with anything. Things rarely went the way we would like them to in the Void. The news of Asa was troubling though. She was captain of Nathara and if she turned Trask down, Nathara could be hit at any time.

"When was this?" I asked.

Challa shrugged. "Who knows for sure. I heard it moments ago, from a reliable source. He acted as if it was new."

"What will you do?" I asked him, glancing at Renlii, who had on her setrak face. She was very good at that. Alone, I could read her well enough, but in public, you could never read anything about her.

"We will move on," Challa said. "Any Station that turns Trask down has a visit from a Corporation. You know this."

"Yes. I know this," I said and took a long pull of krem.

"We are going to a base called Demisha. You know it?" he asked.

"Yes, I know it."

"Captain Blitil has not been approached by Trask and is still independent."

"Damn." I understood his move and thought it wise, but Demisha was far away and I would see them all much less.

"Come with us," Challa said. Renlii squeezed my leg under the table.

"I have no contacts there," I said, but it was half hearted. I knew I would have to go as well. It was too soon for me to make that commitment. Especially after the recent setback.

"*Haachee*," Renlii said. "There are contacts everywhere. One independent Station is as good as the next. Nathara will be hit soon. Time to move on."

I looked down at my krem and knew they were right.

"I have a job I need to do first and then maybe I will follow you there," I said.

"Good, my friend. Follow us," Challa said with a smile. Renlii gave me a smile along with the rest of the crew.

"Why are you sad then?" Renlii asked. "Demisha is a good Station."

"I like this Station," I told her, and then realized I was bringing things down. I gave them all a smile and raised my glass of krem and said, "Fuck Trask."

They all laughed a little and said "Fuck Trask" and drank with me, but then Renlii said, "Yes, fuck Trask, but this is the Void. You change and you survive."

"Yes," Challa agreed. "That is the way. You know this."

"I know this."

Edda arrived with our food and then Bentook arrived. We ate and drank our krem and tried to forget about the move and what would be next. They were all very positive about the future, but it did not have the feeling of true emotion. I could feel the uncertainty and I did not know when I could join them.

They asked me about the job and I told them I was leaving in the morning without giving too many details. As I told them a few basics, the reality of the mission hit me and I could tell they all felt the same. They were pirates as well, but there was more certainty when working with the same group. They trusted Challa and trusted each other and with few exceptions, they had good intel.

I regretted that I had agreed to the job. I had not thought it through and did not trust my instincts. But I was committed now, and if I backed out it would put Sim in a very bad position; and aside from that, you did not ever back out of a deal once the plans were revealed and you committed to it. They would have to scrap the whole project and I would lose a friend.

Throughout the meal, Renlii and I stole glances at one another and all I could think of was that I might never see her again. As soon as we finished eating, we had another gru and faded to the darkness again. When we got out of it, I took Renlii's hand and stood up.

"My friends, I am stealing your crew member. I will have her back to you by morning."

"We are flying out tomorrow as well, Jlaeal. Do not wear her out," Challa said as the others laughed.

Renlii gave Challa a half kidding glare. "You are just jealous that he will spend the night with me, while you all spend the night with a cheap haven girl or with your hands."

Challa laughed with the crew. "Maybe I will get two haven girls and Jlaeal will be jealous of me."

Renlii just laughed as she pulled me by the hand and sauntered out of the Cavern with a stride and confidence no other woman could match. She did not need to reply as they all knew there was no match for her. They had other comments, but I did not hear them. I was focused on her and the feeling of her hand in mine and her smell and her confident smile.

We still held hands as we walked in silence down the hall toward my apartment. With other women I noticed the musty smell of the rock walls and the dirty floors and the people who walked by as we walked through the halls, but with Renlii, all I saw and smelled and thought of was her. Her scent was intoxicating and I felt the warmth and strength of her hand in mine and felt the calm confidence radiating off of her. I caressed the back of her hand with my thumb.

"You are anxious over your mission," she said.

"I am not a pirate. I have a bad feeling."

"Then you should abort."

"Too late."

"You can always abort."

"He has given me his plans and is counting on me. The whole thing falls apart if I back out now."

"You can always abort."

"I gave my word."

That ended the discussion. We were just getting to know each other, but she knew me well enough to know how much truth mattered. Others could lie and back out of a deal, but I did not and I did not trust those who did. If I drank too much gru one night and agreed to partner with the *Kahja* himself, I would do it. Words matter and honor mattered, whatever the cost.

I thought about what she said. She could see straight through to my keel. The mission made sense at the time. Sim had come when I was weak with worry about my finances and future, but I had never done any pirating and it worried me to the edge of sickness. But, I had given my word and he was relying on me. I could not back out now.

"Jlaeal, my love, you are a fool. A good man and a good friend, but a fool. You stick your neck out for friends and you fall in love."

She did not look at me, and there was no question in her voice. It was a statement and she was right and we both knew it.

"Yes. I am a fool."

We continued walking through the hallways, hand in hand, passing through the mass of people, alone in the Void together. The walk from the Cavern to the apartment for passion is always a long one, with thoughts of what is happening and how it will happen, but this walk with Renlii took no time at all. I knew there were people around, but I saw none of them. There was her and there was me. It was us and it was tonight.

Tomorrow I would leave on my mission with no idea of how it would go and no plans on where to go afterward and she would leave for her mission and go on to another Station. But tomorrow was tomorrow and I would deal with that when it arrived.

We stepped up to my apartment door, and I looked into Ren-lii's eyes and all thoughts of tomorrow disappeared. I only had thoughts of her and tonight. I pressed my palm against the pad and the door whisked open and we stepped inside. The door sealed behind us and I took her head in my hands and pressed her lips against mine. She stopped after a while and held me close, resting her head on my shoulder.

I held her tight against me and breathed in the smell of her hair and felt the firmness of her back and the softness of her breasts pushing against me through our clothes. We stood there for a moment without saying a word, feeling each other breathe in and out, and then she raised her head and kissed me.

The kissing turned to a hungry stripping of clothes and touching and a long sleepless night of pleasure. Both of us knew we might never see each other again and did not want to waste a moment in sleep.

After several hours, we lay in the bunk naked and sweaty and out of breath. I was on my back, with her head on my chest and her naked breasts on my belly and her legs wrapped around mine. I stroked one of her arms and her sweaty back and smelled the sweetness of her hair.

"I love this," she whispered.

"I know," I said. "I do too."

"And tomorrow?"

"Do not think of it."

We were both silent again, getting our breath back and enjoying the moment.

"What about tomorrow?" she asked.

"Fuck tomorrow," I told her.

"Fuck tomorrow," she agreed.

I kissed her head and squeezed her.

"And the day after?" she asked.

"Fuck that too."

"No," she said. "When do I see you again?"

I thought of empty promises I could give her, but she would know better. She was not a haven girl to believe whatever *haachee* you told her. She was not one of those girls made for beauty and fun and nothing else. She was smart, smarter than I was, and she knew the way the Void worked and all its ugliness.

"Truth?" I asked.

"Always."

"If both of our missions go well, then I will be here and you will be at Demisha."

"You will stay here?" I felt her tense up a little.

I sighed. *Pada* Trask. The entire Void was in upheaval, and he was at the center of it all, like one of those *pudak* helino spiders. The ones the size of small fighters and moved into large caves and took them over.

"No," I told her. "I will leave after this mission."

"And go to Demisha?"

"If I live, I will meet you there."

She could sense the resignation in my voice. For some reason, I had little confidence in surviving the coming mission. It was all mapped out and settled, but it did not feel right and I never should have agreed to it.

We lay there for a while longer and she raised her head to look at me with her blue black eyes that seemed like an infinite pool of deep water and said, "fuck tomorrow," and she kissed me harder with more passion than she had before.

The room disappeared.

The Station disappeared.

The entire Void disappeared and with it tomorrow and we made love until it was time for us to get up and leave for our missions.

FOURTEEN

A s soon as I lit out the next morning, I crawled into my
rack and slept, but it was fitful sleep, restless and full of waking. After several hours of tossing and turning I gave up and took
a cleanse. I spent the next two days checking through all the systems and making minor repairs, but nothing could get my mind
off the night with Renlii or what would happen at the end of the
wormhole.

I was in a foul mood after leaving Renlii. We had said our
goodbyes at my apartment, neither of us wanting to do it at the
dock. The dock was a place for business, not tearful farewells.
Such things were bad luck.

Instead, we stood at the hatchway for a long time, with my gear
piled at our feet while we held each other. I gave her one last long
kiss before opening the hatch and walking toward the dock. She
walked the opposite direction. I did not look back. That would
also have been bad luck.

I walked through the crowded hallways and tried to clear my
head and get down to business. The job ahead was bad enough
without thoughts of a woman corrupting my thoughts.

Sim and his crew were waiting for me. We went over the plan
one more time. I tried to be cool and professional, but was terser
than usual because of the stress of it all. I think this put Sim on
edge and he kept glancing at me during the meeting, but I assured
him it was fine. After the meeting, we climbed in our ships and
flew out of the dock into the Void and lit out.

I sat in the *Sun*'s cockpit looking at the vidscreen, watching the swirling mass of the wormhole and thinking about the mission. We did everything we could to make the plan tight and complete. Sim assured us that the intel was good. His crew seemed professional. There was nothing else to be done but to fly the mission. It would be fine and we would make it back, or if we did not make it back, we had at least done everything possible to hold a good accounting of ourselves.

I scanned the *Sun*'s system for glitches and everything checked out. We had moments to go before the mission began. I was tense, but not just from the mission. It was the mission and Renlii and Trask and everything else.

The Void was always filled with risk and solitude and death, even when the Galactic Federation was around, but there were fewer Stations then and the dangers were less. The GF would arrest you or confiscate your goods, but they would never kill or enslave you. The Void grew more dangerous after the Fall, but it was still better than the alternative. If you did not take your chances in the Void, then you lived in Corporate territory, following their rules and restrictions, surviving in a world where skill and talent matter far less than politics or bribes. Of course, that was just life in GalactiCorp.

TriKarre was far worse, living under similar rules, but with the additional strictures of the religion of Trill. Although Drakkarans viewed humans as lower than themselves, Trill saw all beings as worthy, so Drakkarans still treated other peoples with respect and patience.

Living under Nallimar was far worse than any other option though. They despised anyone who was not a *pada* Fillonian and treated all other beings as fodder for the Kahja.

In truth, all the Corporations were *haachee* and in spite of the hardships, the Void was the single place left to live with any real dignity. But now Trask had put his chips on the table and got into the game and it was fouling the Void. What he had accomplished with the Corporations was a miracle of subterfuge. The Corporations did not even want the other Corps to exist, much less a company whose sole purpose was buying and selling intel on them.

As I sat thinking about how he gained leverage over the Corporations, the answer became obvious. I had not thought about it much before, but knowing Trask and what he did, it would be easy for him to gain control over them. Corps were run by people, and powerful individuals would do anything to keep their own secret information from getting out into the public, even to the point of making a deal with the Kahja.

Trask probably had information on the CEOs and the Board Members and threatened to release that information. He was blackmailing the people, not the Corporations. I was also sure that he was selling information about one Corporation to another Corporation, information that they did not already have but needed, making his operation a net positive in the viewpoint of the Corporations, rather than a negative. It was a dangerous game he was playing, and at some point one of the Corporations, or one of the CEOs, would decide that the cost of dealing with Trask outweighed the benefits.

In the meantime, we had to deal with all the *haachee* Trask was creating. Stations had always been raided by Corporate Fleets, but it used to be a rare occurrence. Up until the past year, the Corporations were so busy fighting among themselves that they spent little time or effort on cleaning up the Void or fighting against smuggling or piracy. Now that the Corporations had peace deals with each other, more and more Stations were being wiped out, as if a net had been thrown over the Void and was being drawn closed.

I thought back to the time I worked for Trask, back before the Liquidation. My primary job was spying on the other smugglers and syndicates and pirates and anything else off book out in the Void. Trask was fair enough and treated me well and even treated those he captured well. He knew smugglers did not do much harm to the GF. What he was really looking for was intel on people or groups looking to harm the government.

I had no problem with Trask then, but as the GF fell, he had a harder time maintaining the illusion. He was fair in some ways and seemed to take care of his own, but when I found out he actually controlled the crime syndicates, I realized he was not what I thought he was. He was darker. More frightening.

As the GF fell apart, Trask somehow kept his network together. He seemed to be the one man in the galaxy with hard currency to trade and pay his people with. But our jobs within the organization changed as the galaxy spun into chaos. I was sure now that the other spies were sent across the galaxy to infiltrate fledgling governments and Corporations as they began to expand their power. Those of us stationed in the Void were just kept there.

At the end of my time with him, Trask seemed to be more and more concerned with the syndicates and sent me on a few missions to get intel on them. On the last mission, my partner was killed by one of them. I found out later they were doing this on orders from Trask. This is when I realized how Trask viewed the galaxy, as one big game of Empires and my friends and I were just chonns. My friend was a chonn, sacrificed to kill a huicha or shiva, not even a king or queen.

I confronted Trask about it and he admitted to it, claiming it was necessary for the good of the galaxy. He tried to convince me it was all for the GF and his plans to revive it. But I was never a patriot, and when the Fall began I was not surprised by the corruption or the reaction to it. I was not about to stick my neck out for the GF after the fall. And as much as Trask said otherwise, it all appeared as if all his talk of helping the GF was *haachee* and his real plans were for power.

It was the worst time to have met Renlii. There was never a good time for that kind of thing in the Void, but the timing was very bad, with the Corps raiding Stations at every corner and a resurgent Trask gathering Stations like a kid collecting toys.

Fuck Trask and fuck the Corporations and fuck love. They were all like roaming Divoriian trenkas, looking to chew up any living thing in their path. I stopped my line of thinking and realized I had used the word love. It had popped into my head and I knew I was in the deepest of piles of *haachee*.

The control panel and vidscreen flashed red, letting me know I was sets away from lighting in. My gut tightened and I forced myself into easy breaths as I set the system to arm weapons and flip shields to full as soon as the ship lit in. Sim's intel stated that nothing but drones would be nearby, but things did not always go to plan. I powered up the enviro shield on my flight suit, locked myself in and prepared for battle.

As soon as the *Sun* dropped out of the wormhole all the hells broke loose.

Alarms went wild with proximity warnings as energy weapons pelted the shields and missiles headed in. I flipped down seventy-five degrees and set the system for auto heavy evasive maneuvers and locked the weapons on auto while I tried to figure out what the hells was going on. The system started firing off anti-missile drones, energy displacement pods and chaff, but the amount of firepower headed my way was nearly overloading it.

I glanced at the sensor screen and my heart leaped out of my chest. At a quick count, there was a Nallimar medium cruiser, ten fighters and about twenty drones. I caught a glimpse of Sim's ship dodging missiles and energy fire and was glad to see he was still alive.

I must have come out first, as the bulk of the fighters and drones were right on my ass. My defensive system was a Galacti-Corp PK155, upgraded and modified for defense, with improvements to shielding and weapon power. It was one of the more efficient targeting systems in the galaxy, but it was on the verge of collapsing. No missiles had blasted through yet, but the *Sun* was taking one hell of a beating from all the energy blasts.

"Sim. We have to get the hells away from that cruiser!"

By instinct, I had fled from the cruiser and Sim had done the same. It would have been smarter to split up, but Sim chose to fight together. The cruiser was charging after both of us spewing missiles, but held back on the energy weapons so it would not hit her own fighters and drones.

"Lead the way," he said.

I flipped the *Sun* up and back toward the cruiser to catch them all off guard. My targeting system fired missiles at three separate fighters, and my energy weapons took out several drones. My shields were down to about forty-five percent already. The maneuver did not fool any of them and they stayed close on me as I raced toward the cruiser.

The *Sun* was a *pada* good ship and fast and did not slow much in the turn. It was not long before I raced past the hulking cruiser, taking a pounding from a blinding flurry of energy blasts. The fighters and drones were right behind me, but it would take a while for the cruiser to turn around to follow. The big cruisers were not made for quick maneuverability.

I flew erratic as the cruiser fired off its rear blasters and the other ships fired everything they had. My system took out two more drones and fired another missile at a fighter. Two of the missiles had reached their targets, but I was still up against four fighters and who the hells knew how many drones.

None of them were a match for the *Sun* one on one, but it was just a matter of time before they took me down by sheer numbers. My shields were down to eighteen percent. I checked the sensors and saw that Sim was still right behind me, dealing with his own problems, but the cruiser was far behind us now and her weapons out of reach.

The *Sun* took out two more fighters with a missile and beam combo, but there were still two fighters chasing me and at least ten drones. If I was at full power I would have felt better about the situation, but the shields were down to less than ten percent. I hit the brakes and flipped the ship straight up and flipped around in a big circle and maneuvered back behind them, giving the system a clean line of sight to take out a few more drones. She fired another missile and took out one more fighter.

My shields were almost gone. It would be *pada* close. I followed behind the last fighter while my system targeted the last of the drones. I had one missile left in the hopper. The system lined it up for the last fighter.

I started to think I had a chance at making it out of the *chee*.

That was the last thing I thought before a missile broke through the chaff.

The *Sun* ejected me into the Void through a fireball of gas and fire and metal.

Everything cut to black.

FIFTEEN

IRST THERE WAS pain; mind-crushing pain. I could not
scream. I could not move. Red angry colors swam before my
eyes and blended into a swirling motion of agony. I heard distant
voices, as if I was submerged in a lake of water and they were far
away on the shore. I tried to fight through the madness; tried to
focus on shapes and words. The colors began to take form. The
voices grew less muffled. They had a familiar sound to them. I felt
hard hands and then movement, but the world exploded back
into a madness of color and pain and fused into a living creature
that tried to devour me. Just before he took me, something was
placed over my face and the beast and the colors faded and the
safe dark abyss returned.

I floated in endless black, as if I had too much gru and was stuck
in the darkness of the Void. I heard a muffled voice. It was Sim.
He was panicked and I could not understand him.

I realized he was speaking about me and I tried to break
through the darkness. I tried to open my eyes, but it was no good.
I tried to speak, but my mouth would not work. They tried to
move me and an explosion of white pain shattered the darkness
and I let out a scream, but the scream in my head came out as
a faint moan. I heard my name and tried to focus through the
bright light to the voice. A shadow broke through the light and
then there was another shadow.

"Jlaeal, we are on Nathara. Everything will be fine." It was Sim. Then he said, "Do you have anything for the pain?"

Another voice said, "Yes."

And then the darkness came again.

I woke up in blackness again, but there was less pain and confusion to fight through. I did not try to open my eyes. Instead, I enjoyed the stillness of the dark. It felt as though I was lying on a soft rack. There was a solid chirping and voices spoke medical-sounding words, but I could not understand them. I rose out of it enough to begin thinking about where I was and what had happened.

I struggled through the fog of memories and came to the end of them and the battle with Nallimar. I thought of the fighters and the drones and the Cruiser. The memories stopped when a missile broke through the *Sun's* defenses. I clenched my eyes and tried to breathe, but breathing hurt too much and now there was other pain in knowing the *Sun* was gone.

I tried to open my eyes, but the light was too bright and painful. I opened them a little more and light became shadow. I fought to blink away the cobwebs and the shadows coalesced into figures and shapes. I blinked more and willed away the mist and the shapes took form.

I was in a gray lifeless room. Two people stood in a corner speaking in hushed tones. They mentioned a leg and then something else. They approached and I blinked more and they solidified into human women. They wore blue uniforms and I realized they were meds. One of them was talking to me. I could not make out what she was saying and tried to read her lips. She was an older human, with graying, short cropped hair and natural age lines.

"-your leg," I made out.

"What?" is what I tried to say, but it came out garbled. My lips would not work right. My mind told them what to do, but they acted as if they had been drinking. The older woman said something to the other younger woman. The younger woman brought an air syringe injected something into my arm, and then everything came into better focus and I could hear and understand what they were saying.

"Jlaeal, can you hear me? Can you understand?" asked the older woman.

"Yes."

"You are in the Nathara med bay. You have suffered multiple injuries from an explosion on your ship."

"My ship?"

She just shook her head. "Your friend said he left you a message giving details of the incident. After we discuss your options, we will bring you a com unit."

Although I could understand what she was saying, my mind struggled to keep up with the actual meaning. I was stuck on the one word she said. "Options?" I asked.

"We have repaired the superficial cuts and lacerations. One of your eyes was damaged, but we were able to save it. Your vision should be near one hundred percent by tomorrow. You had a gaping wound in your stomach and internal bleeding when you came in. Your friend was smart enough to put you in frozen stasis right after the injury and was able to close the wound. It will take another day to heal completely."

My awareness improved as she went through the list of injuries and I could sense her building up to something.

"The hand and the leg require more work, and we need to discuss your alternatives."

"My hand and leg?" I asked, knowing with some dread what she would say. I looked down as she talked, but everything from the chest down was covered by a blue sheet.

"Your right hand and the majority of your right leg were lost in the explosion."

I should have cried out or screamed or reacted somehow, but there was nothing. It could have been shock, or a side effect of whatever it was they pumped into my system, but I was numb as I lifted my right arm away from the covers. There was no hand. The arm just ended in a stub, wrapped in a clear material, filled with some kind of liquid.

"Your right hand was incinerated. We dressed the end of it and put it in stasis fluid until we could discuss it with you. You have lost your right leg as well. We have dressed and wrapped the ending in stasis fluid until you decide what you would like to do."

I closed my eyes and tried to process it all. No ship. No hand. No leg. I knew what she was getting at, but I did not want to think about any of it.

"We have several possibilities for you, but the cost and times of repair vary, as do the ultimate results."

"What is the cost," I said. "Wait. How much do I owe now?"

"Your friend left enough creds to pay for the procedures already performed and for your stay here for another two days."

At least there was that. No ship, one eye, one hand and one leg. I should have listened to my gut. I knew better than to ignore my instincts and they told me the mission would be *haachee*. And now everything was *haachee*.

"The first option, often preferred by most patients because of the speed of repair, is biomechatronic replacements. Artificial versions of your hand and leg would be near mirror images of your natural ones. This can be done expeditiously and with varying levels of performance, ranging from less than the natural appendages to an enormous enhancement of performance over your naturals."

"How quick? How much?"

"The procedure to replace each limb would be two hours, with full functionality within a day, but rehabilitation and retraining can take weeks."

"And the cost?"

She broke down all the variations on the artificial limbs and went over the possibility of regenerating my old limbs. I have always preferred regenerated limbs, even compared to enhanced limbs. Challa used to make fun of me for preferring natural limbs, but no matter how good the artificial ones are, they are still machines and require maintenance and repairs and constant software upgrades and other considerations, while, if I regenerated my leg, it would always be my leg with no risk of software failure during a fight.

Of course, regeneration took time, and the rehab afterward took more time. Also, unless you were getting an artificial with enhanced systems, regeneration was much more expensive.

I did not have much saved to begin with and now half of it was destroyed with the *Sun*. The other half was safe in my apartment. I had to find a new way to earn creds, or somehow find a way to borrow the creds to buy a new ship, but I was not big on borrowing. Regardless, I could not afford the luxury of spending extra money on regenerated limbs, much less the time required. I needed to get them both fixed and get working.

"Artificials," I told the doctor. "Basic. Operational. Nothing fancy."

"Good. We do not install them here. I can give you a list of doctors who perform these services on other Stations."

I thanked her and asked to be alone to watch Sim's message before deciding where to go for the surgery. The doc left and the nurse gave me a com system and left me alone in the room.

I watched the message with a detached numbness. Sim said he was right behind me when the missile took out the *Sun*. She ejected me in the evo suit just before it happened. By the time the missile hit, Sim had already taken out the drones and fighters that were following him. He mopped up the few that were on me, hauled me onto his ship and lit out just before the Cruiser arrived. He put me in stasis while in transit and then took me straight to Nathara.

He said it was a trap, which was obvious. Nallimar must have caught on to his contact and forced the information out of them and then set the trap.

He said he felt bad about the ship, but there was nothing he could do and that it was a risk we all took. He had just enough creds to pay the doc for the basic injuries she already fixed. After that, I was on my own.

I replayed the message several times and the meds began wearing off and I could no longer keep my eyes open and everything faded to black.

SIXTEEN

T HE NEXT DAY, I lay back in the soft bed, surrounded by sterile gray walls, watching a helidisk game and thinking about my options. I did not watch sports often, but I enjoyed a good helidisk game when I had the chance. It required speed and brute force, like Punchball or Level, but was more of a team activity that required strategy to win.

It was not as popular as other sports, as some complained that it was too slow, but the slower pace allowed for subtle planning, bringing surprises and complications throughout the game. Unfortunately, games available for viewing in the Void were always at least a week old because of the distances, and the scores were often known before the game even started. It was only when spending time planetside in the GC sectors that I got to enjoy the games in real time.

Between the drugs I was on and thoughts of my new life, I was not paying much attention to the game. The doctor wanted me to wait another day before traveling to another Station for the procedure to make sure all of the other wounds were healed. I was already tired of the ionized antiseptic smell in the room and the gray walls and the *pada haachee* nurse who refused to let me have a drink.

If there was ever a time I needed a drink, it was now. If I was able to walk, I would tell her to pleasure herself with her no drinking and head straight to the Cavern. I was in a foul mood since waking and decided it would be fine if I stayed that way until I got my leg and hand back. Maybe even until I had my own ship again.

There was a knock on the hatchway and Aesal stuck his head in. "You have a woman in there or can I come in?"

It was the first time I smiled since the explosion.

"Get in here, *mata*."

He stepped through the hatch and sat next to the bed. He was putting on a smile for me, and even though I did not believe it, I appreciated the effort. I was sick of all the *haachee* seriousness and stern faces.

Aesal grabbed my shoulder in greeting. "I am very glad you are alive," he said.

I nodded and tried to return the motion before seeing the stump at the end of my arm and remembering it was impossible. I set the arm back down and stared at it for a while. I knew I would have a replacement soon, but it would be a *haachee* artificial, not *my* hand. That was gone forever.

"Are you going with artificial?"

"Yes," I told him. "I would rather a natural, but I do not have the time or money for it. I need to get to work and I need to save up for a new ship."

"How much do you have?"

"Not near enough. I could buy a cockpit, but nothing to surround it with and make it fly."

Aesal laughed. He was a good friend and was quick to laugh at a joke, even if they were bad.

"What will you do then?" he asked.

"For a ship?"

"The ship. Creds. Your hand. Your leg. Everything."

"I head to Tarvil Station tomorrow. They have a good artificial tech there."

"How long will it take?"

"Surgery is just a few hours. Couple of weeks for rehab. Then I am done. Fit to work. Fit to fight. Fit to fly."

"What kind of work will you do? Without a ship?"

I shrugged. None of my options were pleasant or very prof-itable. "Find a crew to work for I guess," I said.

"Challa?"

"As a last resort. I am done with pirate work. And Challa is a good friend, so I would rather not work for him."

"I could find you something," he said.

"No GF *haachee*," I spit out. It came out rougher than I wanted, but I was in a foul mood and did not want to hear of the *haachee* GF or his politics.

"You need work and they need help. Why not take their money?"

"Aesal, listen. I like you. You are a good friend, but I am not interested in the GF. You know that. Quit asking."

He looked down and nodded. "What about working for someone who works with GF?"

"Like —" I almost let it out about the meeting with Trask, but bit my tongue. That was not his fault. He did not know about it. "No. Same risks. Same *haachee*. I would have to sit and listen to them go on and on about the good ol' GF. I have you doing that, and that is bad enough."

"It could pay well."

"No. And for the last time, no."

"All right. I will keep an ear out for something else then."

"I appreciate it."

We both sat in awkward silence. Aesal got me fired up with his politics. Now I was in a foul mood again and I wanted him to leave. But then I thought of Renlii and maybe he had some news of her.

"Have you heard from Challa?"

He gave me a sideways smile. "Challa? Or Renlii?"

I laughed. "Both."

"I have not seen them since they decided to base out of Dem-isha."

Demisha was not too far away with a ship, but I did not have a ship now. Even with a ship, Aesal might never see Challa again. I might never see him again. I might never see Renlii again.

"I believe you love her," he said.

I laughed, but it was not real and did not sound real.

"Love scares you."

"It makes no sense out here."

"I know people that love."

"Yes. And how does it end? One of them has to move on to a new Station, or one of them or both are captured, or one of them or both are killed. It does not work."

Aesal nodded. He knew this. We all knew this.

"This was not always true," he said.

I looked at him. He was talking about the GF. It always went back to the GF with him. I was about to argue with him, but he was right.

"Yes," I admitted. "Back then you could."

"Back then, things were better."

"Yes. I guess they were."

He did not say anything. He did not gloat, but I could tell he was happy over his small victory. I had never admitted that things were better under the GF.

"But the GF is not here, Aesal, and it never will be again. Things are the way they are and there is no sense dreaming about the past."

He could see where the conversation was going. He did not like to hear things like that, so he changed the subject.

"What happened with the meeting I set up? The message you sent sounded urgent. You are not here because of that are you?"

"No." I had forgotten about the message. I was tired and did not feel like having a conversation like that, but he deserved to know.

"Your friend Zhaji is working for someone I know, or used to know. Someone very unpleasant."

Aesal looked at me as if I had lost part of my mind in the explosion. "Zhaji works for no one. He is independent like you."

I just shook my head. Poor Aesal. He had no idea, and I could not tell him everything. No one knew about my past and I preferred it that way, so I gave him the limited version. I told him about meeting Trask and the offer for work.

"Why you? How does he know about you?"

I shrugged and shoveled *haachee*. "Because this man knows everything. Because he knew I was in a bad spot. And because this is what he does. He takes advantage of people in bad spots and uses them to his advantage. He plays the galaxy like a game of Empires and we are all chonn. He tells some people he is backing the GF, but his real ambition is power. He is no better than the Corporations."

Aesal stared at the floor, questioning everything.

"Just stay away from him if you can, Aesal. He is trouble. He has great resources and claims to help the GF, but he will leave you dangling in the Void with no evo suit if it will give him an advantage."

Aesal looked up at me. "But still, he helps the GF."

"Yes, he does. But his motives are not true. It is a distraction. A strategic move."

"As long as he helps the GF, I do not care about his motivations or his end game."

I stared at him trying to think of what to say to convince him, but in truth I did not understand him.

"He is one man. If billions in the galaxy rise up against the Corporations and against him, no single person can stop us."

I just laughed. There was no arguing with a fanatic. He was brainwashed and believed and there was no changing that.

"As long as you are walking into the vintoo lair knowing they are waiting for you."

He smiled and stood up and grabbed my shoulder again. "I have things to do. Do you need anything before I leave the Station?"

I needed a large number of things, but none of them were his problem. I thanked him for dropping by and told him I hoped to see him again and he left. There was no other true thing to say when you parted ways. We will either see each other again or we will not.

That is the way of things.

SEVENTEEN

I FINISHED DRESSING as well as I could with the missing limbs. The easiest part was getting the jox on. The shirt was a struggle, but nothing like the pants. I got them on after a fight, but was too exhausted to seal them up. I sat staring at the end of my bad leg. Like the arm, it had a flexible, waterproof mesh material holding the healing stasis liquid to the injured area. It prevented infection and kept the tissue from healing too much or closing itself off, so they could attach the artificial later without any problems.

I went back to work on the pants and sealed the last attachment after a bitter scrap. I leaned back on the bed to catch my breath and stared down at the one boot. I was tired from the battle of getting dressed and the boot taunted me. The nurse had offered help, but I was sick of feeling helpless and wanted to do it on my own. I looked down at my good leg and the boot and decided I was too *pada* proud.

The hatch slid open and Challa stepped in with his instigator smirk. It was *puda* good to see him, in spite of the sadness he hid behind a broad smile. He rushed over and hugged me. Drakkarans were known for being more expressive with their emotions. Challa was good about holding back, but the sight of me in pieces was too much for him and he hugged me tight. I was not used to this kind of thing and endured the awkwardness, reciprocating the best I could, but wanting to get away from him so we could talk.

He finally broke off and smiled at me with tears in his eyes. I gave him an embarrassed smile and he grabbed me by both shoulders. "Jlaeal, my friend, I am very glad to see you alive."

"Thank you, Challa."

He sat down on the hover seat next to the bed. "From what I have heard, you are very fortunate."

"It was a close thing."

"As close as any I have heard of."

I nodded, looking down at my hand, or where my hand used to be. I had thought much about how close it was. The *Sun* had a good evac system and I had a good enviro suit, but it was rare for anyone to survive an explosion like that. The meek suit did what it was supposed to do, sealing over the injured limbs and holding off the bleeding, but many other things could have gone wrong.

I owed my life to that *benetcho* Sim. I had thought much about that the past two days. I was conflicted, I never would have lost my ship and my limbs if not for helping Sim, but he also saved my life. I was furious at him at first, and blamed him for what happened, but I knew what I was getting into. He did not owe me anything. He saved my life and healed me as much as he could. I would say that makes us even.

"You are dressed," Challa said. "Are you checking out?"

"Yes," I told him. "I booked passage for Tarvil later today."

"Aesal told me you were going there."

"What are you doing here?" I asked. "I thought you moved to Demisha."

"I have. The crew is there. Lucky for you I had a meeting here with a buyer."

"I am *puda* glad to see you," I said. "I was going to the Cavern before the trip. Join me."

"That is a fine idea," Challa said. "But you are not getting on some *haachee* transport. I am taking you."

"Tarvil is two days in the wrong direction."

"Bahh," he said with some disgust. "What is two days for an old friend."

I smiled as a warmth rose up inside of me. There are friends you drink with and friends you go to battle with. People tended to fit within one category or the other, but not both. Challa was a rarity in that he was both. The first time we met was in battle and I saw the truth of him. You never really know a person until you are in battle together. Then you find what they are made of and whether they are just good for drinking or good for everything else.

The nurse had set me up with a mobile hover seat for the trip. Challa helped me with my boot and helped me into the seat and I guided it through the hatch and out into the hallway. I breathed in the musty air with relief. It was not fresh air, but it was hells of a lot better than the sanitized acidic smell of the med bay. The smell of the asteroid rock and of sweat and metal was the smell of home.

Challa walked beside me as I coasted down the hallway toward my apartment. He had convinced me that we should pack my belongings onto his ship before the drink. I was anxious for the drink, as I had not had one since before lighting out for the *haachee* mission, but he was right. We would not want to pack my gear and load it onto his ship after drinking gru.

Challa had a few workers load up my gear and my cases of creds. I had heard that Trask was establishing a new banking system for the Stations. The system was similar to the one the old GF used. You just deposited your credits at a UI-backed Station and transferred credits to anyone using the same system. It was good incentive to work on a UI Station. Hauling around hard creds was a pain in the ass and risky. The amount of creds I lost on the *Asron Sun* was rough to think about.

I shook thoughts of Trask's new banking system out of my head. As nice as it sounded, I did not want to be part of his *pada* system. Fuck Trask. Fuck UI and fuck his new bank. It was all *haachee* and a trap. When the Corporations got tired of him and decided to take him out, he and his bank and all the creds would burn away.

The workmen were quick about loading everything onto the

Sh'kurah Nuilla and we locked up the ship and made our way to the Cavern. As we entered, I noticed a different feel to it. There were new faces everywhere and it felt secretive and on guard. They were all talking in hushed tones of conspirators rather than friendly tones of familiar patrons and fellow travelers. Things were changing. With the fall of dozens of Stations and the growth of Trask's agency, people were more nervous, imagining spies and Corporate hacks everywhere.

Challa and I sat at a small table in the back. Edda was taking orders from a table across the room, but she took the time to send a wink and a smile my way. She had chopped off her orange bangs and was growing the rest of her hair out, so she had light-orange stubble all over her head. Her outfit looked like she had taken several ammo belts, dyed them blue and attached them together in one long strand and wrapped it around her just enough to cover up the special parts, leaving the rest of her olive-toned skin in the open for us to enjoy. The ammo belts and combat boots were all she had on. She looked delicious and many in the bar were watching her like a horrig who had spotted its prey.

Challa took notice as well and smiled. "I am glad to see some things have not changed."

"That was not injured," I told him.

Challa laughed. "She is very beautiful."

"Yes, she is."

"We might never come back here," he said. "It might be worth the risk."

I shrugged. It was nice to think about, but my heart was not into it. Even through everything that happened my thoughts were stuck on Renlii.

"And Renlii?"

I gave him a look that he mistook for anger. He backed away from me holding his hands up in defense. "I am not one to bear judgment, friend."

I smiled as he laughed. Edda approached our table with

drinks. She had a smile as she arrived, but with a touch of concern.

"Jlaeal, I am glad you are alive."

I gave her a smirk and a shrug, but my confidence was gone and she could see through it.

"Your friend told me all about it," she said.

"Which friend?"

"The friend you were with before leaving for the mission."

"Ah, Sim."

"What will you do?"

I told her about the artificial and of Tarvil and of leaving Nathara. She seemed upset to hear I was leaving. I thought of the possibility of saying a long and private goodbye to her, but Challa and I were leaving right away and my heart was not in it. Renlii was still heavy on my mind.

"It seems everyone is leaving," she said.

"The Corps have us on the run," Challa said. "Only UI Stations are safe now."

She had not heard about UI, so we broke it down for her. She was flustered by the time she left to take care of other customers, but it was always better to know. Challa and I watched her walk away. She had lost the pleasurable swing to her hips and walked normal like a scared girl rather than a confident woman who knew her place in the Void.

It was like catching a glimpse behind the scenes of a holo show and seeing the real person behind the character. She was not the cocky, sexy waitress we saw in the Cavern. She was scared and doing what she could to survive in the Void, but without any skills other than a charming smile and the swing of her hips. She would be better off planetside or on a UI Station where it was safe.

Challa raised his gru and we saluted one another before downing them. The gru was bitter and sweet and delicious and I savored the burn on its way down my throat before slipping into the darkness. When I came out of it, Challa was already sipping his krem and looking at me. It was the face he gave to new crew members or while inspecting new equipment, like he was trying to look inside and see how my engines were running. I took a sip of krem and avoided looking him in the eye. He broke the silence and asked me the question I had been asking myself.

"What of Renlii?"

I took another sip of krem. It was ice cold and frothy, just the way I liked it. But the krem was just a distraction; something to take my mind away from his question.

"I have no answer," I said.

"You care for her?"

"Yes," although the answer was more complicated than that. I loved her and that was a problem. It was a problem before. Now it seemed insurmountable.

"Thinking of us as anything more than pleasure was a luxury," I said. "It was something I could afford when we were together on this Station and Trask was not stirring up the Void and I had a ship and all my limbs."

Challa looked down at his krem, staring deep into it as if all the answers were somewhere at the bottom of the glass. He nodded with his lips set together.

"We can never really afford love," I said. "Not out here. That is the greatest danger of it and I should have listened to you all these years as you warned against it. The Void tricks you into thinking the cost is low, or even if it is great, that you can afford it and that she is worth it. But she is crafty and a tease and will always change the rules of the game just as you think you have won."

We were at the beginning stages of drinking and I was at the stage of melancholy where I had become a philosopher and felt like I knew all the answers of the galaxy. Challa did not say anything, but continued looking down at his krem.

He looked angry, as if he was sharing my grief at the unfairness of the galaxy so I continued, "I knew what I was getting into. The cost has not changed, but I no longer have what it takes to pay the cost. Before, I could take care of myself. My coordinates were never plotted in, but at least I had the tools to get where I was going. Now — I am a ship without an engine, floating in the Void."

Challa drank the last of his krem with a disgusted look on his face, like something had settled at the bottom and he was forced to drink it. Edda arrived with a new set before he spoke his mind.

"This will be it for us," he told her. "I am flying after this."

"You could always fly out in the morning," she said with a smile.

"I have to get him to Tarvil and get back with my crew or they will mutiny."

Edda put on a pouty face and walked away with the swing back in her step, looking back once to make sure we were watching.

I began to raise my glass of gru to Challa, but he was looking at me with disgust and anger and said, "*Haachee.*"

"What is *haachee?*"

"You are *haachee.* You are full of foul *chee* and your disgusting *haachee* self-pity. I am sick at my stomach listening to it."

I set my gru down and looked at Challa with a rising rage. Self-pity? Fuck him. What the fuck did he know?

But he kept going, "Fuck your missing leg. Fuck your missing hand. Fuck your missing ship. And sure as hells, you can fuck your self-pity."

I kept reminding myself that this was my friend; that I should not hit him or kill him. But darkness began to close around the corner of my vision and the fury was forcing a blackout.

"You are my good friend, Jlaeal, but fuck you if you want to sit in your *haachee* self-pity and feel sorry for yourself. You are alive, *pudak*! You are fucking alive and not dead and that is no small thing."

As he leaned in, I took a deep breath and tried to cool down and force the dark rage away.

"You sit there and feel sorry for yourself and say foolish things like, 'I am without an engine, lost in the Void,' like some panty-wearing artist or a dream boy at a GC University. Fuck that Jlaeal!

I want no part of that Jlaeal. The Jlaeal I know and love would say fuck him, too, and fuck the leg and fuck the hand and fuck anything that would try to stop him!

"Yes, you are right. That is the Void," he continued. "She is harsh and unrelenting and if you sit sulking like you are, she will eat you alive and smile as she spits out the dust of your bones.

"So, you lost your leg and you lost your hand — in a few days, you will have new ones. So, you lost a ship — you will get another one. Or maybe you will not. And if you do, maybe it will not be right away. But you are alive, *pudak*!

"You are alive and nothing has changed but you. If you want to be done with her, be done with her. But do not use *puda* excuses and whine about what you lost. Love her or do not love her. Leave her or do not. But fly true. You wander about whining about no engine and you can ride that transport to Tarvil. I want no part of it, or of you."

He took a large drink of his krem and stared me down, daring me to argue, to flinch or even look away. But I did not argue. The darkness had faded away and I was seeing clear, for the first time since the explosion.

Deep down in my bones I knew he was right. A good friend once told me that many in the Void will shower you with compliments and clap you on the back, but a true friend will tell you when you are a *mata* and full of *haachee*. A true friend will tell you when you are flying into an asteroid field, while the rest of the galaxy will tell you how nice your ship looks. Challa was the best of friends and always told me truth.

I gave him a bitter smile. "Fuck the leg," I said. "Fuck the hand. Fuck the ship, and fuck the Void." I raised my gru to him. "To being alive and to my good friend who tells me when I am *haachee*." He smiled back and raised his glass and we both swallowed the bitter drink and slipped into the darkness.

EIGHTEEN

THE FLIGHT TO Tarvil went by quickly. Once Challa had shown me how *haachee* my thinking was, my mood shifted and I could feel my old self coming back. Life was hard, and if you were not hard to match it, then it would annihilate you. I had lost a leg and a hand, but I was alive and I was on my way to get new ones. I was still worried about life without my own ship, but I would survive. It had been a long time since I was without a ship, but I had skills and connections and would find a way.

Challa offered a place on his team, but I thanked him and turned him down. Working for him would change the nature of the relationship. We would no longer be on an even keel if I worked for him and we both knew it. He would be the captain and I would take his orders. We were used to us both being our own captain, and changing the dynamic would be hard on the friendship.

We joked during the trip and played kalla and Empires and talked about the past. Once in a while, we ventured into the future and discussed Trask and Renlii, but we did not stay on that for long. Neither of us wanted to think about what was coming; the Void was full of change, and we would have to change with it. As far as Renlii went, we both knew if I stuck with her, it would make it harder on both of us, but he did not try to talk me out of it. He knew we were both too far in already, and in spite of the risk for us both, I think that deep down he liked us together.

He did not stay on Tarvil. I thanked him for the ride and for the truth he gave me and he hugged me. The hug put me on edge and he laughed at me, then gave me one last firm hold on the shoulders, boarded his ship and flew out of the dock.

I sat in my hover seat and waited for the dock rep. She was a harsh-looking Drakkaran woman; a devoted follower of Trill, shown by her expansive, untrimmed eyebrows and a beard that had grown down below her breasts. Strict Trillists never cut or trimmed any of their facial hair, letting it grow out to extreme levels. In spite of her tough-looking exterior though, she was kind and efficient and helped me deposit my creds into a Station account. Then, she coded the location of Dr. Quane's med center into my hover seat and left as the seat guided itself out of the dock and into a wide hallway.

Tarvil was one of few Stations in the Void used for its original purpose. It was on a direct pathway between Drakkara and Shiltii, built centuries ago as a trading outpost and neutral meeting place. It was one of the oldest Stations in the Void, but the captain took good care of it. In fact, it was one of the better-looking Stations I had visited.

It had a classic look retained from its construction millennia ago, making it unique and more pleasant than other Station. It was utilitarian though, with very few aesthetic qualities. The floors were synthetic hard wood, made for durability and longevity, but made back when the material was still at least fifty percent real wood. The walls and ceilings were all alidnum synth-steel metal, the thick and heavy kind used long ago. Most Stations smelled of space dust and sweat and mildew, but Tarvil had a fleet of service drones maintaining the facility, leaving it smelling fresh and clean. It gave the place an old Galactic traveler feel, as if the GF still existed and we were all just part of the Cargo Freight Union, on our way to peaceful trade between systems.

The hallways were filled with Humans, Shiltians, Drakkarans, Diviians and even Fillonians. They were business people, traders, negotiators, techs, smugglers, tradesmen, courtesans, guards and pirates; all moving about on their different missions without a second thought about the cripple in the hover seat.

I became more and more aware of my helplessness as I moved through the hallways, jostled by the crowds. My gun was holstered on my left side and I could fire with my left hand, but I was used to two guns and my left did not have the accuracy of my right. It was the first time I was alone in public as a cripple and I felt naked and vulnerable.

I was relieved when the chair finally stopped at a hatchway with a sign reading "Dr. Lix Quane. Biocybertronic Enhancements." I had done some research on artificial doctors and she was one of the highest recommended. She had close to zero bio-rejections and no equipment failures.

I sat at the hatchway, staring at the entrance pad, but I did not go in. The crowd in the hallway pushed past me and jostled my chair. Something deep within me was still fighting against the artificials. I had always looked down on them and did not understand why someone would take an artificial over naturals. I was old fashioned about technologies mixing with organics, because of horror stories from millennia ago and the battles some systems had with tech. That was long, long ago and there had been no problems like that since before the GF, but somehow it still gave me a distaste. Now that I lost my own limbs, and had very few creds, I understood why people got the artificials — sometimes you had no choice.

I took a deep breath and pressed the pad. The hatch slid open, revealing a clean and stylized-looking entry, with real wood floors and real plants in the corners and several old-fashioned seats held up with legs resting on the floors. I hesitated at the door, but then floated inside and the hatch sealed closed behind me. An image of a stern-looking Diviian appeared in front of me. She wore a blue physician's jumpsuit and greeted me with what I assumed was her version of a smile. Diviians did not wrinkle with age as humans or Drakkarans do. Instead, their features hardened, giving them a more severe look. She was trying to look friendly, but it came off as mild professional interest.

"Welcome to BioCybernetic Enhancement Systems of Tarvil," she said. "Are you here for an enhancement?"

"Yes. My doc on Nallimar sent a message. Name is Jlaeal."

"Jlaeal from Nallimar. We have been waiting for you. Please wait here while I finish a consult. I will join you in a moment."

The holo did not wait for a response as it dissolved, leaving me alone in the room with the real wood and the real plants. It was usually hard to tell real plants from synthetics, but I had spent enough time planetside to tell the real thing. The smell of the plants filled the room, along with the smell of the real wood floors. It made the air itself feel different, like there was too much oxygen in a closed atmosphere. Live plants seemed to tighten the room up, making it feel like I was being squeezed out.

I moved my chair off to the side and tried to ignore the tightness of the room. I pulled out my com and sifted through messages. My vendors and buyers were starting to respond to the messages I sent about the loss of my ship. I had some time to work on a solution and hoped to find someone I trusted to take over the routes. They were not happy about the delay, but understood that without a ship, there was not much I could do.

A message had come from an old buyer in GalactiCorp territory who whined about how furious his customers would be and about his loss of income and complained that he would have to hold off on buying his new habi. What a *mata*. I was moments away from spending half of my remaining savings on a new hand and a new leg, with no ship and no prospects, and he was whining about having to wait to buy a bigger habi. I laughed and deleted his *haachee* message. Fuck his *haachee* habi and fuck him.

I put the com away in disgust just as a hatch slid open and a middle-aged woman stepped into the room. She had a face that showed no signs that it had ever smiled.

"Follow me," she said and walked back through the hatch. I guided my seat after her without a word. She did not seem interested in conversation, and I felt the same. She took me down a sterile blue hallway that looked to be made of smooth plasteel, curved at both the floor and ceiling. It felt like walking through a giant tube. She stopped at a hatch to the left and turned to face me. She palmed the hatch panel and it slid open, but she gave no indication that I was to go in. As I approached, she stood in place, watching me, blocking the hallway.

I looked inside the hatch into an office. It had real gray wood floors and real plants surrounding a desk made from gray wood several shades darker than the floor. The walls were a dark fluorescent green seen only in nature. The office as a whole was that gaudy naturist *haachee* I hated. The air went out of me just looking at it, but I coasted into the room anyway. The hatch shut behind me without a word from the *puda* nurse.

The nurse reminded me of a cretch; an old mangy kalca, near its end and tired of life, disgusted with their aches and pains, no longer young and able to chase game. Young kalca were friendly and playful and full of life, but as they aged they grew angry and bitter and bit any creature that came near to them, even their own children. This was the nurse; angry and bitter about life and what it dealt her and ready to lash out at everything around her.

Dr. Quane stepped into the office wearing the same outfit as projected in the holo. She walked behind her desk and sat in the chair without saying a word or even looking at me. She sat up proper and straight with her palms laid down on her desk, and finally looked at me once she was settled. She was cold and all business, but after meeting Nurse Cretch, she seemed almost pleasant.

It was a short meeting with very little talk. She was there to give me a new leg and a new hand and that was it. We went over the options and I picked the ones that were closest to natural as possible, without using all of my credits. She went over the process and explained that the pain would be greater than anything else I had experienced. I thought she was trying to scare me at the time. I am glad I did not realize how serious she was, or I might not have gone through with it, or I might have found another surgeon.

She believed in letting the artificials adapt in a natural process, without any aid of medicines, molecular manipulation or nerve dampening. You woke up with a new arm and leg and experienced every sensation as they learned to communicate and adapt to your body. It did not dawn on me at the time that this was any different from any other method. Her reputation was the best of any other surgeon in the galaxy so I trusted her. Having no experience with the procedure, I thought what she was explaining was the way it was always done, so I agreed to everything and transferred payment from the Station bank, and we got straight to it.

Nurse Cretch came in and took me out of the office, back into the hallway and into a prep room. It was a large blue sterile room with plasteel walls and a blue table with control panels on either side standing upright in the center of the room. The nurse helped me take off all of my clothes. I did not like the feeling of helplessness as she undressed me and liked even less sitting naked in front of her, but she gave no sign of any emotion or response. She helped me stand, with my back against the table as multiple straps came out of the table and locked me into place.

The table rotated until I lay flat on my back, staring up at the ceiling. The straps had me firm in place, so that I could not move any part of my body, not even my head. Then the table injected me with something and everything went black.

NINETEEN

THERE ARE MANY versions of hell in the countless religions across the galaxy. True hell was in that recovery room, on that cold hard table. I cannot remember details of the next two days. I knew only pain. Dr. Quane believed that medicines or unnatural chemicals or molecular modifications or numbing agents of any kind would "adversely affect the artificial limb's ability to form a cohesive communicative relationship with the rest of the body."

I hated that woman with the heat of a burning sun.

I cannot begin to describe the agony of those days. It was like fire. Raging fire from an exploding supernova. Molten fire injected into my veins while someone worked at my limbs with a sonic hammer. But these are just words and do not give a true picture of the real pain.

I was not awake for the actual surgery, when they joined the artificial muscles, tendons, bone and tissue to my natural body. They connected them cell by cell, molecule by molecule, and atom by atom. When I woke, they had given me nothing for the pain. Days after the surgery I was told that two point one percent of those who receive artificials using this method go insane. I was sure at one point that I was one of them.

I was made as comfortable as possible, with Nurse Cretch keeping a close eye on my vitals and washing the wounds and keeping sure of the progress, but in spite of her care, she became the focal point of all my rage.

I could not speak the first day. I could not even think. I was in a world filled with shadows and muffled sound and knew only pain. The second day was not as bad. My world was still pure agony, but the fog started to clear and I could begin to process what was going on.

On the third day, the pain had lessened enough to let me think and speak, but then they attached me to a machine that forced my new hand and leg to move, conditioning the limbs to communicate and work. This brought the pain back like a rushing flood of boiling acid racing through my veins and into my muscles and skin and bones. In spite of this, I could speak and used what energy I had to call them the worst insulting names I could think of, or beg them for meds or gru or turn off the *puda* machine. I begged, I threatened, I tried to bribe, but they did not budge.

By the end of the third day I knew it was no use and stopped wasting my energy on the insults. It was the first night since the surgery that I slept more than five sets at a time. I slept for three solid rotations and woke up to find that the pain had receded down to a nova rather than a white-hot supernova.

I awoke on the fourth day somewhat rested, and cleared the tears and *chee* from my eyes and tried to see. Someone was standing on the left side of my bed, but I could not make them out. I was sure it was Nurse Cretch and several choice words floated up to the edge of my tongue, but then I caught a scent. My heart sped up and I blinked and tried to bring the blurred shape into focus. I tried to speak, but it came out as a steel croak and I blinked away more of the mist and *chee* and tried to clear my throat again.

Then I felt her hand on my arm.

"Renlii," I croaked and tried to say more, but could not.

"Shhh. Go back to sleep. I will be here."

She kissed me on the forehead and closed my eyes. I was excited to see her, but still so tired. With her there, I relaxed and forgot about the pain a little and fell back to sleep and instead of dreaming of molten lava coursing through my veins, I dreamed of her.

It was less than a rotation before I woke up again. This time I looked up at Renlii and forced a smile. The pain was still there, like a laser welder beaming into each new limb, but as I looked at her, and felt her hand in mine, I did not care as much. She was so beautiful and her smile so tender and warm, and looking up at her, I knew that I loved her.

Pudak, I loved her.

She held my hand and smiled down at me and I knew that she felt the same. She had said so, but I did not know what that meant at the time. Now, looking into her eyes, I felt it and knew what it was. Then I sensed something else in her smile. Something was wrong. Something other than me and my pain.

"What is it?" I asked, my voice still husky and deep from waking.

Her smile broke. She was a great setrak player and could hide her emotions better than anyone, but she was breaking and I knew it was something terrible. I squeezed her hand with my good one and rubbed the top of it with my thumb.

"What is it?"

It sounded harsh after I said it, but she knew it was not meant that way.

"Nallimar hit Demisha," she said as tears formed in her eyes.

I tried to think of what that meant, but my mind had not cleared from the pain. I held her hand and watched her cry and tried to think of what to do or say. I had not seen her cry before and I hated it. It was like a punch to the gut. I loved her for her strength and intelligence and everything that made her seem unbreakable, and it tore me apart to see her crying.

Then I thought of what it would take to make her cry and what would make her come to me now and I thought of Challa. My stomach tightened and my breath stopped and my heart felt like it was trying to beat itself out of my chest.

Holy hells.

Not Challa.

"Tell me," I said.

She looked at me through tears and must have realized what I was thinking and squeezed my hand and arm.

"Not Challa."

I closed my eyes and let out a breath, but I knew there was more.

"Who then?"

"The rest," she said as her voice broke. She gathered herself and wiped her eyes. "None of the others made it. Challa and me —" She paused to regain control and took a deep breath. "We are the only ones who made it out."

I wanted to look away so that she could not see me cry, but I forced myself to look into her eyes, to see her, to be there for her. She was blurry through my own tears, but her eyes were closed and a single tear streamed down her cheek. I reached up and grabbed her head and brought her to my chest and held her close and caressed her head. We both closed our eyes and held each other as we cried, neither of us saying another word.

The Void was a fucked-up *haachee* place and it grew darker every day. I had lost more friends in the past year than I lost during the entire Liquidation. I was tired of losing and tired of the fight and tired of the Void.

We held each other tightly and I thought about my friends. I thought about Bentook and Ree and Da'd and Pell and Khiltala. I could think of a hundred different nights spent in the Cavern with them, laughing and drinking and telling stories. They were as close to a family as I ever had and now they were gone.

TWENTY

143

T HE NEXT FEW days were torture, but would have been far worse without Renlii. We did not talk about Demisha or our friends or what happened. She was not ready and I did not want to hear the details. They were gone and we were here and we could do nothing about it.

Renlii never left my side that first day. She even forced Nurse Cretch to bring in another bed so that she could sleep in the room with me. Cretch fought her on it and threatened to call security, but Renlii told her if she did, she would have an unfortunate accident that would leave her dead. Cretch might have been hard and cold, but she was no match for Renlii and was quick to follow her orders.

That day was also when the real work began. They took me off the machine and made me work with the hand and leg on my own, first flexing and unflexing, moving this finger, then that finger, then all the fingers, curling my toes, stretching the leg, bending the leg. It was very difficult work and the pain was excruciating and Renlii was even harder on me than Cretch or Dr. Quane. If I ever complained about the difficulty or the pain or showed any signs of self pity, Renlii would give me a look filled with so much disgust that it shamed me and forced me to get back at it.

I reached a melting point on one occasion and swore at them all, including Renlii and told them all to burn in hells and leave me alone. Renlii and Nurse Cretch sat and took the insults and after I exhausted myself, Renlii started taking off my pants.

"What are you doing?" I asked and pushed her away.

"Checking to make sure you did not lose your *cojos* during the explosion."

I stared at her in fury and then laughed. I laughed so hard I cried and she smiled at me. Nurse Cretch had no sense of humor at all and sat fuming at us both. When I finished laughing I got back to work and tried not to disappoint her again.

By the second day of her arrival, they had me on my feet, learning to walk on the new leg. I could not put all of my weight on it, but I could walk some and began to grasp things with my new hand. Renlii was quiet during the exercises, but did not let me quit until she had to help me back to bed.

She was quiet and dark since her arrival. I knew the death of our friends was the cause of it, but did not press it. I knew she would bring it up when she was ready, and if she never brought it up, that would be fine, too.

Later that night, I rested in bed while Renlii left to get real food. She had to smuggle in the food and the bottle of drin she bought. If Cretch or Dr. Quane caught her, they would have kicked me out. They were getting tired of us pushing back on their methods and would have been glad to see us gone. I did not know what she was doing when she left and when I saw the food and the drin, I fell in love with her all over again. It was the most beautiful thing I had seen since Renlii arrived at my bedside. It was the first real food I had since the operation. It was delicious and the drin took the edge off the pain and I loved it and I loved Renlii for bringing it.

When we finished the last of it, she hid the bottle and glasses in her pack, then crawled into my bed and cuddled up on my left side with her head on my shoulder. I held her hand with my new hand, and in spite of the pain it gave me, I squeezed her hand. She squeezed me back and then ran her fingers along my new hand and along the surgical line at my wrist. I ran my fingers of my good hand through her hair and put my arm around her shoulder and rubbed her back and smelled her hair and kissed the top of her head.

"It happened quickly," she said.

I did not say anything. It was her story and I did not want to ruin it with any *haachee* comments or questions. I continued to rub her back and let her get it out.

"Bentook was in the bay, locking down *Nuilla*. The rest of us were in the bar when the Station alarms went off. There came an announcement that a Nallimar fleet had arrived outside the asteroid belt. The whole Station raced to the docks. It was madness, Jlaeal.

"We fought our way to the dock as a team, but when we got there, there were too few ships and too many people. The ships were flooded as soon as they opened and they could not get the doors shut and were not able to take off.

"It was a hard fight getting to the Nuilla. Ree was struck in the head and then trampled underfoot and died as we watched. There was nothing we could do but keep going."

Her voice had grown husky and deep. She was not crying, but she was deep within herself telling the story, recounting it as if she were making a report, trying to do so without emotion. I held her tight and rubbed her back to let her know I was listening.

"As we drew closer to the *Nuilla*, we saw it rise and take off. Bentook's mutilated body lay where the ship had been. Our fighters were still there, but they were single seaters.

"Challa ordered us to take the fighters and leave him. He forced me into the first fighter while they fought off the crowd. I did not want to leave them, but Challa insisted, threatening to shoot me for mutiny if I did not go. I sealed the hatch and locked myself inside and then I saw Pell go down with a blast to his face."

She paused to take another breath and collect herself.

"When I started the engines, the crowd pushed away toward other ships that were left in the hangar. I continued the startup sequence and Challa, Da'd and Khiltala fought their way to the other fighter. I eased out of my space, but there were so many people on the deck I could not move. After a while, I was able to lift straight up and fly over them.

"Challa and Da'd reached the fighter, but I lost track of Khiltala. I made it out of the bay and saw the Nallimar fleet closing in toward the Station. I flew to the other side of it, far enough away so the Nallimar fighters would not bother with me. I waited to see if the other fighter would make it, but Nallimar fighters had reached the bay and destroyed any ships trying to leave. The assault ships landed and the larger ships were surrounding the Station. A few of the fighters broke off and were coming toward me.

"Then I saw the other fighter launch out of the bay into a swarm of Nallimar fighters. I knew it was Challa. He is a better pilot than any of us and got past the fighters without a scratch. I told him where I was and to meet me, but he told me to go and that he would draw them off."

She lay quiet for a while. I squeezed her hand and held her tighter. She was breathing harder now and I could tell she was fighting the emotions.

"I felt like a coward, but I knew he would not leave until I did. As soon as I cleared the asteroid field, I lit out. I stopped a few times and changed course to make sure I would not be followed. Then I set course for Tarvil. I had no idea if he survived or not, but when I arrived here, I received a message saying he made it to another Station. None of the others made it."

She was quiet again. I should have said something, but did not know what to say. The typical *haachee* ran through my mind, like "it would be alright", or "everything was fine", but everything was not fine. Everything was *chee* and the Void was *haachee* and there was nothing I could tell her that would make it better. I squeezed her tight and held her hand tight in spite of the pain and kissed her on top of her head.

"After I escaped I thought of them and what had happened, but I also thought of you. I wanted to hold you and know that you were okay. I thought if you were fine, it would make things better. That is weak talk though. It was foolish."

"No," I told her. "It is not foolish, or weak. I am beyond glad that you are alive and I am glad you are here. My life is better with you here."

She squeezed me tighter and the room was quiet. I hesitated saying the next thing. I had never said it before, but I knew she needed to hear it and that I needed to say it.

"Renlii, as soon as I woke up to see you I knew that I loved you. It is the Void and it is a dangerous thing to feel and to say, but I love you in spite of what it brings."

She raised her head up and looked me in the eyes. I did not know if it was good that I said it and I held my breath while she looked at me, but then she kissed me and I knew it was fine. It was a long kiss full of love and gentle passion and I decided the Void could burn as long as I had her.

TWENTY-ONE

Renlii continued sneaking in food and drink. We got caught a few times and Cretch yelled at us and accused us of sabotaging the healing process. After several days of this, I decided it was time to leave. She and the doctor warned me that healing would not go right if I left, but my hand and my leg worked well enough. I was using a cane and I was slow, but I would continue to train on my own, away from the sterile room and away from their *haachee*.

Renlii sided with them, but she also knew I had made my decision and could not be persuaded. She stood by, saying nothing as I packed what little gear I had.

I walked toward the exit with a limp, pushing a hover cart full of my things. Renlii tried to help, but I wanted Cretch to see that I was able to do it on my own. I pushed the cart out of my room and down the hallway toward the exit. Cretch followed, telling me how stubborn I was and what a fool and a *mata* I was all the way to the main entry area. After a long and slow march to the front hatch, I reached up and put my good hand on the panel and the hatch slid open.

"You might never heal right," Cretch said, while I stepped into the Station hallway.

Renlii followed me out and I raised my new hand in Cretch's direction and forced it into a rude gesture.

"Look at that," I told her, "I guess it works well enough."

As the hatch sealed between us, I felt a warm glow at her look of horror.

"How long have you been planning that exit?" Renlii asked.

"A while." I smiled. "Where to?"

"Follow me."

She led the way as I limped down the hallway, pushing the cart. In spite of the pain and the limp, it felt good to be in public, away from the *haachee* clinic and the *haachee* nurse. My guns felt good against my hip and I felt ready to face the Void and everything she could throw my way. I had work ahead to get up to full thrusters, but I hoped the worst was over.

It was refreshing to see the people in the hall and smell the air of the Station, a mix of cleaner, synthmetal, synthwood, sweat and body odor. Funny, the things you miss. It was not that I enjoyed the smell of sweat and body odor, but it was better than the antiseptic smell of the med bay.

The apartment Renlii rented was small, but there was plenty of room in the rack for the both of us and there was a cleanser unit and a refresher unit. It was all we needed.

When we got inside, she locked the hatch and I parked the cart and we attacked each other and made love for several hours. Renlii had stayed with me at the med center, but it was not a good place for pleasure. It was not private and the mood was not right with Cretch sticking her face in the hatch too often. Pleasure was difficult with the leg and the hand, but it was still beautiful and soon I forgot about my new limbs and Nurse Cretch and everything else in the Void disappeared.

Much later, we decided to go out. I had been cooped up for too long and wanted to go outside and see more of the Station and have a fresh, hot meal.

The doctor had recommended I use a cane for a few days, but I ignored her on this as well. I limped some and it was painful, but

I wanted to get used to walking normal and wanted to show as little weakness as possible.

Renlii took my new hand in hers and we walked side by side through the crowded halls. The Station was engorged with travelers and refugees. The smells of wood and synthsteel and cleanser I experienced when I arrived had been overwhelmed by body odor and bad breath. We passed through the steady stream of people like fish traveling upstream. Once in a while someone would knock into me and throw me off balance, but Renlii helped me recover and we kept moving.

We took a long walk and explored the entire Station before stopping somewhere to eat. The layout was different than Nathara, which had a central hub where all the merchants and the havens were. On Tarvil, the shops and merchants and havens were spread out all over the Station, giving it a busy feel throughout.

We passed a few eateries that did not match our moods, but then found Trill's Delight, which was perfect. A hard-line Trillist might have been offended by the name, but for everyone else it was flawless. Trill had actually encouraged the drinking of krem in moderation. In fact, a common Drakkaran belief was that Trill himself created the first brew from the fields of his home village before he received his enlightenment.

Trill's Delight had a dark atmosphere that fit the style and taste of Drakkara, with floors made of real nalasa wood from the home planet, carved with intricate relief carvings detailing the history of Drakkaran travel throughout the galaxy. The tables were carved out of the same native nalasa wood. Each table had a unique relief carving telling the history of a different planet in the Drakkaran core system.

The walls were lined with thick hand-carved wood paneling showing scenic images of Trill and the history of his discovery of krem. Booths lining the right wall were covered with an ancient-looking leather. The bar took up the wall on the left. The lighting was darker than the rest of the ship, but not so dark that you could not see who you were talking to. It all made me feel like I was back on Drakkara.

Renlii knew without asking that I would love it and pulled me inside. The bar was half full, with just the right level of noise so that we would not have to yell at each other for a conversation. As Renlii led me past the full room, I noticed stares and odd looks. They could have been watching her, but I suspected they were staring at the strange couple holding hands. Couples were a rare thing in the Void and couples holding hands was unheard of.

Renlii led me down to the farthest booth. As soon as we sat down, a husky Drakkaran came to the table dressed in the priestly robes of Trill.

"Peace to you, travelers. Welcome to Trill's Delight, where the krem is icy cold and the food is steamy hot. No guarantees on the taste — but the temperature will be just right."

He gave a hearty laugh at his own joke. We could not help but laugh with him. His strong accent revealed him to be from the rural areas of the back side of the home planet.

"Krem for you both?"

"Yes, please." I said. "And food. What is good?"

He detailed a long list of savory-sounding food, but I settled on the konkerian steak and Renlii had the schinly swimmers.

As the waiter left the table, I caught Renlii watching something behind me, then I heard a voice say, "You owe me a gru. Several in fact."

It was a familiar voice and I laughed and struggled to turn and get out of the booth. Detsch was an old friend, a young smuggler I had known for ten years. He was a human from one of the central GC planets. He was short, thin and far from intimidating, but he had a big set of alidnum balls on him that got him into more close calls than I could remember.

I forced myself off the booth and grabbed both of his shoulders as he grabbed mine and we smiled at each other.

"I am glad you are alive," I said.

He returned the greeting and gave me one final slap on the shoulder.

"Where've you been, old man?" he asked.

"Come join us." I turned to the table and went to sit down. "Renlii, meet one of the most dangerous smugglers in the galaxy."

She was already standing, towering over him and gave him a smile as they locked wrists.

"I will watch myself," she said.

"Oh, not dangerous to you. Dangerous to himself."

Detsch sent a rude gesture my way as I slid in to make room for him. He brought his own food and drink over to our table. He was drinking krem and gru and was already a couple in. We decided to join him with the gru and ordered three for the table.

After we shared the first one, I gave him a better introduction to Renlii and we started catching up. He had a nice set of routes going, but things were tightening up for him like they were for everyone else. He complained about this and I started to smile.

"What's funny?" he asked with a scowl. He had a quick temper and was quick to fight, even with old friends.

"Calm down," I said with a laugh. "I was just thinking of you now compared to you in the old days. You are getting old."

He looked at Renlii and then at me, holding on to his scowl. I think if Renlii were not there he would have hit me.

"Renlii, let me tell you about this man and how he got his start," I said.

I grabbed his shoulder and gave him a wink. He could not help but smile and took a swig of his krem. There were few who knew how to handle him, but I had learned that you had to assure him you were playing and that things were all right before going on with the joke.

Renlii smiled at Detsch and looked at me with shining eyes.

"Detsch started working with pirates before he was even old enough to join the Corporate fleets. They were a mean bunch, with no rules among themselves and no loyalty. After just three years, he decided he had had enough."

"Two years."

"All right, two years. He installed remote disablers on the worm drives of each of the ships in his crew; he is very smart with these things and was able to install them without his crew detecting them. It also did not hurt that he was often the one inspecting the ships."

Detsch let out a laugh and took another drink of krem, still proud of himself after all the years.

"So, he waits and waits for the right moment. Then came an easy hit, just a small convoy of TriKarre cargo vessels. The convoy did not have much security and by the end of the mission, they captured two 2B vessels full of vesh and krem. Detsch was assigned to fly one of the vessels and they were all to meet at a pre-designated Station to sell the ships and cargo."

"I am guessing neither reached their intended destination," Renlii said, smirking at Detsch.

Detsch laughed. "One did not. As we approached speed, I shut off their drives and left without 'em."

"You left them stranded?" she asked, looking at me and wondering what kind of friends I had.

"No, no. I'm a *benetcho*, but I'm not a complete *mata*. I was tired of 'em, but I di'n't want 'em dead."

"How did they escape then?" she asked.

"The disabler was set to release after an hour. I figured that was long enough for me to get away, but not long enough for 'em to get captured."

"Did they seek you out?" she asked.

"I hear they still are," he said and we laughed with him.

We talked more about him and his business and then he asked about me and I told him about Sim and the battle. It hit me as I told him the story that we might be able to solve some of each other's problems.

"You say business is slow?" I asked.

"Yeah. Lost a few routes."

"Supply or purchase?"

"Both."

"What if I could give you some of my contacts and routes. Would that be worth something to you?"

"'Course. What're we talking?"

I went over the routes I had that were still available. I had lost some and had found other traders for others, but I had a few left that were waiting on me. The negotiations did not take long. I was reasonable and I liked him and I knew he would give me my share, so we settled on ten percent of the profits over the next two years. Then we settled the deal with a wrist lock and a shot of gru and I felt good that the routes were not a complete waste and I would get something out of it.

"Now that that is settled, we just need to find jobs," I said, winking at Renlii.

"First thing is getting Challa's fighter back to him," she said. "He is selling both and getting a larger ship again."

"You work with Challa?" Detsch asked.

"I did."

"You don't anymore?"

I looked at Renlii and she nodded and did not say anything. Detsch caught this.

"Wait. What happened?"

I waited for Renlii to say something, but she was quiet, looking into what was left of her krem.

"Challa's crew caught it," I said.

"*Chee.*"

"Challa and Renlii got out in fighters. The rest are gone."

"Bentook?"

I nodded as the waiter arrived with another round of gru and krem. He could sense the seriousness of the table and did not say anything. I watched Renlii. She had not said anything for a while, but now, she looked up at both of us grimly and raised her glass of gru.

"To Bentook and Ree and Da'd and Pell and Khiltala. They were excellent and loyal crew mates. They were my friends."

Detsch and I joined her and drank our gru and fell into the darkness. When we came back out of it, our food was waiting. It was steaming hot as promised. It had been weeks since I had hot food and it looked more delicious than anything I had seen in a long time.

"Jlaeal, this has been fun, but I got a meeting I gotta to run to," Detsch said as he stood to leave.

"How long will you be on board?" I asked.

"I leave tomorrow."

"Then come back when business is done," Renlii said. "We plan on staying a while and swimming in krem and gru."

Detsch laughed and said he would. He turned and took a step, but then stopped and came back.

"Renlii, you lookin' for a new crew?"

"I have not started to search yet, but I am available."

Detsch nodded and looked at me and then her. "Either of you know Captain Echta?"

I shook my head. Renlii had not heard of her either.

"She's an old friend. Older than Jlaeal even," he said with a smile. "I think she's looking to expand."

I looked at Renlii and raised my eyebrows. Renlii looked at Detsch as if trying to read into his soul.

"I would like to meet with her," she said.

"She's the one I'm meeting with. When we're done, I'll bring'er back here."

He left and we dug into dinner. The waiter had undersold it. It was not the best food I had ever had, but it was *pada* good and I enjoyed every bite.

Renlii and I talked about the possibility of her joining Echta's crew. We had finished the meal and were drinking more krem when Detsch came back with Captain Echta. She seemed solid and fair and we knew some of the same people. We dove deeper into the gru trips, which grew longer and longer and before the night was done, Renlii was part of Echta's crew.

The Void was a dark place, but the good people in the Void

were like shining stars breaking through the darkness, making life good and worth living. We started the day in love, but with few prospects and a bleak future, but things had turned around and there was hope.

Sometimes the Void beats you down to the point where you think there is no hope, but you can never give in or she will find a way to make things worse. You cannot win against her, but you can survive, by ignoring the pain and hardships and working in spite of it and living every day and enjoying the things that are good.

As I drank and laughed and talked with my friends that night, I kept looking at Renlii, knowing that she was the brightest light in the Void to me and I could not bear life without her.

TWENTY-TWO

I WOKE UP alone. I lay in bed and thought of Renlii, wishing she was there. It was funny how things had changed. I had never wanted any woman to stay in bed past the pleasure portion, and there I was missing Renlii and unable to sleep with her gone. She was out on her first mission with Echta. I was not worried about her. I just missed her. I knew it was a waste of time to stay in the rack, so I crawled out and started my exercises.

My hand and leg worked well now, but I still had a couple weeks of hard work before they were back to what they once were. Between sets I caught a look at myself in the reflective screen. Sometimes, that was all it took, a quick look, a glance into your own eyes, to come to an epiphany. I had enjoyed my time with Renlii, but had used it as an excuse to put off moving forward. I loved her and that was a new experience and I had focused everything on that, but now that she was gone, I had time to think about where I was going.

I had been independent for so long that the thought of working for someone else filled my stomach with alidnum and gave me the cold sweats. But sometimes in life, you have to do things you do not want to do. I could either sit around and feel sorry for myself, or I could get back into the fight.

I was about to start another round of squats when the hatch beeped and someone started banging on it and yelling, "Get up, you lazen helo-thumper."

I laughed and rushed for the door, palmed the hatch and there, with a wide grin on his face, stood Challa. I reached out for his shoulders, but he pulled me in for a back-crushing hug. This time I did not fight it, and for once I enjoyed it. I let it linger a while and then broke away and grabbed his shoulders.

"I am very glad to see you alive," I said.

He had tears in his eyes as he nodded. He grabbed my shoulders and gave me a serious look. "I am very glad to see you, my friend."

Challa was a poor setrak player and showed his feelings freely. His smile was real and his scowl was real and his anger was real. A smile broke back on his face and he slapped me on the shoulders and I knew he would be alright.

"Look at you," he said and laughed. "Let me see them." Before I could even react, he took my hand and inspected it, turning it over and feeling at different spots.

"It looks like your old hand. How does it work?"

"In a few more days, you will not be able to tell the difference," I told him.

"And the leg?"

"The same."

"Good! Then you can join me for a drink!"

"*Puda* right!"

He gave me time to take a cleanse before we left and we headed to Trill's Delight. Challa picked a table near the middle of the room and we sat down. I always picked a side table or something in the back so I could watch what was going on in the room and feel that at least my back was safe, but Challa preferred to sit right in the center, so he could "feel the temperature."

Renlii and I had made Trill's Delight our regular place. It did not have the exotic servers of the Cavern, but it had a good feel to it and the drinks were good and the food was good and the crowd was usually good and without the type that was looking for a fight.

As soon as we sat down, the waitress was at our table. She was a young Drakkaran and kept her face clean of the normal Drakkaran facial hair. I found it unusual and refreshing, but in spite of that abnormality, the place made you feel as if you were on Drakkara itself, inside a krem bar in the home capital. We both ordered krem and I started it off with Challa.

"Renlii told me of Demisha."

He sighed and looked at the table and then at me.

"You could not wait for me to finish one krem before starting?"

He was right. Puda. "I guess my thirst for news was greater than my thirst for krem."

He smiled. "Well, that is thirsty indeed. Never have I known you to crave anything more than krem, except maybe women."

I laughed with him as the waitress brought the krems back.

"Are you eating?" she asked.

"Yes," I told her. "Menas. Messy. With gremacas and tomas. And a side of shredded loches."

"You?" she asked Challa.

"Menas. Clean. With gremacas and cheese; no tomas."

She walked away without a word. She was a very cool waitress, showing little warmth, which was a different feel from the other waiter.

Challa raised his krem to me saying, "To our friends who have joined the Void."

We saluted each other and took a long pull of the icy cold drink. It was from Drakkara, of course, and it was very good. You could not name your bar after Trill and not serve real Drakkaran krem.

We sat quiet for a time and reflected on our old friends. I thought it best to let him begin, especially after I ruined it earlier. I did not know whether he wanted to discuss it or not and decided I would not push it again.

He broke the silence after another long drink of krem. "I have been on two Stations attacked by Corporations," he said. "I hope I never see it again."

I nodded. I had been on one, and that was where I met Challa. It was not the worst thing I have experienced, but it was high on the list. I gave Challa a moment to continue, but I could tell that he did not want to go into details.

"I am glad that you and Renlii both made it out," I said.

He nodded and took another drink.

"Where will you go?" I asked. "What about here?"

He shook his head and gave me a sad determined look. "I am through taking risks I should not take. No more swimming upstream for Challa."

"What does that mean?"

"I will find another ship, rebuild my crew and I will base out of a UI Station."

I almost dropped my krem. Challa and I had always seen eye-to-eye on things in the Void, but this was a quick turn.

"You are siding with Trask?"

"No, my friend, I am siding with Challa."

I shook my head. It was a sad thing to hear.

"Listen, we both choose to live in the Void and we both know that in the Void, we change with it or we die."

This was true. It was a fundamental truth of the Void.

"It is time," he said. "Look at how many Stations have gone down in such a short period. We ignored this for a while, but then Demisha, now Nathara — what choice do we have?"

"Nathara?" I looked at him in shock. I had heard nothing of Nathara. Challa looked up at me in alarm as it hit him.

"Oh. My friend. I am sorry, I assumed you had heard. It happened a week ago."

"*Chee.*" I had nothing else to say. My stomach rose up to my throat and I fought the emotions. I thought of the captain, whom I knew well. I thought of my friends there. I thought of Edda and wondered if she got away.

"You see what I mean?" Challa said. "Everything crumbles around us. Everyone who does not side with Trask is destroyed. I am tired of running. I am tired of fighting this battle. We cannot win."

"*Chee.*"

"Yes — *chee*. The whole Void is *chee* and *haachee*. But at least on a UI Station I will be safe and my crew will be safe and we can continue our work."

I sat dumbfounded by it all.

"Jlaeal, I know there is something personal between you and Trask, but it is time to put it aside."

I looked up at him in surprise.

He laughed.

"You are no stranger to me. I can read you like a deck of setrak chips. There is a past between you. I can hear it in the way you speak about him. And further, if it were not personal, you would have already gone with the safe bet."

I shook my head. I thought all the cards were hidden and close to the chest, but Challa knew and I wondered who else did.

"I used to work for him —"

"You do not need to tell me," he said.

"I know. But you are my closest friend and you should know. I worked for him, back during the GF."

Challa gave me a look of complete surprise, but did not say a word. The statement was loaded and he knew what it meant and I did not have to say anything more about what I did.

"I know the man," I continued. "He is brilliant. No, beyond brilliant. By far, the smartest man I have ever met. But I have seen how he uses and manipulates people. He is dangerous and I do not trust him. I have watched my friends die for the furtherance of his plans."

I leaned in closer and lowered my voice. There were ears everywhere and what I was about to speak would get me killed.

"He runs the syndicates, Challa." Challa turned his head, processing what I was telling him. "All of them. We are all meant to think they are independent, and to some extent they are, but if Trask tells them to do something, they do it, or the other syndicates take them out. That is truth."

Challa took another long pull from his krem and finished it off just as another round was brought to us.

"You know this?" he asked.

I nodded. "I know much about the man. He holds power over the Void more than anyone knows. Taking over the Stations is just his next move. He is more dangerous than the Corporations. At least they come at you straight ahead with shields on and guns blazing. Trask will come at you with a warm smile, while one of his people slits your throat from behind."

Challa sat and processed this, saying nothing.

"I cannot back him. I have seen too much."

Challa shifted in his seat and leaned in closer. "It is no longer about backing him. It is about backing yourself, making the safe bet and watching out for your own ass."

I shrugged. I did not want to think about it, but deep down I knew my options were shrinking. And now I had Renlii to think about, which meant I had to think clearly and without emotion.

"You do not need to work for him again. You do not need to get involved. But you do need to take the safe bet. He is not worth dying for."

Deep down I knew he was right and I should take the safe play, but I could not do it. Not yet. I thought again of Nathara and looked at Challa and we both took another long pull from our krem, and in spite of the early hour, I wanted a gru.

"How is Renlii?" he asked. He was good at changing the topic at the right time, just as he had won his point. I smiled.

"Good. She joined a salvage team led by a woman named Echta. Have you heard of her?"

"I have heard of her."

"We met her through a trader friend of mine. He recommended her and I trust him."

"Good. She is very skilled. I was sad to lose her."

"I am sure. You always seem to find a way though. I am sure you will be fine," I said with a wink.

"She sent me a message that the fighter is here. I am going to sell it and put the money toward a larger vessel."

I nodded and sipped at the krem.

"And you two. How are you two? It seems you have made your decision?"

I laughed. "There was no decision to make. I woke up and she was sitting at my bed and I knew. For better or for worse, we are both in it."

"For worse. You know where it will lead."

"You are the one that encouraged me to stay with her."

"No." He shook his head. "I just wanted you to make the decision with all sensors clear, not in that *haachee* dark cloud you were hiding in. I knew it was too late even then, but I wanted the decision to be yours."

I nodded and took another sip of krem.

"What will you do?" he asked.

"We will base together and live together and see each other when we can and hope that the Void is merciful."

"You know she will not be."

I shrugged. Challa shrugged, but he wore the saddest face I had ever seen him wear.

I laughed. "I have not died, Challa. I am still here."

"I know. But life is already hard. I think this will make it much worse for the both of you."

"Yes. And much better. Both at the same time."

He shrugged again and raised his krem with a forced smile. "Well, here is to love and the Void and life being wondrous and *haachee*."

I laughed. "To wondrous and *haachee*."

We saluted each other with the krem and drank the last. We drank the rest of the day, exchanging stories and jokes and lies until we both passed out. When I woke the next morning he was gone.

TWENTY-THREE

CHALLA GAVE ME much to think about. The changes in the Void would be permanent. I did not trust Trask and would never work for him again or his *haachee* outfit, but I did not want to get me or Renlii killed by a Corporate fleet because I was too stubborn to change.

Renlii was not scheduled to come back for a few days. We had several things to talk about when she got back, including finding a safer home. I was also restless about my dwindling savings and about work and about being trapped on the Station without the ability to light out whenever I felt like it. I used my days alone to send messages out about work and to talk to the few contacts I knew on the Station.

I had sent messages out before the surgery, hoping for a quick recovery, but I had not received any bites for work yet. If I wanted to try my hand at pirating again, I could have worked right away, but I was not anxious to pursue that again. I was good at smuggling, good at networking and finding opportunities, and good at getting past Corporate security, but I was not the only trader that liked to work alone. Most traders did not like to split their profits.

I went to Trill's Delight again and sat at the bar. I was sipping on a krem, thinking of what else I could do to find work. Sitting at a table in a corner was safer, but now that I was looking for work, safety was less important than sitting where I could talk to the bartender and listen to gossip.

Having my back to the crowd made me nervous. I scanned the

place again. It was empty except for a few travelers, but it had a growing buzz to it, as if things were about to get busy. A man walked in and searched the bar, as if he was looking for someone. He looked like a trader, with meek pants and a meek shirt, matched with hard hide boots and a tan jacket that matched his shaggy light-brown hair.

He did not search long, before strolling over to the bar as if he had found what he was looking for. He played it cool and did not look my way, but I knew I was his target. He sat down two seats to my left and ordered a krem. I hoped that it was business, but kept my guard up just in case. While the bartender poured his drink, he watched carefully, as if he was afraid the bartender might slip him. The bartender set it down in front of him and he took a long drink, then set it back down and turned to face me.

"You Jlaeal?" he asked.

"We know each other?" I had already set myself in as good a position as possible, holding my krem with my left hand, with my right hanging down close to my gun. I had worked on my draw with my new hand. It was still not where it should be, but it would be enough if it came to it.

He was relaxed and did not show any signs that he was there for trouble, but some of the best draws were that way and seemed very cool until they shot you. He had the appearance of someone who did not care about his looks or what people thought of him. He had an accent I had heard a few times, that I guessed was from some less populated area in the TriKarre territory.

"I'm looking for a secon'. Hear you be a good man to have at my back."

I grinned. "Depends on who sent you."

He smirked. "He sai' he was an ol' frien'. Tra'er named Mik."

I smiled but did not drop my guard. Mik was an old friend. We met after the Liquidation and hit it off right away. Like Challa, he told things the way they were, without any flattery or *haachee*. If Mik did send this man my way, I could trust him, but I had to make sure that was the case.

"Who are you? And how do you know Mik?"

I relaxed enough to take a sip of the krem, but not enough to take my hand away from the gun. Anyone could say you shared a friend, but all it proved was that they knew who your friends were.

"Name's Kep."

Under normal circumstances, we would have locked wrists, but the point of locking wrists was that you trusted the other person enough to take your hand away from your gun. He could sense I was not ready yet and did not force it.

"We were compe'ors for years and hate' each other 'til we were in a bar on Xtil Station one night. We're both alone, sittin' at our own tables. He walk' up to my table carryin' two krems and two grus. He set down across from me and says, 'I'm tire' o' hatin' you. We're gonna drin' this together and much more 'fore the night is over. Either we will be frien's by the end of it, or one of us will be dea.'"

I laughed. That sounded like Mik. He could not stand hating someone unless he knew for sure it was worth the effort.

"We spent the night drinkin' and laughin'. We' been frien's ever since. We even sen' each other business when we're too busy to take it oursell'es."

"A friend of Mik's cannot be half bad," I said with a smile.

I pulled my hand away from the bar and reached out to him. He smiled and we grasped each other's wrist. It was an old tradition, but one that worked.

We spent the next hour telling each other stories about Mik and then about ourselves and how we got to be where we were. Then, we got to my final story, which was about losing my ship and two limbs.

"An' now you wanna work," Kep said.

I nodded. "You have something?"

"Yeah," he said. "Lookin' for a par'ner. Well, I'm in charge. It's my operation, but like I sai', I need a secon'."

"What happened to your last one?"

"Always work' alone 'til now."

"Why now? Expanding?"

He nodded and took another sip of krem. "Of a sort. Got a bi'er ship but same routes. Bi'er shipmen's an' hopefully more profi's."

"So what would the second do?"

"Watch my ass."

"You are tired of looking after your own?"

"You tryin' to talk me out of hirin' you?" he asked.

I laughed, but was not sure he was kidding. He was hard to read. And there was something I did not trust about him, but on its own that did not mean anything. Some people were just like that when you first met them. He seemed arrogant and full of himself. That might have been why Mik did not like him at first.

"No. I just like to know what I am walking into."

He looked at me with caution. "Mik sai' you were careful. Tha's what I wan'. You and I both know the galaxy ain' what it was ten years a'o, or one year a'o or even a month a'o. Thin's are tigh'er. Tougher. We have frien's dyin' every 'ay now in Station rai's."

"True. How will a partner help? It will not stop the Stations from getting raided, or Corporations from boarding your ship."

"No. But a secon' can help me keep an extra set a eyes out. You know there are more eyes out there now, lookin' for us, trackin' us."

"I know this."

"Even planetsi'e, there's no safe por' any more. Vendors I once truste' have turn' on their own travelers."

He was right. Corporations were offering bigger rewards and freedom from prosecution if the vendor reported on a smuggler. Things were not what they used to be.

"While I ma'e the deals, when I dock the ship, when I offloa' or uploa', I want you to keep an eye out for anyone too intereste'. I will do the same, but you know how' is. Sometimes you're 'ealin' with the business si'e of things, and ge' distracte'."

"Right," I said, "so you want someone on security."

"We both will, but it'll be your main focus. You'll help with other details too, but I wan' you doin' research on our conta's. I'll as' my people and you'll as' yours, so we have double the intel. And, you watch my back while I'm distracte'. Easy enough, no?"

"Sure," I said. "What about the pay?"

"I figure, twenny percen' of the profi's, plus I pay for room, boar' and drin's while planetsi'e."

We talked it over some more and went into more details. I had to know what the costs were to make any kind of good decision. In the end, we settled on twenty-five percent, which was not bad. He was leaving for Drakkara the next day and wanted me to go with him. I still had reservations though and did not want to commit fully until I saw him in action.

"I do not like stepping into a full relationship without checking out the goods first," I said.

"What are you thinkin'," he asked.

"I think you and I should make this trip a trial run. We work together under the agreed conditions. If we like each other and work well together we keep going. If not, we part as friends."

He said nothing. He looked at me with an unreadable face, then let slip a grin and reached his arm out.

"Agree'."

I smiled and took his arm and we both ordered another gru. I was not anxious to leave Renlii and hoped she would make it back before I left.

When I got back to the apartment, Renlii was already there. I took her in my arms and we kissed and held each other. Then the kissing turned to groping and then other things. It was a while before we even said anything.

"Do you trust him?" she asked while we lay in bed naked, wrapped around each other.

"No."

"Then why do you go?"

"I agreed to a single job. A test. Trust comes with time and experience. At the end of the job, I will either trust him or I will not."

"Or you could be dead."

"That is always a risk."

"And when you come back?"

I told her about Challa's visit and his decision to move to a UI Station. She did not say anything right away. She was silent, thinking, then, "We should follow him."

"What?"

I sat up and looked at her.

"I do not trust this Trask any more than you do," she said. "Especially after the stories you have told. But sometimes you must move with the flows of the Void. There are times when fighting is suicide. Sometimes it is worth it. But fighting this has no value."

"What about freedom?"

"How long will we be free if we stay on a non-UI Station?"

I had no answer for that. It would not be long.

"My gut says you are right. I do not trust it lately though."

"Your gut has been right all along. You just choose to ignore it."

I looked at her again. Was she trying to start an argument?

"What did your gut tell you about joining with Sim?" she asked.

I did not want to answer. She was right and I did not want to say it.

"You kept saying you had a bad feeling. You ignored it and you lost your ship and other things."

I agreed.

"So," she said, "your gut was right, but you ignored it. My gut says we should go to a UI Station where things are safe. Your gut agrees. My mind does not like it. I want nothing to do with that man or his organization, but we will go to one of his Stations and stay away from him."

I did not say anything. She was right but I could not force myself to say it. I looked into her eyes though and thought of her safety and the decision was made.

"You are right. We will go. I will finish this job with Kep and you will wrap things up with Echta and we will follow Challa."

She took my face in her hands and looked into my eyes.

"I know this is not easy for you, but it is right. You know this."

"Yes, I know this."

She kissed me firmly with passion. I thought we would stay there all night, but she surprised me by getting out of bed.

"Where are you going?" I asked.

"We are going to go out and enjoy each other's company in other ways. I want to go out and celebrate our last night together on a free Station."

She pulled me out of the rack and we both took a cleanse and got ready. I got out of the cleanser before she did and made a few secret arrangements, then we put on our best clothes and headed out.

She kept asking where we were going, but I wanted it to be a surprise and did not tell her. She would put on her angry face like she was annoyed that I was keeping it secret, but I could see through the anger and knew she was having fun.

While wandering the Station while Renlii was away I had found a club like you would find planetside on one of the GC core planets. It was in the storage section of the Station, near the docks. From the outside, it looked like a warehouse entrance. There were two large loading doors, so large you could fit my old ship through them.

A large Diviian stood at the doorway. He was exploding with muscles, had guns strapped to each leg, and guarded the entrance with extreme vigilance, as if he were guarding a vault filled with gold. I found the password from the bartender at Trill's Delight and when I gave it to the giant, he opened up a secret, smaller door and let us inside.

Renlii was on guard as she approached the guard, but as soon as we were safely inside she dropped her restraint. She grabbed me by the arm and held on to me, staring around her in wonder, like a kid seeing magic for the first time.

The club was a shining, glowing tribute to the old clubs from the prime GF days. The floors seemed to open up to the Void, making it feel as if you were floating in space. It was disorienting at first and took a while to get used to. The booths on both sides looked like small asteroids, but they were fitted with comfortable leather disguised to look like rock. The seats floated in place, but once you sat down, it drifted up and down and side to side on the wall around the other booths, as if you were part of a large asteroid field.

A bar at the end looked like it had been carved out of an asteroid, but it was one of the few things in the club that stayed in place. A large asteroid stage floated above the bar, as if it was a piece broken off from the bar itself. A Diviian woman sang, while a group of musicians stood behind her playing real instruments. Little glowing balls of light drifted throughout the club, changing colors as if they were little stars that grew in intensity for a while, building to a supernova explosion of light and then fading again.

An attendant gave us anti-grav belts when we walked in and brought us to our booth. As soon as we sat down it began drifting around the other booths along the wall. The club was filled with peoples from every end of the galaxy, dancing on the ground, in the air, the walls and even the ceiling. The music was loud, but you could still hear the laughter and people having fun, as if there were no problems anywhere in the Void.

The waitress came over as soon as we sat down. All she had on were tiny white panties, with a matching white anti-grav belt and an old white enviro helmet, open on the front and one side. There was a small army of male and female attendants throughout the club, all wearing the same outfit, as if they were ancient naked astronauts mining an asteroid field.

We drank fine drin that night and ate seafood from Diviia and when we were full, we ordered gru and drank until we felt very good. Then we turned on our belts, stepped out of the booth and floated on air as if we were walking in space. It was difficult to control where you moved at first and we had fun with this as we floated the wrong way and bumped into people, but we got the hang of things after a while and learned to move and dance to the music.

It was good to hear Renlii's laugh and see her shining smile. I fell in love with her all over again. She was beautiful and a delight and every one of her laughs made my heart burst out of my chest. We stayed at the club for hours, drinking and dancing and kissing among the stars, until all we wanted was to be alone and in each other's arms and then we left.

Neither of us slept at all that night. We kissed and touched and enjoyed each other until we were both exhausted. Then we lay naked in bed, holding onto each other and talking about a future together, hoping the Void would let us love each other without further harassment.

TWENTY-FOUR

I ARRIVED AT the dock the next morning tired and hungover, even after glephash. Kep's ship was half again as large as the *Asron Sun* and was not much to look at. She was called *Diviian Princess*, but it was hard to imagine how she got the name. The ship was gray synthsteel mixed with rust and remnants of an ancient paint job. She was an old cargo ship, made by Pibco, a company once known for building quality ships, before it was swallowed up by a larger but now extinct Diviian Corporation.

"She don' look li'e much, but she does alrigh'."

Kep had arrived behind me.

"As long as everything works."

"She wor's jus' fine. I woul'n' want to get into i' with a Corpora'e flee', but if we do, I don' figure it would matter what kin' of ship we ha'."

I disagreed, but smiled at him and did not respond. The *Sun* had helped me out of more scraps with Corporate fleets than I could count, and if she were not in top shape, I would not have had a chance. In fact, if she were not in top shape during the last battle, I would not have survived.

Kep showed me around the outside of the ship, going through the engines and external mechanics. None of it was nice to look at, but it all seemed operational.

"Come in. She loo's be'er insi'e."

I followed him up the ramp and through the hatch and he sealed it shut behind me. It was clean and everything was in order, but unimpressive. He showed me around and we went over the specs and mechanics of everything. I felt better afterward, as he had made solid upgrades that could help us in a jam. She did not have much in the way of weaponry, but she had a thick hide, decent shielding, and a good engine. We could not fight our way out of a battle, but we might be able to run.

The last thing he showed me was the little closet of a room where I would sleep. I set my pack down and turned to Kep.

"What kind of schedule do you like to keep? I should have asked that yesterday."

"You look tire'."

"I am. I am used to sleeping as soon as I light out, so I did not sleep."

"That ain' the way I wor' it. This is the mornin', so I plan on wor'in', plannin', ge'in' to know each other."

Some runners adapt to whatever Station they are on and do not change that schedule until they arrive at a new destination. I was always of the theory that once you left a Station you hit the wormhole and could just sleep for a couple of days. I never had a problem staying up all night and hitting the rack as soon as I lit out.

"Shoul'a aske'. Sleep or no', you're here to wor'."

"It will not be a problem."

"Goo'. Now le's ligh' ou'."

Kep had me pilot her out of the dock so he could see what skills I had. The ship handled rough, but she was not as bad as she looked. I took it slow and easy on the way out, but once I cleared the bay, I played with her to see what she could do.

"Wha'ya think?"

"She does fine."

"Fine!" He laughed and I smiled. He was proud of the ship and there was no point in arguing, but she was not in near as good of shape as he thought she was. I cleared the Station's gravity pull, set the coordinates and lit out.

Kep and I used the two-day trip to Drakkara to get to know each other and to go over the details of his operation. I was not impressed with him. He was cocky and sure of himself and was the type that did not ever see any wrong in his own actions. I enjoyed his company back when we drank, but I could not see us becoming good friends or long-term partners.

I wondered about his relationship with Mik. I sent a message to him right after the meeting asking about Kep just to make sure his story held up. I was curious to see what he had to say. I did not talk to Kep about plans after this trip. There was no point until I decided I would work with him again.

He did seem to want avoid as much risk as possible, which was a good sign. There are as many different methods of smuggling as there are ships in the galaxy and no way is wrong until you get caught. Whether or not you get caught depends on what risks you decide to take, how much planning you do and how smart you are.

The trip to Drakkara seemed low risk. We would land in a city on the back side of the planet, pick up krem and take it off planet. Kep had a license to ship goods within TriKarre as long as the goods did not leave their territory. This is what all of their licenses required, but it was rare for them to confirm where the goods ended up. Kep delivered only a small portion of his krem to an outpost on the way to Nejune, but his contact there always reported that all the krem was delivered. So as far as Drakkara was concerned, all krem was accounted for.

In spite of all this, I knew that every route in the Void held risk and that things were changing and more dangerous. On top of that, I did not know how he handled his contacts or operations planetside and as I got to know him, I started to worry about it. I was there to keep my eyes out for trouble, but the trouble could be Kep.

When we arrived in the Drakkara system, Kep took the controls and had me look out for signs of trouble. Security forces surrounded the ship and went over our licenses, but this was standard and his licensing checked out and they let us through without trouble.

We flew around to the back side of Drakkara to the city of Jphentia. Drakkara began calling it the backside because the front side was more advanced, but off-worlders called it the back side because of the stark geographic and landscape differences. While the rest of the planet was green and lush, the back side was a hot barren wasteland of mountain and rock and contained the nastiest creatures of the planet.

In spite of the relative harshness of the back side, I still enjoyed it. There was a peace that came with the open spaces that the Drakkarans left unmolested. Their respect for the planet and its beauty was a sharp contrast to other Corporations and a reminder of who they were as a people.

By their nature, Drakkarans were peaceful and believed in the power of nature to heal. It was ingrained in their systems from millennia of belief in the tranquil teachings of Trill, but I believed it was part of their natural instinct; non-Trillists were just as peaceful as followers of Trill.

Trill and TriKarre, Inc. were one and the same thing. TriKarre was owned and run by the Church of Trill and its CEO was also the head of the church. It did not make much sense to the rest of us, but to the Trillists and natural-born Drakkarans it made sense and had worked for centuries. Trillists are peaceful and pacifist by nature, and so the Corporation was peaceful and pacifist, but if you crossed them, you were crossing Trill, and they harbored no mercy for that.

Kep always did his business on the backside, away from the capital and the busiest sections of the planet. Security was more relaxed on the back side. Security surrounding the capital and the holy sanctum of Trill was intense by any measure and the farther we kept from that place the better.

Kep flew low over the city toward the port. It was nice to enjoy the view and not have to focus on flying. Drakkaran architecture was some of the most beautiful in the galaxy. They designed their buildings to blend in with its environment. In the Capitol, the buildings were made of wood from the ancient forests which surrounded it. The trees used for buildings were thousands of years old and were a solid and hearty wood, able to withstand centuries of abuse from the sun and weather. Each piece of wood held bas-reliefs which blended together to tell a story or create some kind of unified message. The Drakkarans were proud of their history and never tore down their buildings unless it was necessary for safety or by decree of the Church.

In contrast, the buildings in Jphentia were constructed out of the red rock taken from the hillsides and mountains that surrounded the city, making the buildings look as if they were carved out of the mountains themselves. Like the Capitol, the buildings were carved by hand with exquisite craftsmanship. Although they were made with hundreds or thousands of individual stones, they showed no seams or cracks and appeared as if they were carved out of a single stone. The buildings flaunted scenes of nature or history or scenes telling stories of Trill.

We passed over a residential district, which blended into a business district and then came to the krem district. It was a fraction of the size of the one at the Capitol, but it was still immense, with thousands of large buildings spanning mylons in every direction. Demand for real Drakkaran krem from the home planet was more than they could produce realistically, so entire swaths of the krem districts of the major cities were eaten up with warehouses and distribution centers. It was by far their biggest export and their most profitable.

Port Sec had already been prepped by System Sec that we were on our way. Kep angled the ship to the expansive opening at the top of the port and hovered over the lip while they did a thorough scan. These scans told them everything they could want to know about the ship and anyone on board. By the end of the scan, they knew who we were and our entire history and the history of the ship and had a full inventory of everything on board. But a good smuggler knew how to hide things on their ship and had a fake travel history in place. There was always a way.

"*Diviian Princess*, you are clear to land. Section five, space fourteen."

"Copy," was all Kep said. He was very professional with his flying and did not joke or flirt as I did.

He lowered the ship down into the port. The port was always busy, with ships leaving and arriving and customers, buyers and traders conducting their business on every level of the large structure. The building itself was an incredible feat of engineering and was beautiful. Like the other buildings, it was made of red stone and molded together seamlessly, with bas-reliefs in the stone going down representing old Drakkaran parables of Trill, or his followers, helping travelers and wayfaring strangers. The depictions going up portrayed ancient parables warning of the dangers of travel and advising caution and wisdom when traveling to strange lands. It had an old-world charm that I loved so much in Drakkaran culture.

Kep guided us down through the hundred levels of the port to the designated pad near the edge of an immense landing field at the bottom. As soon as the ship set down, he sent a message to his contact that we had arrived. We hit the release on our seat harnesses and I followed him to the main hatch to check in with Port Sec.

When the hatch opened, a traditional-looking Drakkaran woman was waiting at the bottom of the ramp with a security drone at each shoulder. TriKarre was smart in placing orthodox Trillists in the security divisions of the company. A purist would never take a bribe or betray the company.

We stood at the top of the ramp and stepped aside as one of

the drones flew into the ship. The other one stayed at her shoulder, with its guns locked on us.

"Fkasha," Kep said to her. "Peace to you."

She did not look all that pleased, but returned the standard Drakkaran greeting, "Peace to you, Kep."

She looked in my direction and her look brightened. "Peace to you, Jlaeal." I did not recognize her at first, but then realized I had dealt with her several times and she was very pleasant. She was sometimes cold, but always fair and truthful.

I returned her smile, "Peace to you, Fkasha."

"Where is the *Sun*?"

"In the Void. Pirates took her."

She nodded, somber. "I am sad to hear of it, but I am glad you are alive."

I had decided to revise the story and blame pirates for her loss. It was my fault as much as Sim's, but piracy was at the core of the loss and it sounded better to say that pirates took her, rather than admit to being a pirate.

Fkasha turned back to Kep and the light in her eyes died down. She did not care for him and did not try to hide it. I was already nervous about the deal, but after seeing her reaction to him, I felt a rising panic. We were legal, technically, but if he had crossed someone, things could go bad fast.

"Pickin' up krem from Laughin' Boar. Takin' it to Bal'ash minin' Station in the Nalla sec'or."

"We have this on record. How much of the krem will remain there?"

Kep looked shocked.

"All of i'. Tha's wha' I'm license' for."

She nodded and gave me a quick glance. I did not like the way this was going at all. I could not tell if this was a normal occurrence for Kep, but she had never grilled me to this level.

"Yes. That is what the license says. All of it."

The drone flew back out of the ship and went back to hovering at her shoulders while she held her stare at Kep.

"Have I ma'e a mistake, Fkasha? If I di' somethin' wron', or somethin' to offen' Tri'arre or Trill I'll fix i.'"

"TriKarre is Trill, Kep. Remember that. Just make sure the krem reaches Baltash and all will be satisfied."

"O' course."

"Standard package while you are here?"

"Jus' a refuel," he said, showing signs of relief.

She made a notation on her pad and left the ship, giving me one last glance that gave me a cold chill. It might have been my imagination, but she had sadness in her eyes when they fell on me, like she was seeing me for the last time. Kep was on someone's bad side and now TriKarre had him on their radar. I knew then we would be lucky to escape the planet.

TWENTY-FIVE

I T SEEMED LIKE many rotations before the vendor came. It was longer than I had ever had to wait, but his contacts eventually arrived and we traded the Drakkaran creds for a ship full of krem. They were not friendly and I watched them load the last pallet onto the ship with a growing apprehension. I thought about leaving Kep and striking out on my own, but it would not help. They would still arrest me. I would just have to ride it out.

We said our goodbyes to the krem vendors and sealed ourselves back into the *Princess*.

"Friendly guy," I said.

"He use'a be a lo' nicer. Ge'in' more and more pissy."

"What happened?"

Kep walked straight to the cockpit and I followed behind.

"No' sure. Maybe I sai' somethin' to piss him off."

We sat down in the cockpit seats and began the startup sequence.

"Did you?"

"Who knows. Does i' ma'er?"

"Hells yes it does. What if he decides to report you and make a bonus out of it?"

He waved me off, as if I said something absurd.

He opened the com to the tower, "*Diviian Princess* seal' and ready for ta'eoff."

"*Diviian Princess*, stand by."

The com system went silent as we waited for clearance to take off. Another bad sign.

"Something is wrong," I said. He lifted a finger to his lips and entered a command on his console.

"Blocker's on. Can' hear us. I don' like it either."

"I have never had to wait like this."

He nodded. There were little beads of sweat on his forehead.

"Be rea'y," he said.

I knew this guy was *haachee*. Should have listened to my gut. I ignored my gut before and lost the *Sun*. Now I was about to lose more. I thought about getting off the ship and making my own way off planet, but it was too late. Whether I liked it or not, we were in the *chee* together. I strapped in as he lifted his finger to his lips and entered a command on his console.

"Tower, are we clear?"

"Hold, *Diviian Princess*. We are scanning now. You will be cleared at its completion."

Kep looked at me with a look of hidden dread. We did not have a lot of moves here. Security had enough weapons and droids on the dock to blow us to hells before we ever left our pad. All we could do was sit and wait and each moment of waiting was like an eternity. I thought of all the ways it could go down and all of them were bad. There were ways it could go well for us, but none of them seemed realistic at the time.

"*Divvian Princess*. You are cleared. Please use flight path Five A for exit."

It felt as if a Jintaran Helo had stepped off my back and I let out a deep breath; Kep gave me one of his arrogant winks. The ship lifted and Kep maneuvered her to window Five A, which was lit up green on the vid screen. I turned the sensors on before we even cleared the dock, suspicious that more dangers were ahead.

"See anythin'?" Kep asked.

I started a tight scan and saw that it was clear outside the dock. I expanded the scan to a wider net and did not see anything that looked like it was waiting for us.

"Nothing suspicious. Just commercial traffic."

Each Corporation had a different way of dealing with trouble.

GC and Nallimar took care of things right there on the dock to avoid any additional hassle. But TriKarre liked to do things by the book, even though they created the book. Loading goods onto a ship was not illegal. You had to make an attempt to smuggle the goods off planet to break TriKarre law, so they waited until the ship left the port, so they could charge you with smuggling. Then they guided the ship to the awaiting fleet, or if you resisted, they obliterated you.

We both knew this and that leaving the port meant nothing. We were not out of the wormhole yet. Every muscle was tight as I watched the scans, but the sensors showed no signs of trouble as we cleared the port. I looked at the vid screen and could see nothing on them either.

"I thin' we're clear," Kep said.

"Not until we light out. Anything can happen until then."

"Ahh. Don' be so down."

The sensors were a flurry of activity, with cargo ships flying in and out of the busy dock and ships flying across the city on various errands. The ship's system had a different symbol for cargo vessels and personal vessels and TriKarre Security. I set the sensors to mark any TriKarre Security in red and auto-amplify so that I could spot them easier.

We were far above the city now and angled to exit the planet on the far side, away from the heaviest security. I was sure Kep knew that the fastest route to light out was on the front side, but he was trying to avoid the busiest activity, which I did not mind.

A ship outlined in red came onto the sensor field and before I could say anything another one popped on. Both were angling our way.

"Two sec ships coming straight at us," I said.

"*Chee.* You sure they headin' to us?"

"Yeah. And a third just came up behind."

"*Chee.*" Kep wiped the sweat from his forehead with his forearm just before it dripped into his eyes.

"*Diviian Princess*, this is TriKarre Security. Head to Security

Station T-Five. Coordinates have been sent to your guidance system. Any deviation will result in immediate termination. Turn all shields off. Comply and respond."

"*Chee*. Wha' now?"

"Comply. Turn the shields off."

"I will no'. I' rather die on this hulk than go to a damn prison Station!"

Kep was a complete *mata* and I was tempted to turn him over and hope for the best. "Just comply," I told him and signed in pirate code that we would not be complying.

He just nodded. A fourth ship arrived and they surrounded us, with one in back, another in front and the other two rotating around the ship. Kep looked at me for a beat, shrugged, brought the shields down and opened the com.

"This is *Diviian Princess*. Shiel's down."

"Copy, *Diviian Princess*. Do not deviate."

"Copy."

Kep shut down the com and keyed on the sound buffer system.

"Wha' now, smar' guy?" he asked.

"I think we can both agree this hulk will not get far in a fight with them."

Kep showed a flash of anger, but then laughed.

"Give me a bit to think this through."

"You go' abou' three bi's before we clear air and another five before we're a' their station," he said.

I expanded the sensors beyond the planet and out to the system. Station T-Five was past the first moon and farther into the system. We would have to clear the system to light out, but at our speed that was a good ten minutes of fly time. I scanned the system and ran calculations.

"Runnin' out o' time," he said.

"Hold on, *pudak*," then, "Wait. Wait. I got it."

"Qui'. We're hittin' space."

"Start fluctuating the speed. Just a little, up, down and start acting like the controls are fighting you. Just a little."

"Alrigh'. Fine. Wha' then?"

He started doing as I said, making slight adjustments to the speed and direction back and forth. He showed his skill as a pilot, as the movements were very subtle.

"We are going to have problems with one of our engines. I will fix it so that it will start smoking, meanwhile, you act as if the computer is fighting you on the controls and overcompensating. Slowly increase the struggle until the engine begins to smoke, then pour it on. Fight with the controls and make it look like we are losing control. Keep them on the coms and let them listen in. Ask for help. Meanwhile, gradually increase the speed of the ship."

"Thin' i"ll work?"

"You have to sell it."

"Bu', will I' wor'?"

"It has before," I said as I unstrapped myself from the seat and got up to go to the engine room.

"This is complete bli'ze'."

"You have a better idea?"

Kep shrugged.

"Just keep an eye on what I do to the engine. Keep heading straight to the station, build up speed and at the right time, kick the shields on and punch it."

I made my way to the engine compartment and tried not to think about how blitzed it was. I had done it before, a long time ago, but on a ship and pilot I trusted. You can adjust the mixing ratio in the engine and make it smoke, but that would be too obvious. I would have to turn the engines off and on to sell it, otherwise their scanners would be able to tell that the engines were running fine.

I recalibrated the right engine to burn at the wrong rate and then withheld the fuel mixture so it could not burn right if it wanted to. I played with the mixture and the burn at an increasing rate and listened in on the com system.

"*Diviian Princess*, maintain speed during approach."

"I'm tryin," came Kep's voice over the speakers. "Havin' problems with the righ' — fuck!"

I had cut off the right engine on him at just the right moment. I watched the monitors and saw that he took advantage of it and started spinning the ship and slowed her down.

"Level off. Maintain speed."

I changed the engine mix, fired her back up and smoke poured out of her.

"Tryin," Kep said. "Righ' engine. Havin' problems. Jlaeal, wha' is i'?"

I could see that he was increasing the speed in spite of the engine going in and out, but he was very subtle about it. He was a *pada* good pilot.

"*Diviian Princess,* if you do not level off and maintain speed, we will be forced to —"

Before they could finish I broke in, "Kep, I think the engine firmware is corrupt. It will not shut down and is self-adjusting the mix."

"Try manual reboo'."

"Diviian Princess, you will level off. Now!"

"You fuckin' bastar'! I can'! Jlaeal? Try the reboo'."

"It ignores all commands. Try the main system. Shut her down. All stop and we can do a manual reboot."

"TriKarre? You hear what he just sai'?"

"Yes. We hear you."

"We're gonna try a manual reboo'. Means the engines'll stop and we'll coas' and then we'll try to reboo'. In the meantime, sen' some help jus' in case i' don' work."

There was silence on the other end. We passed the main fleet and were heading toward the Station, but were well over approach speed and the speed was climbing. The ship was still flying erratically, and I continued to turn the engine on and off. Smoke continued to pour out of the back.

"*Diviian Princess*, change your course to the following coordinates to meet with a Cruiser and repair ship. Once you are headed toward those coordinates, shut down all systems and we will board."

"Copy, TriKarre."

Kep shut the com system down and called me on the in ship system, "Now wha'?"

I looked at the sensor map and sent Kep the coordinates I was looking at. For the most part, you needed to get out of a system to light out, but once in a while, there were spots in-system which allowed for a wormhole. The coordinates to the nearest area of clearance was just three minutes away, but with the fighters on us and the cruisers nearby, that was a long three minutes. Kep sent a private message, telling me to fix the engine at his signal. I kept playing with the engine until Kep's voice came over the com system.

"Now."

I normalized the mix and reset the levels at default on the system and raced back to the cockpit. He had flipped the shields on and punched the accelerator and the security ships went into full attack mode. By the time I got up to the cockpit, we were racing to the gravity hole and Kep was dodging energy blasts from the fighters.

"Take the weapons!" Kep yelled.

I kept the weapons on auto but adjusted the focus from the nearest ship, to scatter shot. The *Princess'* guns were weak, but shots to the pilots' screen could create a distraction. Kep maneuvered the ship like a drunken racer, so that few blasts hit the bulky ship where it mattered, but the shields were weakening and each blast increased the odds that we would lose them altogether. Then a loud explosion shook the ship.

"They go' through. Righ' engine gone."

We started spinning for real this time, but Kep increased power to the other engine and used the spin to dodge the fire. Two of the fighters switched from energy blasters to tactile guns and shrapnel started pounding the armor in the aft section. If not for the ship's well-armored ass, we would have been sucking space.

"Light out!" I yelled at Kep.

"We're no' there ye'!"

"Just do it!"

If we tried the wormhole at the wrong time it could rip the ship apart, but we were out of time. If the hole did not crush us, their weapons would. Kep hit the command and a wormhole opened. It did not look right and I held my breath as we flew in, not knowing whether it would hold or not.

I looked over and Kep had closed his eyes as soon as we entered the gray swirling cloud of the hole. It had a bluish tint that I had not seen before and I was worried it would collapse. The fighters had veered off behind us. I held my breath as I watched the timer. When it hit thirty I took in a huge breath. Thirty was the threshold and we had made it.

I clapped Kep on the back and smiled. He opened his eyes and looked at the clock and leaned back in his seat and laughed. Kep was a *mata* and *benetcho* and put me in a hells of a bad spot, but he was a hells of a good pilot and we made it out alive.

TWENTY-SIX

I LEFT THE cockpit and went to the cleanser to wash my face. I was furious at the situation and wanted to cool down before confronting Kep. After a lifetime of good trades and good experiences on Drakkara I was burned could not go back; not without a new ID and a good facial mod, or a more permanent change. He had done permanent damage to my reputation and my value. I did not think that he knew we were walking into something like that, but I was sure he knew things were starting to go bad and he thought my reputation would help him or delay the bad things.

I dried off and went to the front of the ship, but he was not there. I looked at the ship sensors and saw that he was in the back section in the engine room. When I found him back there, I was tempted to take a swing but did not.

"You arrogant *mata*," I said.

"Wha'?" He put down his tool and stood to face me.

"You knew things were going bad there. You knew what we were going into."

"You los' your hea'. Why woul' I go there if i' was goin' ba'?"

"You knew things were going bad and took me hoping my relationships would make things better."

"*Haachee!* Why woul' you thin' tha'?"

"Things were obviously bad. How could you not know things were going bad? You said they were getting less friendly."

"Well, I di'n' thin' they were tha' ba'. How coul' I?"

"Anyone would know. The signs were all there as soon as we

arrived. How could you not know? Unless you are completely oblivious you would know."

Kep stood in place staring me down. I waited for him to take a swing, but he did not.

"You arrogan' pri'. You thin' you go' all the answers?"

"I have more than you."

"Where's your shi' then, you *mata*?"

It took everything in me not to take a swing, but I knew that would not solve it, and maybe he was right. I did not have all the answers. But I knew a far sight better than he did. The argument continued for several more minutes until I realized there was no point. I decided he was telling the truth, at least, that he did not know things were going bad. He could never see that he made mistakes and he was as bad at reading other people as he was himself.

I gave up arguing with him and we talked about what to do next. Supplying the Drakkaran Station was out now and going straight into GalactiCorp territory with a damaged ship brought too much attention. The best way to raise a red flag about your ship was to fly in looking as if you just came out of a fight. We decided to stop at a Station and repair the damage before doing anything else.

We broke the wormhole several times at random places to change course and make sure we were not followed, then we headed to a Station called Luhantu in the space between TriKarre and GalactiCorp territories. From what we could tell it was small and not much was there, but they did have a repair facility. Kep and I did not talk much after that. We spent the rest of the trip in the engine room, making what repairs we could, mostly in silence.

Luhantu Station was extremely small and more rust than metal. There was just one engineer available, so it took us three long days to get the ship fixed. I finally received a response from Mik that warned me off of working with Kep, saying he had worked things out with him, but he still did not trust him and did not recommend working with him as he was a loose cannon. He did not send Kep my way and assumed that Kep overheard him telling another friend about my need for a job.

I almost backed out of the deal with Kep after reading the message, but I decided to see it through. As much as I hated going through with it, and although his dishonesty about Mik gave me an out, I could never stomach the idea of backing out on my word. It had almost got me killed before and would probably finish the job this time, but at least I had my honor – and the creds.

I sent a message to Renlii, telling her what happened on Drakkara and where we were and that we planned to go through with the sale. Right after I sent my message I received a message she sent a week ago telling me their group had attacked a Nallimar convoy, but it was a trap. Just a few of them survived and they were still trying to get away from the security fleet when she wrote the message. They were able to light out, but the fleet was hot on their trail.

My heart was in my throat as I read it and I had to blink back tears. They had been chased by the fleet for two days and she was not sure they would make it. She said goodbye as if she would never see me again, saying how much she loved me and that life was much better in the Void with me, no matter the risks or the pain from thinking of me so far away.

I read it again and wiped the tears away. I felt like a *mata* for crying. I was not used to that kind of thing and was glad Kep was not on the ship to see it. She closed by saying that if they did survive, she would go back to our Station and wait for me and that she did not want to separate again. Whatever we did in the Void from now on would be together.

I wiped my eyes again and tried to swallow the lump in my throat and read the message again. I read the message a dozen times before Kep came back.

"How goes the repairs?" he asked.

"I think he might be finished tonight."

"Goo'. We leave as soon as he finishes."

I nodded, but I was not looking at him. I was still thinking of Renlii and was not focused on our conversation.

"Wha' happene'?"

I looked up, realizing I had not hidden things very well.

"I need a krem first," I told him. "We can talk over krem."

He smiled again and said, "Soun's *pa'a* goo'."

I poured each of us a krem and told him about Renlii and that she was on the run from Nallimar.

"*Chee*," he said.

I nodded and took a long pull from the krem. There was not much else to say.

"How many Stations you fi'ure were rai'e' las' year? In the whole galaxy?" Kep asked.

"Just a few."

"An' how of'en di' the Corps trap frien's of yours on a rai'?"

"Maybe once. They were not always successful on their raids, but getting trapped the way they are now was a rare thing."

"Thin's ha'e ne'er been this ba'. Even after the Fall. Wha' the hells' goin' on?"

"Trask," I said.

"What is Trask?"

I explained to him about Trask and Universal Intelligence and what he was doing to the Void.

"Why?" he asked.

I shrugged. "Power? Control? Why do the Corporations fight for more territory?"

We sat there for a while and sipped our krem.

"To fly straight with you," I said, "if I thought I could help her, I would leave you here."

He took a long drink and stared at the krem before saying anything, "And go where? Soun's like one o' Tras's Stations is the way to go. You gonna sign on with him?"

I shrugged. "For now, we have a delivery to make and I will help you finish this job. After that, I find Renlii and we will find a UI Station."

"Le's ge' pas' Nejune firs'. Then worry about the nex' mission."

"Right."

"To Nejune and profi's and survivin' to the nex' mission," he said and raised his krem to me.

I saluted him back and we both finished our krem. About six krems later, repairs were finished and we lit out for Nejune.

Kep and I went over the plans several times during the trip. We were prepared as much as we could be, but the bad feeling I had before Drakkara was still there.

TWENTY-SEVEN

NEJUNE WAS ONE of GalactiCorp's key planets in one of their core systems, with a population of over fifty billion people. It had defense platforms placed in strategic spots throughout the system, and a fleet with hundreds of warships, all on full alert looking for danger. After the Drakkara disaster, I was relieved when we made it past the final checkpoint and began the descent to Nejune.

Kep took the *Princess* through the atmosphere and guided her down toward Jinton, one of the planet's larger cities. It was night on that side of the planet and the entire skyline glowed with flashing artificial light from giant vidscreens and holo units playing endless advertisements, the lights of which reflected off the massive shiny synthsteel buildings.

GalactiCorp viewed architecture with a different eye than other Corporations. Each building showed pride in technology and size and power, rather than history or nature. They were made of the latest blend of metals and synthmetal, and they did not believe in sprawling out into the countryside. Power was exhibited through colossal constructs reaching into the sky as if they meant to punch through the atmosphere into space.

"JPS, this is *Diviian Princess*, requestin' permissio' to lan'. Sendin' I.E. now."

"Approach using the course provided while we scan your ship and process your request."

Kep brought the ship in low and soared around several of the largest buildings toward an enclosed port made of white polished alidnum. In the dark of night, it looked as if GC had taken down a small sun and planted it in the center of the city. It was not the largest dock I had ever seen, but it was close. A constant stream of ships flew in and out of the massive structure, like echas streaming in and out of their home mound.

"*Divvian Princess*, you are approved for landing. Level sixty-five, pad five-one-three. Follow the flight path indicated."

"Copy. Proceedin' on course."

We flew through one of the gaping entry bays into the immense port. In the very center of the port sat a slender and clear control tower, rising one hundred levels from the ground to the ceiling. All the pads were on the outer edge of the inside walls. Between the landing pads and control tower, the dock was open and divided into invisible, electronically controlled flight lanes.

Kep knew his way around the bay and quickly found our pad. He could have let the computer take over and land, but like me, he did not like to risk it. The ship's systems were always fine for easy jobs, but if something came up, like security ships, it was better to handle it in manual so that changes could be made quicker.

Kep guided the ship into the pad and landed it smooth and easy. We had both already stashed our weapons in hideaway holes in the cockpit. I hated leaving my guns behind, but they were outlawed in the Corporations. Kep left me in the cockpit to finish the shutdown sequence while he went to the main hatch to greet the dock rep. By the time I completed shutdown, the scanning drones had boarded and were finishing up their work. As I approached the hatch, the drones zipped down the ramp to the representative. The rep said one last thing to Kep and walked away with the drones at each shoulder.

"Everything clear?" I asked.

"Yeah. Ba' news on the deal though."

"How bad?"

"Jus' a delay. He says we're too la'e to do i' tonigh'. We're meetin' in the mornin'."

"On the scale of bad, that is pretty low on my chart."

"Yeah. There's a goo' gues' house down the roa'. I'll book us rooms and we'll make a nigh' of i.'"

"I could use a good meal. And some krem. Or what goes for krem around here."

"Righ'. Le's get our packs and lock up."

We got our packs, sealed the ship and had a GC-Ride pick us up and take us straight to the guesthouse. GC-Rides were always obnoxious, with display ads and holo ads running over every inch of its interior. I tried to ignore them and watch the city pass by, but it took serious concentration.

The buildings of the GC core systems were the most obnoxious in all the galaxy; not the ugliest, but certainly the most obnoxious. Metal and synthsteel and clear alidnum were all you could see in any direction, aside from the unending ads running all over them. There was little to no sign of any creative intent other than big and shiny and attention-grabbing.

The car slowed to a halt in front of one of the least objectionable-looking guesthouses. It was not elegant, but it looked clean and had enough amenities to make it an enjoyable stay, including a pool, a rain room, virtual centers and relaxation pods. Kep explained all of the amenities with some excitement, but I was more interested in finding a place with a good Grontok steak and a cold krem.

The guesthouse was similar in style to the rest of the city, with plain synthsteel and some minor paint overlay, but it lacked the usual display ads. Inside, was short-haired carpet that felt an inch thick when you walked on it. Art screens on the walls displayed traditional paintings that changed to fit the weather and mood and time of day. They were tasteful and of the same theme, creating a story of sorts as you walked through the place.

As soon as I arrived at my room, I took a long hot cleanse, got dressed and sent a message to Kep that I was heading out to get food. He did not answer right away and I did not wait around for him. I assumed he was visiting a Haven or bringing women to his room. In spite of the horrible buildings and gaudy décor, GalactiCorp was the best Corporate territory to travel in, because of its relaxed view toward the pleasure trades, like Havens and alcohol and drugs and every other enjoyable thing. As long as they controlled its production and distribution and were able to profit from the venture, they kept it legal.

The patron downstairs gave me directions to a place that he claimed had the best steak in the city. I traveled there in a GC-Ride, but the place was *haachee*. It was far too upscale and had the gaudy GC style and taste and I did not fit in there at all. I tried a couple more places until I found the right one.

The exterior of the Grontok Savor was synthsteel like the rest of the city, but it had a worn and rusted look to it, as if it had been there well before the Liquidation. The age was just part of the marketing scheme, but it still felt right. Inside, the walls had a rusted look too, as if it was built centuries before the development of non-rusting synthmetal. The room was dark and smoky from jak sticks and korgas and a real fire burning real wood in an old stone oven back in the kitchen.

A patron at the door asked if I wanted a seat, but I declined and made my way to the bar. The bar was ovoid in shape, enclosing the bartender and the drinks. It was made of dark echa wood at its base and the top of it was made of thousands of grontok horns pounded together to form a single smooth piece. It had the look of something unique and genuine, but I had been to one identical on Dellinar. There were never any truly independent bars or eateries in GalactiCorp. They were all part of the Corporation, designed to create the illusion that they were unique and special.

The bartender came over as soon as I sat down. He was the type you would expect in a place like this; tall and attractive, with a slight rugged look, as if he raised the grontok himself and knew how to take care of himself in a fight. He was about as rugged and real as the rusted walls and belonged on a vid screen rather than a grontok range.

"Drink?"

"Krem."

"What kind of krem. We have fifty," he said with pride.

I nodded and held back a sneer at his smugness. There were different brands of Drakkaran krem out in the Void, but they were all going for the pure krem flavor. Some did it better than others, but they were all true krem. In GC territory, there were ten different categories of krem, with a spectrum of flavors in each category, each of them moving farther and farther away from true krem. The only variation that came close to real Drakkaran krem was naga, which was all right, but just a pathetic mockery of the real thing.

"Naga," I told him. "Natural."

He nodded and went to pour me the krem. He had a look of disappointment, which did not surprise me. GC residents prided themselves on their knowledge of krem and the ability to determine the different variations and tastes, and their idea of a good "krem" was harsher and more bitter than real krem. Anything like the real krem was considered amateurish and they did not respect it. It was the opposite in the Void and in the other markets, but in GC territory the marketing team had spent decades convincing their people that GC "krem" was the best and Drakkaran krem was old fashioned.

The bartender brought over the naga and asked me about food.

"Grontok steak, cute cut, juicy, with finla stems and baked goush."

"Cream and butter?"

"Yes. High."

I sipped the naga for taste and found that it was not horrible. When the grontok arrived, it was beautiful and cooked perfect, a light shade of black and crisp on the outside, but red on the inside and bloody, with very light, blue marbling. I cut into the steak and the juice trickled down onto the plate and mixed in with the finla stems and gourd. Sometimes, it was worth the sacrifice of real krem for a good grontok steak. They had grontok in the Void, but it was never the same as eating it fresh on the planet where it was raised. Eating grontok planetside was like drinking real krem on Drakkara.

After finishing the grontok I had another round of naga, but stopped after two. I never drank too much while in Corporate territory. You never knew when security forces were keeping an eye on you, or were looking for an excuse to haul you off and confiscate your ship.

Before Renlii, I would have spent the rest of the night looking for a woman to share the night with, but now things were different and I was not sure what to do with myself. On top of that, something in me told me that I needed to stay sharp. So instead of staying out, I ordered a Ride and went back to my room and hit the rack.

I woke up early the next morning, took a quick cleanse and packed. Kep had still not responded to any messages. It was still a couple of rotations before we had to meet the contact at the ship, but I was surprised he had not responded. My experience with him so far, was that he was an early riser.

I took my pack and went to his room. An alarm started going off in my head when I did not find him there. I tried to convince myself that he was sleeping off a rough night somewhere else, or maybe back at the ship. I decided to look for him at the ship, but I decided to move on with more caution.

I took a GC-Ride to the port using an alternate I.D. If the Ride did a facial scan or gen scan it would give my correct identification, but the alt I.D. would still buy me some time if it came to that.

I directed the system to take me to the port, but did not instruct it on which pad to travel to. It was a long ride there and I kept checking for new messages from Kep. The long silence increased the alarms in my head.

A touch of ice rose up from the bottom of my spine and twisted its way up to my head as the Ride approached the port. I could see Security ships in the distance, hovering outside near the entrances. It was not unusual for Sec ships to patrol the entryways, but I had a bad feeling they were there for us.

I did not stop the Ride, but instructed it to enter the port, giving it step by step instructions so it would not know the final destination. We entered the huge bay doors and sent it up to level sixty-five, flying past the long line of starships at that level. There were more Sec vehicles in the distance and as we drew closer I realized they were parked at our pad.

"Slow down!" I told the system. "Half speed. Continue down the aisle," I said.

The car slowed and continued past the *Diviian Princess*. Two security vehicles were parked at the pad and several officers stood at the main hatch of the ship. Two attack drones flew patrol around the ship. Another officer came out of the hatch and signaled to one of the others.

As we flew past the security vehicles to the other side of the ship, I saw Kep lying face down on the pad in a pool of blood; half of his head was missing. A security drone hovered over, like a hunter gloating over his kill.

"Keep going," I told the ride. "Maintain speed. Go up to the next level."

The car continued to fly past the rows of ships as I forced down the panic and tried to figure out my next move. I knew they would be looking for me by now. I could not go back to the guesthouse. I was lucky they had not already tracked me there. I was also lucky they had not tracked me to this Ride. If they were serious about finding me they could reset all the Rides in the area for facial or gen scanning and then they would have me.

I had not done business on Nejune and had no contacts. My face and name and genetics were all over the security scanners by now and I had nowhere to go. I searched through my system and found an ideal part of town to travel to and entered the coordinates. Then I sat back and watched out the screens as we left the port and entered the city again. I kept a lookout for security forces, but saw none. I was in it deep this time, *chee* piled so high I could not see my way out.

TWENTY-EIGHT

T HE GC-RIDE DROPPED me off in one of the lower parts of the city. It was not so low that I would be attacked as soon as I arrived, but it was dangerous and I felt naked without my guns. There were fewer patrols and security officers in the lower sections though, and almost no cameras. The Corporations did not care about protecting the lower areas, so although I had to worry about some of the locals, at least I would not have to worry about Security forces.

As soon as the Ride left, I walked down the block at a quick pace and zig zagged my way deeper into the lowest parts. It was a stark contrast from where I stayed the previous night. The buildings were hundreds of years old and had not seen anything beyond basic repairs since the Liquidation. Rust grew on most of the structures and some of the buildings were not even made of metal, but of mixtures of natural elements, showing them to be very old.

People on the streets were scarce and the few that I saw looked at me with suspicion. I walked deeper into the low areas for close to a rotation, hoping that if Sec came after me, they would not bother going this far in. Once I felt I had put enough space between myself and the drop-off location, I ducked down an alley and hid behind an abandoned and rusted-out hovercar. I sat in silence, watching the street to make sure no one followed me and that I was safe. The alley was full of garbage and filth and smelled like hard-baked piss and *chee*, but there was no one around, no windows in the alley and no signs of any cams, so I felt safe.

I pulled my system out and did an electronic sweep for cams and did not detect any. It was a small system and not always reliable, but it was all I had and had to trust it to some extent. I crouched down further behind the car, making sure I was hidden from the street and opened my pack and dug out my emergency kit.

Every smuggler carries a kit, just in case. Mine had a facial mod pill and a matching GC ID kit for a man named Hiff Klimina and enough creds to get me off the planet. The creds would do me no good though, unless I could find a pilot willing to take me.

I heard footsteps on the street and stopped what I was doing and waited. The footsteps grew louder and I focused on staying quiet and took in silent breaths until the footsteps faded away. When I felt safe and heard no footsteps, I swallowed the mod pill.

They take a while to kick in, so I went over my ID, making sure I remembered the name and history attached. There were cheap pills and good pills and the ones I had were supposed to be very good; at least, they were not cheap.

The conversion process from a good mod pill was a painful one, but when it was done, no person or system could recognize you, even with a good facial recognition scanner. A full molecular scan would reveal your true identity, but the new face would be fine for getting around on the planet. Getting off planet and back into the Void was another matter.

I had used mod pills in the past, but you never get used to the pain that goes with it. I felt the pill begin to work and I set the ID packet down and braced myself. Some pills put you to sleep for the duration of the transformation, but I knew if I was ever in a spot where I needed a mod pill, I would need to be awake to spot trouble.

My vision began to blur and I shut my eyes and then the pain hit, as if someone heated up two dull knives and shoved them into both eyes at the same time and pushed them deep into the sockets. Then the pain in the cheeks hit, then it struck my jaw like a sonic hammer and my entire face lit on fire, as if I was back on the *Sun* when it exploded. I nearly blacked out when the fire spread from my face to my entire skull.

If someone shot an ionic torch at my head, it would have been less painful. I leaned against the car and tried to listen for anyone coming down the alley, but it was no use. I could not see or hear or feel anything but pain. I did not scream or make a sound, but it was not easy and I was close to passing out.

I am not sure how long the pain went on, but it eventually eased off. I opened my eyes and the light of the sun was like a million tiny needles plunging into my eyes. I shut them and blinked the tears away and tried to adjust them to the light by easing them open a bit at a time.

The pain continued to drop off and I sat back up and massaged my jaw, then my cheeks, then my nose and my forehead, and then my scalp, then I started all over again. If you did not massage the face after everything set, it created problems with restoration when the pill wore off.

When the pain was down to a low ache I dug a fresh shirt out of my pack and changed, then set my system to reflection and looked at the new face. It was strange and unrecognizable; even the eye and hair color was different. I took a small set of cutters out of the pack and began chopping the hair closer. It was not quite a buzz, but when I was finished, it was very short and lay flat on my head.

I looked at my image again. The pills did a fine job and no one would ever recognize me. They were designed to last for three days, unless I took an extender pill which would give me another three days.

I put everything back into the pack and glanced around the car. The alley was still empty. I stood up and walked to the corner. The air was fresher at the street and it was nice to breathe it in. Nothing in this part of town smelled good, but the street was better than what I had been smelling in the alley. I looked around to make sure no one was watching, then stepped out and walked to the south west, away from my drop-off point and toward the main city center.

I walked for over a rotation looking for a place to rest and put a plan together. It was a long walk, down streets with rough and desperate-looking people who eyed me like I was a grontok steak. I felt helpless without my guns, but tried to show confidence and did not back down from any of the stares. They needed to know that I was not afraid of them, and might have a few surprises for them if they made a move. You could not fake this look. It was something you earned by experience, and I was not bluffing. If any of them did make a move, I would fight hard and dirty and use tricks I learned from years of training and actual fighting. If they did take me out, they would have a lifetime of scars to show for the effort.

The walk helped to clear my head. I thought about who could help, but it was a short list, not knowing anyone on this planet. I did recall a conversation with Aesal and remembered that he did some business on Nejune. The problem would be reaching out to these people, or reaching out to Aesal without alerting GC security.

As I drew closer to the city center, the faces softened and the streets grew busier, with ad screens and security cams popping up with greater frequency. After a long walk, I found a decent-looking krem joint and stepped inside. It was a rough place, made up of repurposed junk and metal parts found around the slums. It had a feel similar to some of the bars in the lower Stations in the Void, which put me at ease.

I sat at the end of the bar, where I could keep one eye on the other patrons and the other eye on the door. The bartender was short and fat, and looked as if he had given up trying to impress anyone about five weeks ago. His hair was unshaped, he had several weeks' of facial hair and his clothes had not been washed for days.

"Wha'ya wan'?" he asked.

"Naga."

He brusquely grabbed an almost-clean cup, turned to a series of valves behind him and filled it to the top with foamy naga. He dropped it in front of me and said, "Six cred."

I gave him seven GC creds and told him to keep it. He did not acknowledge the tip at all. He just took the creds and put them in the cred drawer and went back to watching the game on the screen.

The naga had too much foam and a bitter taste to it, but after the morning's events, it still tasted *pada* good. I drank half of the cup in a single go and set it down. Now that I was inside a building with my back to a wall, I tried to relax and get my head clear to figure out my next move.

I took out my com and prepared a message to Aesal. Galacti-Corp scanned all messages within their territory, so I had to be careful. I logged into a pre-made GC account for Hiff Klimina on the local network and in the alert line wrote a code that let Aesal know it was me. Then I told him I could not come to the meeting and was stuck on Jinton/Nejune on business. I sent this to his secret GC account and finished the naga.

"Another naga," I said to the bartender. He waited until the current play ended and broke away from the vidscreen long enough to pour me a refill of foam and naga. I gave him another seven creds and he went back to his game.

Unless Aesal was in the GC, it would take at least two days before I heard back from him, but it could take much longer. Corporate accounts could be used on Stations, but not while in ship or transit, or while in another Corporation. The message would have to be picked up on the Station network and sent to him and that would take time.

I sent a message to Renlii, saying I hoped her trip went well and that I would be delayed. I tried to explain by code what had happened, but could not give her any details. I sent a message to Challa and a few other friends, telling them in code that I needed a contact here, but revised it to tell them to let Aesal know. This way, if they could not help me, they would make sure Aesal was told.

Even this ploy was dangerous, as all messages using the GC system were scanned, and if their security forces were able to link that Jlaeal knew Challa or Renlii, then they could figure out that I sent the messages and trace it back to me.

After sending the last message, I decided to move on. I left half of the naga on the bar and walked out. I hated to leave krem unfinished, but staying in one place too long was a bad idea. The krem tasted like junto piss anyway.

I kept walking south and west, but never in a direct line. I visited bars here and there and tested their krem and checked for new messages. The krem was all *chee*, but it was cold and better than nothing. I kept on the move as much as possible. My com system was able to scramble my location, but GC security was always changing technology and if they wanted me bad enough, I was sure they would be able to crack my system's security.

Toward the end of the day, I decided to find a place to hole up in while I looked for a pilot. I needed a hard-cred guesthouse that was not too seedy, was not too serious about their security and was not connected to the main GC security network.

I was about halfway between where I took the mod pill and the main city center and the guesthouses were getting to the right level. The worst ones had no vidscreens and no pricing on the front and were just as willing to rent by the hour as by the day. I would never get any sleep in one of those, and if I did sleep I would wake to find my things stolen, if I ever woke at all.

Closer to the city center, there were places with flashing screens advertising their prices and what few amenities they had. I picked a place that had a decent look to it, with no visible cams on the outside. Once inside I confirmed that they were not on the security grid and did not charge by the hour, so I rented a room. I was able to get one on the second level, in the corner near to the street. I did not want to be surprised by security. If they did come, I was *chaf*, but a room with an escape route gave me at least some chance at survival.

The room was clean enough, with a vidscreen and plenty of channels, but the cleansing Station was public to the whole floor and had no lock. The room had a lock though, and a bed with covers that looked clean enough, so I decided it would work.

It was a far cry from the room I left that morning, but at least I had a safe enough place to rest. I set the proximity alarms on my system so I could sleep and then spent the rest of the night thinking of Renlii and hoping she was safe and wondering if I would see her again.

TWENTY-NINE

I SPENT THE next two days asking around about independent traders. It was never easy to find information like that, especially while trying to keep a low profile. Any business that sold non-GC goods did not broadcast that information, and none of those businesses had a direct relationship with the trader. The trader always worked with a distributor, who then sold to the businesses.

I found a bartender who I thought might be willing to talk, but he told me to come back later that afternoon, which meant it could go one of two ways. Either he would help me and talk like he said he would, or he would turn me in for the reward. It was a risk to go back and I had not decided whether it was worth it.

As soon as I left that bar, I received a message from a strange account. A code word in the heading let me know it was from Aesal. I did not expect to hear back so soon. The message said there was another party going on that night at a bar called the Thirsty Croshe and that they had a very good selection of minshi there. It did not say who to meet or what time to be there. I responded by saying it was a long time since we last saw each other and I had changed my style, which let him know in code that I would be there, but had changed my appearance.

I ran a search for the Thirsty Croshe and found it was on the other side of the city center and was too far to walk. I did not want to risk a Ride, but with the ID and facial mod, I decided it would be safe enough if I did not do it too often. It was a long ride to the bar. I imagined dozens of ways of getting captured in the ride or ways the meeting could go bad. It had been a long time since things were this out of control.

The Thirsty Croshe had a perfect setup for clandestine meetings, whether for business, for love or for revolution. It was nothing special from the outside, just a typical bar specializing in varieties of minshi, but inside, it was so dark it was hard to see; I had to stand at the door and wait for my eyes to adjust. When the dark eased into sight, I could see it was a place of leather and real wood, like a Drakkaran bar or some place outside the core planets, not something typical for GalactiCorp. Large high-backed booths lined both sides of the room, and an oval bar made from solid natural wood sat in the middle.

I was not sure how the contact would find me, but I sat in a booth farthest away from the door and looked toward the entrance, so I could see everything going on. A cute waitress, wearing short shorts and a tight see-through tee shirt came to the table.

"Wha'ya drink?"

I gave her the smile I used to flirt and charm. "I heard you have a good selection of minshi. Give me a vinti. Dirty."

"What kind?"

"What do you like?"

She shrugged, not caring to flirt or play. "Bolinta is good."

"Bolinta then."

I was used to more flirtation, but then I remembered that I was not Jlaeal. I was Hiff. And Hiff was not attractive by any definition. In fact, with his acne scars, brownish gray eyes, and short chopped and patchy hair, he looked *pada* ugly. I smiled as she walked away, thinking what a difference appearances made, especially in GalactiCorp.

I should not have ordered something as strong as vinti. I had not had minshi in a while and was worried how it would hit me. I had been drinking naga all day, but you could drink it all day without much effect. I was looking forward to the vinti though. I did not drink minshi often, but when I did, I preferred the smoky flavor of a solid vinti.

She dropped the drink off and left without comment. I took a sip of the Bolinta and let it sit in my mouth to taste it before swallowing. It was good. It was strong and had just the right blend of smoke and herbs and there was no harsh burn on the way down. I decided that I liked the feel and the flavor and should drink more of it in the future.

I caught movement at the front door and spotted a woman stepping inside. She stayed by the door while her eyes adjusted. She was past middle age with a look of middle management. She wore her short-cropped hair in a conservative style and an outfit to match. She was a little overweight, but carried herself with confidence and purpose, comfortable with the world and her role in it.

She strode to the bar and ordered a drink. The bartender slid her a minshi clean and gave a quick glance in my direction. Middle management did not look like the GF conspirator type, but they were perfect to handle that type of work. She strode straight to my booth carrying her drink, which I noticed she did not pay for.

"Hiff?" she asked while standing at the booth.

"Yes," I said. "We have a mutual friend?"

"Yes." she said. "He says you had something to tell me."

"Mirishma Station," I said.

She nodded and said, "Kalhaff's."

I smiled up at her and indicated she should join me. Aesal and I first met on that Station and at that bar. It was an easy enough code, but one that worked. We would need to change it after this, if we ever saw each other again. A code was good once. After that it was burned and you could not trust anyone with it.

She sat down and stared at me with a look that bore straight through to my core. She set her drink down and continued staring, either expecting me to say something, or trying to make a decision. I took another drink of my Bolinta.

"Our friend says you're in trouble."

"Yes. I need travel arrangements."

"What's your destination?"

"Anywhere in the Void. Any Station works. I can handle things once I make it out there."

She took a sip of her drink, not taking her eyes off of me.

"Do you have proper identification?"

"Yes."

"Will you be recognized by security forces?"

"No."

"Then take commercial."

I could not decide what her play was. She knew why I could not take commercial, or she should know, if she knew what was going on. Commercial travel would have high security, including gen scanners, which would spot me right away, mod pill or not. Security would just have facial security scanners for those entering a port by a GC-Ride. She knew this.

"You know I cannot take commercial."

She sat regarding me for several moments. I thought she might walk away.

"Do you have any creds?"

"Not much on planet," I admitted. "Five thousand."

She grimaced at the mention of five thousand. It was not a horrible figure, but it was a big ask on my part. Smuggling a fugitive off planet and out of the system was no small matter.

"I can pay more if I am taken to Tarvil."

"You said you could go anywhere."

"True. If they are willing to do it for five thousand, I will go wherever they happen to be going in the Void. If they would like more creds on delivery, I need to go to Tarvil."

She took another sip of her drink.

"Why should I help you?"

The conversation was starting to piss me off. I was not sure why Aesal had sent this arrogant cretch my way, but I could tell already she was not going to help.

"I thought our mutual friend sent you to help."

"We have reason to deal with one another on occasion, but I don't work for him. I don't have any debt to him and I certainly don't have any debt to you. What you ask is difficult and holds risk for those willing to come to your aid. So, once again, I ask you, why should I help you?"

The whole thing had been a waste of time. Either she thought I would have more money or Aesal had not explained the situation, or this whole thing was some kind of setup. I finished my drink and set it down and stood up.

"It sounds like you will not," I said.

I walked to the bar, paid for the drink then made for the doorway. Middle management stayed in the booth and did not even turn to watch me leave. I understood where she was coming from. If they were not close, then she owed him nothing and she owed me nothing. But she could have mentioned this to Aesal and not wasted either of our time. Now our code words were *haachee* and I could not trust any more contacts from him and I was *chaf* again.

I slammed the door open into the open air of the busy street and blended in with the crowd, wondering where the hells I would go from there.

THIRTY

I WOKE UP with a start the next morning at a light knocking on the hatchway. I leaped out of bed and grabbed the alidnum pipe I had found the night before. It was not much, but it would do some damage and could help me get away. I hit the panel to see who was outside the hatch. Middle management stood outside the door, looking down each end of the hallway with impatience, as if Sec troops would appear any moment. I opened the hatch, pulled her in, threw her onto the bed and shut the hatch again.

"What do you want? How did you find me?"

She did not look surprised or angry at being thrown around. She just sat up on the bed and straightened her outfit. I did not bother holding the pipe at her. If she wanted me dead, she had plenty of opportunities. I leaned the pipe against the wall next to the door and I noticed what she was holding. It looked like a system pad, but it was thicker, and had several satellite nubs attached to it.

"What is that?"

"A com device. Someone wants to talk to you."

"Who?" I asked.

I had a bad feeling about the whole situation, but did not interrupt her as she got up from the bed and placed the device on a table. Whatever *haachee* I was in, I was in, and I might as well see it through. I spent the rest of the previous night haunting bars around the dock and could not find even a hint of help. I did not like that she knew where I was, but if she wanted to hurt me she could have done it already.

She slid her finger across the top and stepped back to give me an unimpeded view. A holo of Trask appeared above the pad.

"Fuck me."

"Jlaeal. I hear you are in need of assistance."

I laughed. I should have known. I was in a bad spot, but getting help from Trask was the last thing I wanted. It was like making a deal with ghajhi.

"All roads lead to Trask," I said.

There was a slight delay between what I said and his reaction. Com devices did not have a delay and did not require equipment of such bulk and I wondered what the thing was. Trask gave me one of his ironic smiles. The lady stood to the side with her hands clasped in front of her, showing no reaction to our conversation.

"Your name came to my attention when Melia sent in a report of your meeting."

"You work for Trask?" I asked her, and then realized it was a *haachee* question. "Of course you do. The entire galaxy does, or will - that is the goal, right?"

There was never any point in saying anything like that to Trask. He never reacted to any goading.

"Why are you in GC territory?" I asked. "I know you have your deals, but entering GalactiCorp seems high risk —"

"I am not in GalactiCorp territory. I am on my Station."

I stared at him and then at Melia.

"You brought me an autoresponder?" I asked. "Why not just give me a message?"

She did not respond, waiting and staring at Trask, or his projection.

"Jlaeal," Trask said, "this is not an autoresponder, this is an experimental com device. I am showing a lot of trust in letting you see it."

It took me a moment to gather my thoughts before I could even respond.

"Impossible."

"New advances in my research division have made it possible. While the Corporations work on new methods of destroying each other, I have worked on this."

It was a hells of a weapon to have if your business was information, or for any business for that matter. The ability to communicate across the galaxy without delay could change everything for the one who had it. The fact that he would even show it to me came as a surprise. Of course, it could be a trick and the device could be *haachee.*

"You have come to the end of your rope. You have no ship, you are wanted by local authorities, you have no contacts, are running out of creds and have no feasible way of escaping GalactiCorp territory. If you do reach a Station, you have few ways left of supporting yourself."

That tightly summed up my situation. I did not want to think of things as that bad, but they were. I had no luck finding a pilot to take me off planet and my mod pills would only last a few more days. If he did not supply me transport, I would have to risk public transport, which would probably lead to capture.

"That about sums it up," I said. "But I always find a way."

He smiled. "Yes. You do. However, this time might be different. Things in the Void are not as they used to be."

"Thanks to you."

"Thanks to the Corporations."

"So you say. What do you want?"

"I want you to work for me."

"We had this conversation already."

"Things have changed. You are in greater risk of danger than you realize. Things are coming to a head."

"I do not want to work for you, Trask."

"You would have your own ship again, funds to operate, enough intel to provide an element of safety."

"Fuck that," I said. I knew I should have kept my voice down, as the walls were very thin, but I had had it with him. "I told you we do not see eye to eye. You know how many of my friends are dead because of you?"

"You do not under —"

"I understand that life out there was already hells and you are turning up the fires and throwing my friends in to feed it."

"Jlaeal, that is far from the truth."

"Somehow I doubt that. I would rather end up in a GC prison hole somewhere than help you take over the Void." I turned to Melia. "Take him out of here. We are done."

"Melia, wait. Jlaeal—"

"You have five seconds."

"I will get you off planet. No strings attached."

Melia stood next to the device, looking at me in shock.

"Why?" I asked.

He was close to giving me a straight answer. I could see it on his face. But then he closed his mouth and considered and said, "Because I owe you that much."

I did not know how to respond. I still did not trust him but if they could get me off this place and on a Station, then I had to take the chance. There were always strings with Trask, but I would fight that battle when it came.

"Fine," I said.

"Good," Trask said.

He seemed to show some relief, as if he was worried that I would not take the offer. But he should have known I did not have a choice. In fact, I had growing suspicions that he put me in this position in the first place.

"Melia will provide you with new IDs. GalactiCorp has changed their protocol and yours are outdated. A smuggler who operates for us will supply transport off planet and deliver you to a UI treaty Station."

"Fine," I said. I would take his help, but I would show no appreciate or gratitude. He was right. He did owe me and I would take this from him and then he could go to the hells.

"I would advise you to stay at UI Stations and avoid the others. The Corporations are planning a massive push."

"I will take that into advisement."

Trask knew I would not be moved. He shook his head before signing off.

"Farewell, Jlaeal. Good fortune."

"Right."

His image disappeared and Melia picked up the device. She looked flustered and ill at ease now that he was gone. We went over the plans to get me to the ship and they seemed solid enough. I could see she would rather see me in a GC prison camp than help me. She was a cold-hearted cretch and I did not care for her either, but I had no choice but to trust her to get me out of the system and into the Void.

Things were bad. If Trask was right, the end of the old life was in sight, but I could not think beyond getting off the planet and back out into the Void.

THIRTY-ONE

A COUPLE ROTATIONS later I was flying with Melia to a warehouse on the other side of town. It was a distribution center for GalactiCorp filled with housewares. I caught several of the workers watching as I walked through the towering aisles of crates, as if the place was more important than a simple distribution center. They nodded to Melia like she was the queen of the hive. I got the feeling that a number of them did more than warehouse work for her. She took me all the way to the back of the warehouse and through the loading dock to a side room where she closed the door.

"Get inside." She pointed to a medium-sized crate. I might have fit inside if I held my breath and shaved more hair off of my head.

"In there?"

"You want off planet? The case is lined with material that will give a false reading to anyone that scans it. As long as they don't stop the truck and open the case, you'll be delivered safely inside the ship."

"How about a bigger case?"

"This is all we have. You're fortunate we have this."

I did not like any of it, but it was their trip and their rules. I tried to put myself in their place and knew I would not put up with some big-mouth *mata* giving them *haachee* about their operation, so I stepped inside.

"How long will I be in here?"

"That depends on various factors. We load the hauler and head straight to the dock. If we don't run into trouble, then it'll be quick."

I nodded and crouched down, but decided I had to ask.

"Do you work for Trask? Or are you part of the GF?"

She gave me her first genuine smile, but did not answer. She hit the button to seal the crate and I was locked inside.

I began sweating right away, either from the stress of the situation or the heat in the box, or both. I heard Melia giving commands and then felt the crate move. I was jostled around and knew I would be sore for weeks, but if I made it out, it would be a small price to pay for freedom.

It was a hard time in that little box, cramped into such a tight position, sweating, muscles aching, and not knowing what was going on. I listened to everything outside, trying to keep track of what was happening. I could tell when the crate was loaded onto the hauler. I felt it when the hauler took off and left the warehouse. The hauler did not have any force compensators and I was pushed down to the floor and against the back wall of the crate. I focused on keeping my stomach calm as the hauler moved up and down and side to side with traffic.

By the time the hauler made its way back down, my muscles were cramped and the box smelled of musk and sweat. It was not a short ride and I was tense and powerless. I did not like cramped quarters and liked the helplessness even less. The whole situation was *chaffed*.

I felt the hauler slow to a halt and knew it was being scanned. All the big docks used giant scanners that could see everything inside the ship and all of its contents. They could also scan the genetic coding of any person inside and match it against IDs in their system, but as long as the crate tricked the scanner as promised, it would be fine.

The hauler held its place for longer than it should have. I tried to stay calm, but knew it was not good. I heard the door open, followed by footsteps and voices inside the truck. I took in a deep quiet breath and tried to empty my head and calm myself, but there was nothing I could do but be quiet.

I heard the sound of crates opening. Security picked haulers at random to spot check and I hoped that this was all that was happening. If they sensed something odd with the driver or the scanners, and decided to check all the crates I was *chaf*.

The voices grew louder and clearer.

"Crate one-five-six."

"Over here."

"Open 'er up."

There was a zip sound of the crate lid sliding open and then, "Fine. Close 'er."

"Crate one-seven-two."

"Right here."

"Open 'er."

They were doing random spot checks. As long as they did not pick mine, I would be fine. They opened containers for what seemed like a full rotation. I was drenched in sweat and the crate smelled awful, like I had been stuffed in there for days. It was getting harder and harder to breathe between my tension and the stuffiness in the box, but the voices drifted farther away and I relaxed. But then they drew closer again and I closed my eyes and took a deep breath and held it. They opened one more container close by, but then they walked away and I heard the door close and I could breathe again.

I breathed in and out several times to get my heart rate down and I felt the truck moving forward again. The worst seemed to be over, but it was not really over until I was out of GC space and back in the Void.

The hauler went on for a little while and then stopped again. After several sets I heard the door open and I heard more talking. They were loading the cases out of the hauler. I hoped mine would be among the first, but it was a long time before they hauled it onto the ship.

There was more talking and then the ship was closed up and

I breathed a sigh of relief. It was not over, but I was through the worst of it. The pilot would not release me until we lit out, but the waiting was easier. Unless security stopped us during flight, we would make it.

It seemed like rotations upon rotations before anything happened again. With the ship's compensators, I could not tell if we took off or lit out, or what the ship was doing, but I knew that unless things went to sudden *chee*, I would be free soon.

After another long wait, I heard footsteps coming toward the box. I was exhausted and hurting and drenched in sweat, but I tried to prepare myself for a fight just in case.

The top zipped away and I tensed, preparing for the worst, but a man dressed like a trader stood over me. He was shorter than me, with blond hair down to his neck, meek pants, and a t-shirt, with gun holsters strapped to both hips. His hand rested on one of them as he looked down into the case.

"Come on out. We lit out a while back."

"Thanks," I said with a hoarse voice and tried to stand. It took effort and help from him and it came with a lot of pain.

"You look like you just played a full round of Punchball."

I laughed in spite of the pain. It was good to be alive. It was good to be talking to a trader. It was even good to be taking his *haachee*.

"I feel like I was the punchball," I told him.

He chuckled as I made it to a standing position and stretched and moved around to get the blood circulating.

"Yento," he said and reached a hand to me.

"Jlaeal," I said and locked wrists with him.

"First thing to do is get you a cleanse," he said. "For both our sakes."

I laughed and stumbled out of the crate and followed him to the cleansing room. In spite of all the aches and pains, I felt *pada* good. I made it out. I was alive and I was free.

❖

I felt even better after the cleanse. I would be traveling for a couple of days, but I was free and out of GalactiCorp and heading toward Renlii. As soon as I got out and dressed, I found Yento and asked how updated his network was.

He smiled. "I work with Trask, so I even get updates in Corporate territories."

He was reclining on a couch in a lounge in the center section of the ship when I came in, but he stood up and walked over to a refresher unit.

"He can he do that? I would think they could track it."

He pulled out two cups and poured krem into one of them and my mouth began to water, hoping it was the real stuff.

"Krem?" he asked.

"Hells yes," I said.

He handed me the first cup and began pouring the second.

"I don't know how he pulls off half of the things he does," he said.

I took a long drink of the krem and closed my eyes and savored it.

"Yeah," I said, opening my eyes to see he was sipping on his own krem.

"Feel free to link to the network."

"I appreciate it, and I appreciate the ride."

He waved his hand as if to wave away some pesky insect.

"Not a problem. I owe Trask and he said he owed you. Happy to help."

I set down the krem and linked my com unit to the network and looked for messages.

"Heard you had some bad *maja* down there."

"You could say that," I said. I took another drink while the com downloaded a patch of messages. "I partnered with a man I should not have, and things were catching up to him."

He nodded and watched me go over the messages. There were several new ones responding to my call for help.

"Make yourself at home," Yento said. "Come to the cockpit when you're through. Give you breakdown of where we're headed."

"My thanks," I told him.

He left the room and I skimmed through the messages and opened one from Renlii. She and Echta's team lost their pursuers and made it to Yymna Station. She said it was flooded with refugees because the Corporations launched a full invasion. Echta was forming a new group, but was going to operate out of a UI Station. Everyone was going UI. She said she would find passage back to Tarvil and meet me there and from there we would meet up with Challa.

"These are the most trying of times, my love," the message said. "And yet, while we feared that loving another would create another burden when things went bad, I find it a relief knowing you are out there and that you love me. I wish I could help you. I wish I could be with you. I hope to see you soon on Tarvil."

I sent a response, telling her that I was fine and that I would make my way to Tarvil and that we would not break apart again for anything. I also told her not to wait for me, that if things were that hot, she should take my remaining creds and go to meet up with Challa and I would find her.

I sent responses to the other messages and let them know I was fine and had made it out. I finished the last message and enjoyed the rest of the krem, happy to be alive and happy that Renlii was fine. The krem was icy cold with perfect flavor. I savored each sip as it ran over my tongue and down my throat.

She was right about love and the Void. I was wrong to think that it would be a burden. During the darkest of times on Nejune, my concern for her did not make things worse. In fact, when I thought of her, it made life better, to remember the light in her eyes and her voice like music playing, or think of her warm breath on my skin as she kissed me. Whatever was happening in the Void, life was good with her at my side.

225

THIRTY-TWO

IT TOOK JUST a one day for us to get to the Shrkl Station. It had a much different feel than the independent Stations. On approach, things were much tighter, like entering Corporate facilities, with full ship scans, including biometric and cargo scans. But once inside, it felt like things did before the pressure began and security was not anything beyond what I was used to.

Shrkl had once been a mining Station, but was abandoned after all the hunjl was drilled out of it. Years after it was forgotten, a small group of traders took it over and turned it into a Station. The top section of the rock once housed the hangar, offices and operational center of the mining operation, but now held apartments and shops and eateries. They were still in the process of converting the tunnels below the Station into additional apartments and shops.

What made this Station stand out more than anything was not the physical structure though, it was the demeanor of those on board. Everyone in the Void had grown strained and panicked with the idea that their Station would be raided at any moment. They looked at each other with paranoia, wondering who on board might sell the Station out to the Corporations. I felt none of that fear on this Station. It was the old feeling of safety I used to feel before the Corporate raids.

It also felt as if everything was new and fresh. The air was fresh and the dock was so clean it was gleaming, with Sethorian synth-steel floors that looked brand new and gray walls with fresh paint.

We were standing in the dock next to a ship owned by a friend of Yento named Pol.

"He wants a ride to Tarvil," Yento said to Pol.

Pol was a young smuggler, a Shiltian, born and raised on the Shiltii home planet. He had a thick accent and a no-*haachee* attitude found with those born in horrifying slave conditions. He was an old friend of Yento's and he thought he might be able to help.

"Tarvil?" Pol yelped. "Tarvil next on Nallimar hit list."

"What?" I said.

"Tarvil gone. Forget it."

"Renlii is there."

"Renlii gone then."

Yento looked at me with compassion, but did not say a word.

"What about it, Yento? I have eighty thousand creds there. They are yours if you take me there to pick up Renlii."

"No chance, friend. Trask and I are even as far as I am concerned."

"Eighty thousand?" Pol asked.

"Yes. Eighty thousand. Yours if you take me."

"In, out," he said. "Things rough, I leave. No wait."

"Fine," I said.

"Why not just send word and have her find passage here?" Yento asked.

"She might not have time. If word has spread about Nallimar, she might not be able to find passage off."

"That is a big risk. I think you should just tell her to use your creds to get off if it means that much. For eighty thousand, she can find a ride out."

"Maybe," I said. "But if Pol takes me, I know she has a ride out."

"We leave now," Pol said.

"Fine," I told him. "Yento, I owe you. Anything you ever need, let me know."

"Fly safe," he said. "See you 'round the Void."

I grabbed both his shoulders and he grabbed mine.

"Come," Pol said. "We leave. Now."

"Fly safe, Pol," Yento yelled. Pol just waved at him as he boarded the ship.

I followed Pol up the ramp into his ship. As Pol went through the startup sequence, I sent one last message to Renlii letting her know I was coming and to have all the creds ready at the dock when we arrived. I told her if she could find passage off the Station before I got there, she should do it and find a UI Station and I would find her. I closed the com system and looked out the screen as we blasted out of the dock.

Love does wild things to a man. I always voided as much risk as possible and kept things on an even deck, but there I was, flying into certain death, with little hope of either of us surviving. But, if there was any chance at all of saving her, I had to take it. Everything else was *haachee*.

We arrived to chaos. The dock was in near riot, packed with people trying get a ride on any ship, at any cost. Pol had trouble landing with the huge crowds, but as the ship lowered, they cleared from the ship. It was a close thing as he set down, with a few of them close to getting scorched by the engines.

"Trill Fuck!" Pol said. "This madhouse."

I watched the vidscreen as crowds rushed the ship and tried to fight their way on.

"You message friend. I not stay long."

"I already messaged her. No response so far."

"I wait five minutes, then I gone."

I tried to message her again and tried calling her, but she did not respond. My heart pounded like a pulsating air grinder as I looked at the crowd, wondering how she would break through. Then she sent a response.

"*Chee*! She is stuck at the entrance to the dock. Security will not let anyone else through."

"We go then."

"She has the creds! You want your creds?"

"Fuck creds. We leave now." He began to set the ship to launch, but I held onto his arm.

"Just hold on. I will go get her. Just wait five sets."

He looked at the crowds and the panic and just nodded his head. I did not know whether he would wait or not, but I was not leaving without Renlii. I ran to the hatch with both guns drawn. Before leaving Yento's ship, he had given me a new set of blasters, similar to the ones I had. I assumed they were another gift from Trask.

I turned on the com system. "Pol, I am opening the hatch. Set shields and close her up as soon as I am out."

"Copy," he said.

I palmed the hatch release and the ramp began to lower to the deck. I had my guns pointed toward the crowd.

"Back up!" I yelled. "Back the fuck up!"

The crowd saw the blasters and held back. A few had guns of their own and looked like they were close to firing at me to get on board. I stepped onto the hatch when it was halfway down and yelled back, "Now, Pol!"

I jumped off the ramp and the hatch closed again. The shields turned on right after and one poor *benetcho* lost an arm as he tried to push his way onto the ship. No one else tried after that.

I pushed and shoved my way through, and took several shoves and punches myself. It was like the days back on Belarioos when the riots began, everyone for themselves, kill or be killed. My earpiece was already on. I called Renlii and she answered.

"Renlii!"

"Jlaeal, just leave."

"Not without you. Where are you?"

"I am in the dock, but a long way from the ship."

"I am heading your way. We will get there together."

"No. Get on the ship!"

Someone shoved me hard from behind and I turned and laid them out with a punch in the hard knot in his throat.

"I am not going without you."

"You are a *pada* stubborn man."

A Diviian woman would not move out of my way, so I shoved her hard out of the way and did the same to the man standing behind her.

"That is why you love me."

I heard her laugh and then grunt. She was fighting for her life just as I was. I had set my com to search for her signal and I could see that we were getting closer.

Someone pushed me from behind and I almost fell down, but I grabbed onto someone's arm and leveled out. They shoved me off of them and I pushed past.

"Jlaeal, I gone." It was Pol.

"Pol, wait. I have her. Just wait."

"No. Fleet just light in. I gone."

"Pol, just wait."

He did not answer. I stopped and looked back and saw his ship rise from the deck. Some of the crowd were too close and the ship's backwash melted them to slash. It rose and flew out of the bay doors and into the Void and my heart sank into my stomach. I looked at the rioting crowds and knew I had no advantage over them, no way of escaping, no way of saving us.

I felt a hand on my shoulder and turned around with arm raised to swing, but it was Renlii. I grabbed her in my arms and held her as tight as I could and kissed her hard and the swirling madness of the rampaging crowd disappeared.

I broke off the kiss and looked into her eyes and it broke my heart knowing I did not get to her in time. We were both stranded and Nallimar was on their way.

"He left," I told her. "We have no way off."

She put a brave face on and smiled and kissed me.

"You should not have come," she said.

"*Haachee*," I said.

I kissed her long and hard again while the crowd pushed and shoved and fought their way past us, but they were in the same spot that we were in as the last few ships rose from the deck.

2 3 1

THIRTY-THREE

T HE LAST TWO ships were heading toward the exit, abandoning the crowds to their panic. Someone collided with us and we broke apart into the frenzied crowd. I grabbed Renlii's hand and fought through the crowd toward the hallway. I had no idea where we would go, but the dock was the worst place we could be.

We made it two steps when an explosion knocked us both to the ground. My ears rang and it felt as if the whole dock was covered in flames. It cooled down again and I rolled over and looked back to see that the last ship heading out sat on the deck in flaming ruins.

The dock guns sent a stream of blasts toward the entrance as a heavy transport flew in, but the guns were no match for the ship's armor or the ship's blasters and soon the dock guns were smoking slag. Another heavy transport followed the first in and they crushed dozens of people who could not clear the space before they landed.

Renlii was the first to stand and she pulled at my arm and helped me up again. The rest of the crowd rushed toward the exit and we ran with them and were pushed and jostled from every side. As we made it out of the dock Nallimar Invader troops flooded out of the ships and onto the deck. More assault ships landed behind the first two. All who surrendered were rounded up and forced into a corner of the dock. Anyone who didn't surrender or who had a weapon was killed on sight. More assault ships landed behind the first two.

Nallimar Invader troops are the elite troops of the security fleet. They wore black armor from head to toe which was resistant against energy blasts of most blasters and was strong enough to fend off bullets from most guns. They were very difficult to kill unless you hit them up close, or in one of the very few weak spots.

Renlii and I ran down a hallway, surrounded others speeding in panic from the invaders. None of us had a plan or any idea where we were going. There was no point in running, but we all wanted to live and none of us wanted to be slaves and so we ran.

"Come," Renlii said. We were still holding hands as she pulled me down another hallway.

"Where are we going?"

"Away from them!" she yelled.

The sounds of blasts and explosions and screams around us were deafening. Gunfire took chunks out of the Station walls and blaster fire ricocheted and people screamed and yelled and panicked and fell dead around us. The floors were slick with blood as we ran, and some people froze in fear or ran toward the troops or away from them or just fell down crying. We ran toward the end of the hallway where it intersected with another hallway, hoping to get farther away, but Invaders rounded the corner and dropped down into a crouch and fired.

Renlii and I dove to the floor with guns already drawn and fired back. People around us were shot and fell to the floor, but others were fighting back like us. Twenty different guns and blasters fired from behind us at the Invaders. I felt the heat on my back from their fire, and we stayed close to the ground.

I picked out a trooper on the left and hit him several times, but it did not get through the armor. Shots exploded all around me, hitting walls and the floor and other people, but we kept firing. Renlii was a *pada* good shot and had already found a weak spot in one of their armor and took him out.

I ignored the smell of burned flesh and melting synthsteel and focused on the one Invader. I aimed for his eye slit, where the armor was the weakest, and fired several more shots. A shot broke through the eye piece and it ricocheted inside the helmet, melting his face and head into slag. The rest of the troops were already dead and the crowd began stepping over us to get to the end of the hallway.

While others rushed forward, Renlii and I got up with caution, looking down the hallway through the smoke and haze to make sure the Invaders were dead. We let the crowd push ahead of us, letting them take the brunt of the risk, and then we followed them to the end of the hallway and turned left, away from the docks and the troops.

As we ran down the hallway we felt safe, but it was a brief reprieve. A firestorm of blaster fire came from behind and people dropped all around us, some dead, some injured, some knocked unconscious. There were screams and moans and shouts at people to move or shoot or get out of the way.

I grabbed Renlii's arm and took her down a hallway to our right, away from the crowds and the gunfire. The crowds were thinner and the sound of blaster fire was farther in the background.

"Where are we going?" Renlii asked.

"I have an idea," I said.

I knew several Station Captains who had survived raids. Corporations always took the command center first, but Captains knew this and set up backup plans for themselves. Some of them added the same safety measures in their own apartments as they did in the command centers, with heavy armor and heat shields to hide the apartment from scanners. Some built escape vessels into the side of their apartment. A couple of them built in little vaults that were safe from sensors, hidden from sight and filled with food and supplies enough to last until the Corporate troops left the Station. Of course, this assumed the Corporation ever left the Station and did not destroy it.

I knew where the captain's apartment was and hoped we could get in somehow and see what tricks she had built in. We ran down another hallway and turned left again. The large crowds had disappeared. There were a few people in the hallways, but they were running in panic. I stopped at the captain's hatchway. It looked like all the other hatches, but on closer inspection it was more fortified.

"What is this?" Renlii asked.

"Captain's quarters."

"What are we doing here?"

"Sometimes the captain builds a few extra surprises in their quarters."

"You know this captain?"

"A little."

I touched the door alert panel and then knocked.

"Captain. Let us in. We have creds."

"I doubt creds will make a difference now."

"Creds always make a difference," I said. Renlii was looking around both directions, blasters in both hand, watching for troops. I knocked again and hit the panel.

"Captain, open up."

"I doubt she is even in there."

"Maybe," I said. "Step back."

We stepped to the other side of the hallway. I aimed at the lock and shot several blasts into it. It did not do much, but with concentrated fire it started to burn through. It took a few sets but I held true until it melted through the hatch. I blasted several other spots where the exterior locks would be and it shook loose.

Renlii stepped up to the left side of the hatch with her blaster raised and I stepped up to the other side and slid the hatch open. Blaster fire exploded out of the doorway and into the hall.

"Captain! Jlaeal here. We have met. Renlii is with me. We have creds."

"What do I need with creds?" she yelled through the door.

"If you survive, they would come in handy!"

A few traders turned the corner and ran down the hallway toward us. We aimed our guns at them as they ran by and they did not give us any trouble.

"Let us in," I said. "We can make a deal."

The other side was quiet, and then she said, "Come."

I pushed the hatch open all the way and stepped into the entry with my arms raised. She had every chance to shoot me, but did not. She stood at the other end of the room with a blaster pointed at my chest. Next to her, a hatch hidden in the wall stood open, revealing a cockpit.

"You have room for two more in there?" I asked.

She looked into the cockpit and then at us.

"You have the creds?" she asked.

"Renlii?"

Renlii stepped inside and pulled the anti grav pack off her back and set it down. She opened it and pulled out a large sackful of creds and slid it over to the captain. She could have taken us both out then. We were open and helpless against her, but it was worth the risk. Dead was better than getting caught by Nallimar. I stood at the door and looked either way down the hallway to make sure no troops were coming. Several troops rounded the corner and I fired and ducked back inside the hatch.

"What about it, Captain?"

She picked up the sack of creds and nodded. "Yes."

"Get in and get her started," I told her. "We will fight them off until she is ready. Renlii, hold onto the creds until she lets us in. Copy, Captain?"

"Copy."

She handed the creds back to Renlii and stepped into the cockpit and began the startup sequence while we went back to the door and tried to hold off the invaders. We peeked out of the entry and popped off a couple of shots. The troops dropped and returned fire. We darted out and fired again to give the captain time. We were doing fine, but then a round of blasts came at us from the other side. I stole a quick glance and saw that more troops had arrived at the other end of the hallway.

"How goes it, Captain?" I shouted.

"Nearly set," she yelled back. "Get in."

I pushed Renlii toward the ship and backed toward it myself. Then a massive explosion went off behind me and threw me to the ground. Everything was a blur as smoke and fire filled the room and all I could hear was a loud buzzing.

I looked over to Renlii. She was lying on her back on the floor with her eyes closed. I tried to roll over, but could not move. I blinked away more smoke and tears and saw shadows come in through the doorway and the Invaders stood over us. I tried to reach for my gun, but could not move. Then a trooper raised a small shock gun and fired and everything went to black.

THIRTY-FOUR

I WOKE UP to darkness and pain and a solid ringing in my ears. The ringing receded and melded into a mumble of hushed voices. There was a putrid smell of musk mixed with piss and *chee* that made my stomach turn. I opened my eyes to overwhelming light and shut them, then covered them with my hand and opened them again to give my eyes a chance to adjust.

"You were better off asleep, old friend."

It was Challa's voice.

I removed my hand and squinted at the harshness of the light, but could still see a little. I was lying on hard synthsteel floor, in a corner of a very large room, packed from one end to the next with men of all races who were naked and dirty and bruised. Challa was sitting next to me. He gave me a conciliatory pat on my shoulder.

"I am not sure I am glad you are alive," he said. "We would all be better off dead."

There was no smile, no mirth at all. Like everyone else, he was naked. His left eye was swollen shut, and he was so covered in bruises, that he looked like he played a game of Punchball and forgot to wear the armor. I looked down and realized I had nothing on and looked as roughed up as he did.

I tried to sit up, but fell down again. I tried again and Challa helped, but it took effort.

"What happened? How did you get here?"

"That —"

"Wait," I interrupted. "Where is Renlii?"

"Be calm, Jlaeal." He rested a hand on my shoulder. "Take a breath. Remain seated, or they will beat you again."

I looked around again and knew. We were on a Nallimar prison ship, or rather, a slave ship. The entire room was untreated dark-gray Sethorian, with no furniture and no place to sit. All the lights had a reddish tint to them, to better match the lighting on the Fillonian home planet. It was hard to get used to and made it difficult to keep your eyes open for very long. The room was about twenty centems warmer than what was comfortable, which was a more natural climate for Fillonians.

There was a long line of grilles on one side used to evacuate your bowels and a trough on the other side where food was released onto the floor. It looked like the type of room used to transport kliphon or grontok, with no effort at keeping the animals comfortable. I had heard horror stories about the Fillonians' treatment of slaves and I was seeing it first hand.

"Where is Renlii?"

He shook his head, indicating he did not know.

"Was she killed or captured?"

"I have not seen her. They keep women separate."

My heart jumped up through my throat and tears came to my eyes. I wanted to cry out. If she lived through the blast there was no telling what she was going through. There were horrifying rumors of Fillonian treatment of slaves, including rapes and tortures and experiments. The lucky ones were killed. I would rather she died in the blast than suffer any of that. Challa moved closer to me and put his hand around my wrist.

"Be strong. You are alive. Perhaps she is alive."

"I would rather she was not."

"No. That is wrong. If she is alive, there is hope. She will endure and we will live and life will go on."

I did not want to argue with him. I did not want her to suffer, whether we lived or not. She was better off dead.

"How are you here? I thought you were on a UI Station."

He patted my wrist and looked at the rest of the crowd.

"We based off of a UI Station, yes. But we still bought intel from non-UI sources and that intel was bad. We were ambushed by Nallimar and they took our ship. Everyone else was killed. They knocked me out and took me here."

"Fuck Trask and his *haachee* UI."

"Yes," he said. "Yes, fuck Trask, but times have changed. He has won."

It was a hard drink to swallow, but he was right. Trask had won.

"The Void is harsh and unyielding," Challa continued, "and you cannot bend her or break her. You bend with her or she will break you. I bent and found a UI Station, but I did not bend enough and she broke me."

"Fuck the Void."

"Yes," he said. "Fuck the Void, but here we are. We are both broken, but we are not dead, are we?"

It took me a while to answer. I did not want to answer. I wished that I was dead and that Renlii was dead rather than going through the horrors of Nallimar. I wished that Challa was not alive as a slave either.

Then I looked around and thought it through. They would not rape Challa because he was part Drakkaran and they did not care for that, but they might torture him and they were sure to put him to hard work. They might want me for pleasure, but I took it as a good sign that they had not already. I hoped the best for Renlii, but decided it was better not to think about it. There was nothing I could do and thinking about it turned my stomach.

"What good is being alive," I said, "if life is nothing but torture and slavery. That is why we went to the Void in the first place, to get away from slavery. Now we are captured and are true slaves."

"You are wrong. We are not dead. We are not yet slaves. We are prisoners."

I could not figure why Challa was arguing this, but then I noticed what he was doing. He had been moving his fingers in the old pirate code and I had not noticed. I caught myself watching his hands and tore my eyes away so that I could see it in the periphery.

Challa continued the conversation, discussing philosophy of the Void and other encouragement, but told a different story with his hands. They spoke of working with the other prisoners to escape and taking over the ship or dying in the attempt. Life is for living and he would rather die fighting his way out than live as a slave for Nallimar.

I laughed. Challa shushed me and looked at the doors into the room, but I could not stop.

"Quiet," he said. "Or they will beat us again."

I stopped laughing, but gave him a big smile and patted his knee. Challa was a real treasure. The Void could burn in hells fire and he would look for grontok to roast or would look for a new galaxy to fly into.

"You are right, my friend. The Void is harsh and we should bend with her," I said this to him and messaged with the hands and said I was in. Of course I was in.

"But you cannot bend too much," I said, "or you will find yourself sitting in some *haachee* desk in GalactiCorp or TriKarre, filing *haachee* reports for your *haachee* manager."

I said this all while asking in code if he had a plan and asked who else he had talked to. He had not talked to anyone yet. He wanted to formulate the plan with me and then begin recruiting. I looked at the room. There were humans and Drakkarans and Diviians and a few Shiltians. It was a pretty pathetic bunch, all miserable and battered and naked. They did not seem like much for fighting, but the desperate never do.

"Look at them all," I told him. "We are already part of Challa's crew."

He gave me a confused look and looked around the big room, not getting it.

"We all wear the same uniform, my friend. You should be happy."

He looked around at all the rest of the naked peoples and

laughed loud and hard and had to put a hand over his mouth and quiet himself. After he had stopped, we continued our conversation the way we had before, trading coded talk while talking out loud on the philosophy of the Void.

He was right that the Void was harsh and unyielding and that you should bend with her, or she would break you, but she had broken both of us many times and we always came back and faced her and stood tall and told her we were ready for more.

Fuck the Void. Fuck her unyielding nature. We would not bend. Not today. We would fight and free ourselves or we would die. Let those *haachee* Corporate hacks bend to her and let her bend them over. We were tired of bending over for her. Fuck her. Today, we fight.

THIRTY-FIVE

W E FOUND OTHER prisoners who knew the smuggler code. If they did not know the code, we moved on and did not bother with them, but if they did, we explained our intention to escape. Word spread and several hours later I was sitting next to a man named Julls, who had been captain of a Battle Cruiser in the GF fleet. He was older than most of us and would not be worth much in hand to hand fighting, but he knew Fillonian battle strategy and it would be good to have him lead the fight.

I brought him over to Challa and the three of us discussed the battle plan in code. It was very simple and had little hope of succeeding, but Challa and I did not have anything better and agreed that we would move forward with it. We spread word of the plan and encouraged those who wanted to fight to move toward the hatches slow and with caution so they would not create suspicion.

We all knew the dangers of our plan. We knew our chances were slim and that a great number of us would die, or all of us would die. We were naked and had no weapons and the prison rooms were built with vents to pump in sleeping gas or poison gas in the case of problems. If things did not happen fast, we would all die; but the alternative to fighting was worse and we preferred death over that.

There were two hatches that opened into the large prison room we were in. Each hatch led to a small clearing room, which then opened to a control room. When troopers entered or left the room, they entered the clearing room first, waiting for the rear hatch to seal behind them, then they entered the next room. The one exception for this was when a mass of troops entered the room in an emergency and both hatches were left open to allow for the steady stream of security personnel.

Challa and I sat close to one of the hatches. There were dozens of other prisoners between us and the hatch. For the most part, they were in on the plan. Challa gave me a scowl and I nodded to him.

"You are a piece of foul horrig *chee*," Challa yelled at me, "and I would not want you on the bottom of my shoe, much less to be trapped in this room with you."

"Fuck you, Challa. I am tired of your smell and your mouth."

"At my worst, I smell like a Drakkaran. You smell like a *haachee* human."

I stood and put my finger in his face. "I would rather smell like *haachee* than a dirty, hairy Drakkaran."

He stood up with a furious glare and got very close until our faces were close to touching.

"How did you ever happen?" I asked. "No human would ever want anywhere near your mother's hairy smelly Drakkaran hole."

A few smugglers near the other hatch stood up to watch us fight. Meanwhile, the hatch near us opened up and two Security Troopers dressed in their dark-green armor marched toward us with their ugly-looking jada sticks. Two other troopers came in behind them and shoved the other prisoners back down onto the floor. The hatch had opened to let the troopers in and closed behind them, which was not good.

We kept arguing as they entered and acted like we did not see them. I could see the other hatches in the room open and more troopers filed in. The troopers got close to us and did not say a word, but I could see that he was getting ready to swing his jada stick. Fillonian jada sticks are made of solid alidnum and are hard as hell and could knock you out or kill you with a single hit. One of them swung his stick at Challa and the other swung at me.

I dodged the stick and tackled the trooper to the floor and

began choking him at the open joint in his armor between his shoulders and head. He hit me with the stick as I choked him and it felt like he broke one of my ribs, but I kept holding on and ignored the pain.

Fillonians have thick scales instead of skin, and it worked as a natural armor and trying to choke one was like trying to punch a hole through a wall with your fist, but soon I was surrounded by other prisoners. One of them ripped the helmet off his head and another slammed the stick into his skull several times until we knew he was dead. I looked over at Challa and his trooper was dead as well and prisoners were racing to attack the other troopers streaming in through the now-open doors.

All the prisoners were up on their feet attacking the troopers and forcing themselves into the hatchway and using the jada sticks to hold the hatchways open. I joined in the crush as we all pushed and shoved the men ahead of us through the hatch. Several of the men up front had jada sticks now and a great battle was taking place at the hatchway. I could see that the troopers were trying to seal the outer door so that we could not get out, but jada sticks were jamming the hatches open and a growing pile of bodies prevented them from closing.

The last of the troopers near the hatchway were dead and we pushed to get out of the prison and through to the control room. Prisoners ripped armor off the troopers and tried to fit it on or kept it to use as a weapon. The prisoners in the front had fought their way through the outer door, but they did not last long. More troopers waited in the control room with blasters and killed us by the dozens. But by force of numbers, we were able to push through and overwhelm the troopers and kill them and take their blasters.

I was still in the middle of the clearing room when gas began to fill the prison.

"Gas!" someone yelled. And then a chorus of voices began to yell, "Gas! Gas!"

The prisoners at the other hatch did not have the same luck in getting through and both of those hatches were sealed tight. At our hatch, we all climbed over the dead troopers and dead prisoners and pushed into the outer control room to make way for those behind us. Some of the men tried to shut the gas down, but control of the prison had been overridden. The hatch leading out to the hallway had been locked by the central control and we were trapped again, but those with blasters fired them at the hatch and began to slag it.

It did not take long for the blasters to melt through the locks and we pushed the hatch open to find dozens of troopers waiting for us in the hallway. Our blasters took out a few of them, but we did not have enough guns and the troopers made short work out of those who held them. But the prisoners were desperate and those still in the room with the gas pushed hard and forced us forward into the troops with guns and we fought them hand to hand, pushing farther into the hallway and again we overwhelmed them by our numbers.

We were naked and bloody and in pain, and our numbers had thinned dramatically, but we were fighting for our lives and did not care about risk and did not feel the pain and fought like wild animals defending their homes.

I was in the hallway with a blaster. We pressed forward to both ends of the hallway, but troopers fired at us from both sides. I dropped and fired back as others around me were shot and blood pooled all over the floor. More prisoners ran over me toward the troops, but they were shot and killed before getting far. Those of us with guns lay down and fired at the troopers and if one of us was shot, someone else picked up their gun and continued the fight.

I fought my way down the hallway, crawling over smoking bloody bodies, using them for cover, always targeting eyeholes in the troopers' armor and sometimes making a kill. I looked over and realized Challa was by my side and we were inching forward together. More prisoners knelt behind us and fired at the troops, and some ran on ahead in a blind rage to fight them hand to hand, but they were shot before they got anywhere near the troopers. Those running blind served as a distraction though, while we shot at the troopers with our blasters.

Time ran slow as we fought, but we reached the end of the hallway and killed the last of the troopers there as more troopers came down each side of the next hallway. I looked behind us to the end of our hallway and saw that we had taken the whole thing. Captain Julls had broken into the prison across the hall and taken out the security and we had more prisoners joining the fight.

The hallway was filled with unarmed and naked prisoners, but more and more of us had blasters and some wore the armor from the troops and now we had a secure position. We fired around the corners at the other troops and held firm while we waited for orders from Julls. We were tired and covered in blood and scared and wanted to wait, but we knew we had surprised them and had to move fast to take the ship.

Julls put the men with helmets and armor up front and we continued to push forward and less of us died. Inch by inch we gained ground, until we took another hallway and released more prisoners. Then we took another hallway, gaining ground and taking over more sections of the ship and freeing prisoners from every section.

With each prison we freed, our numbers swelled, but all I cared about was finding Renlii. In each prison we opened, I looked to see if there were any women, but we took the whole deck without finding a single female. I started to get worried that they were kept on a different ship, but I knew it was a *pada* big ship with many decks and I held on to hope that she was on board.

We began to get a feeling for the horrors of Fillonia as we cleared our deck. For every prison we freed, we found other, smaller rooms, where some of the strongest or higher-ranked men or Drakkarans or Diviians or Shiltians were raped over and over by the troopers during their down time. It was a horrific thing to see and while some of them were freed, others just wanted to die.

The Fillonians were very rough with some of them and they were so close to death that we put them out of their misery. I thought of Renlii as we came across these horrors and I hoped she was better off or just dead.

There were thousands of us now and hundreds of us were armed. We had taken an entire deck, but there were dozens of levels with levels below and above us and we were at a point where we needed to split our forces.

Captain Julls led a group going up and Challa and I led another group moving down. Our group used the same strategy as before, taking the lower deck one hallway at a time, but we learned that this deck was very different than the one before. We made quick progress in taking the deck, but none of us would ever look at Fillonians the same again and what we saw brought new ferocity to our fighting.

The bulk of their troopers had been used up in the deck above and now they were on the defensive and we attacked them while they hid in side rooms or behind barricades. Those of us who survived and saw the side rooms would never be the same.

I was in the middle of a fierce gun battle in a hallway when Challa came up behind me and pulled me away from the fighting. I argued with him until I saw the look on his face and the horror in his eyes.

"Is it Renlii?" I asked.

He shook his head and pulled me back to another hallway and guided me toward an open hatch. One of our men was sitting on the floor outside of the hatchway sobbing; another was across the hallway, losing what little was left in his stomach. Challa guided me in through the hatchway and I felt the urge to retch.

The entire galaxy knew of the Fillonians' cruelty and thirst for blood, but none of us ever imagined anything like what we saw. It was a torture chamber, with men and women secured to tables or beds, or hung from the ceiling or walls. They were naked and held in humiliating positions. One male human was chained from the ceiling, held by hooks plunged through some of the worst parts of his body. They had removed one of his eyes, but kept it attached to its nerve endings and stretched it out far enough so that he could see his own face and held it in place with a clamp. Then they removed his tongue and then other pieces of his face and mouth while he watched with his own eye.

There were men and women, humans and Drakkarans and even a Shiiltian in this room. Each one had gone through a unique and horrifying display of torture. A line of seats sat against one wall, as if an audience watched the horrors as they took place.

We were conflicted on what to do with the victims. We rushed to take them down, but this put some of the victims in even more pain. We put most of them out of their misery, but some were not too bad and we took care of them as best we could.

The entire deck was full of larger rooms of torture like the first one we found, but there were other, smaller rooms for private pleasure, rape rooms like in the decks above, and experimental rooms, where unthinkable things were done to people, like arms replaced with biomechatronical ones that the person could not control.

We found a Diviian who had no control over any part of his body and it seemed they forced him to do horrific things to his own friends while other Fillonians watched. This was a side of Fillonian psychology we had never seen or heard of before.

Finding these rooms renewed our energy. We were full of rage and revenge. It was a struggle to hold our soldiers (as soldiers they had become) back from the fighting and to keep them organized. Some became feral and hyper aggressive, but these men were the first killed by Nallimar troops and we got the rest of the crew back in line.

The final surprise on that deck was the surgical room. We did not know what it was at first. We thought it was just another room for experimenting or doling out a different type of torture, but after seeing those who had gone through the surgery, we realized it was the worst torture of all.

The prisoners were brought into the room and implanted with a thought inhibiter which prevented the person from ever disagreeing with a request or command. Those implanted would dig out their own eyes and hand them to you if you asked, or they would work hours and hours and days upon days without rest until they passed out or died. They still controlled their own thoughts, but had no control whatsoever over their actions.

No Fillonian slave had ever escaped that we had heard of and now we knew why. We were all committed before, but after seeing that room there was no question at all among any of the crew. There was no more thought or discussion of taking prisoners or being taken alive. We all knew, every one of us, that we had to kill them all or die trying.

THIRTY-SIX

THERE WERE NO prisons on the next deck, just storage rooms and sleeping quarters for crew. We found food supplies, but much of it was Fillonian and inedible, although we did find enough decent food to spread around to the crew. We had not realized how hungry we were until we found the supplies. We ate on the run and felt better after the food and were reinvigorated for more fighting.

In another room we found clothes collected from prisoners, stacked in a giant pile. We did not have time to find clothes that fit because of the fighting, but we threw on what we could, and put on what armor we could find and continued forward.

The next room we came to held all of our weapons and this is when things really began to turn. There was no way of finding your own gun and we did not try, but we distributed the guns to any prisoner that did not already have one and sent a few dozen men with weapons to take to Captain Julls and his team.

We lost some men on that deck to traps and to the few troopers stationed there, but it did not take long for us to clear the entire deck and move on to the next. Resistance increased on the next deck and we found ourselves fighting inch by inch, hallway to hallway again.

The first prison we broke into was filled with women. They were smaller cells than in the male sections and had a softer floor and somewhat better facilities, so that the women did not get as damaged and would be worth more. Fillonians did not view men and women as equals and although they looked down on all other races, they looked down on women more, especially humans.

To a Fillonian, showing strength was everything and the stronger the person subjugated, the greater the power. They sent strong male prisoners to hard work camps or mines or factories, but the strongest males were used for pleasure before the hard work. The weaker women were sent to work, regardless of beauty and those who were powerful and fighters were used for pleasure.

On the male prison level, in addition to the "pleasure" rooms, we found rooms where the strongest or greatest in political or economic stature were held alone and prevented from hard work or tortures, so that they could be sold for more creds to Fillonians with power or wealth. In the same way, women were held in large prisons holding hundreds of them crowded together, but the best of them, meaning strongest or more powerful, were either taken to private quarters of the commanders or set aside to be kept in good condition for their sale or taken to smaller rooms as a reward to the troops. This is also how they punished prisoners who resisted or fought back too hard.

I stepped into one of those rooms and saw a tall woman curled up naked on the hard synthsteel floor. The Fillonians did not tie up those they forced into pleasure, preferring instead the struggle and combat of the resistance, especially when taking warriors. This woman was beaten and bruised and bloodied beyond any recognition and beyond any other person I had seen so far; well, any person I had seen alive. But this one was breathing.

"Medic!" I yelled. "This one is alive!"

I looked at the broken body and a sudden jolt went through me. I looked at the face again. It was swollen and red and purple and hard to recognize, but I knew her.

Renlii.

I knelt down to her and screamed out.

"Get a medic!" I yelled at the man next to me and he disappeared out of the room.

Others streamed into the room. I took her in my arms and

held her while the rest of the men moved on to keep fighting and release other prisoners. She was not bleeding bad, but I was worried about a head wound or internal injuries and did not know if I should wait for the medic. There were few of us that were trained as medics or doctors, and the good ones had stayed in the med bay we found and were treating the worst of us there. There were hundreds and hundreds of wounded there with those who survived the Fillonian torture, and we did not have enough doctors for everyone.

"Oh, dear, Renlii," Challa said and I looked up to see him in the doorway. He was a blur through the tears in my eyes, but I still recognized the look of horror on his face, worse than I had seen from anything else that day. "The cretch-fuckers. The horrific *benetchos*. They will burn in all the hells."

I could not look at him. I could not say anything. There were no words or thoughts. I wished that we had both died on Tarvil. It would have been far better.

"Take her to the med bay," Challa said. "I will lead the fighting."

I looked at Renlii and knew that he was right. The medics would never make it down here. She was covered in blood and filth and very damaged and it broke my heart to see her that way and she would not get any better in here. I picked her up with all the gentleness I had, hoping not to break her further, and carried her out of the door and down the hall and up to the next level. Some offered to help and to hold her for me, but I would not let them touch her.

I carried her into the med bay and looked for a doctor. They were all busy, until I found one of them trying to keep one of our fighters alive and he recognized me and sent me over to a med table. There was a cleansing Station at the table and I washed her down and treated what wounds I could while waiting for the doctor. She had injuries everywhere. I could not stop the tears as I worked on her and thought about the hells she went through. I was worried about her internal bleeding, but I also thought that, depending on what she went through, death might be a mercy.

The doctor came rushing to the table. He was a shorter Drakkaran, young and shaven of all his hair and beard. He examined her with a scanner first.

"How bad is it?"

He ignored me and continued scanning and then turned to leave.

"Where are you going?" I asked.

"I need more equipment."

I let him go and waited again. It was a long wait and I continued cleaning her wounds. The doctor finally returned with several pieces of equipment and another doctor.

"She has dozens of broken bones and internal bleeding in her head and other areas. It has been untreated for too long already. It could cause permanent damage if we do not work on her right away."

He said all this as both of them prepared the equipment and began to work on her.

"What can I do?"

He finished entering a few commands on the first piece of equipment and handed it to me.

"Hold this over her head."

I held it over her head as he showed me. He made a few adjustments and I held it there while the other doctor used the other tools to repair other internal bleeding. I watched with impatience as they did their work and hoped they could save her. All I could think of was whether there was something I could have done to save her or prevent this from happening.

Of course, the answer was yes. Everyone else had gone to UI Stations early on. If I pushed to go to a UI Station rather than keep fighting against Trask, she might be all right. Then again, Challa was here. Who the hells knew. It did not matter. We were here now and there was nothing we could do to change that.

They finished with the machines and closed them up. One of

them took a blanket and covered her with it and the other took the tool from me.

"She will be fine," the doctor said as the other one hurried off to help another patient. "Physically, she will be fine."

"What do you mean, physically? Is her brain damaged?"

"No. No. As I said, her physical body is fine, but she has been through much. Too much. This is hard to come back from."

"What can I do?"

He looked at me with pity and shrugged. "Just be there. Whatever she wants or needs. Even if that means leaving her when she wants you to leave."

He said nothing else and left me alone with Renlii as he rushed away to work on another patient. I was used to seeing her strong and powerful and full of life and it was hard to see her the way she was. I felt a mix of pain and sadness and fury all at the same time. I thought about what the doctor said and it set off a tempest of rage and I wanted to rush back into the battle, but I could not leave her side.

She was deep asleep, but gave a slight shiver so I held her hand tighter and kissed her forehead. I pushed her around on the table and found a private room and laid her in the bed and sat down in a chair beside her and watched. I sat next to her and held her hand and watched her sleep. I thought of Challa and the battle. I wanted to be with them, to kill every one of them, but I could not leave Renlii. My place was there with her. And I knew Challa would give it to them. He would introduce them to all the hells of the universe.

THIRTY-SEVEN

CHALLA AND CAPTAIN Julls continued the fight while I watched over Renlii. Julls died during battle and Challa took charge and they accomplished the impossible; he took over the entire ship and cleansed it of all Fillonians. Every single one of the cretch fuckers was killed and every single one of us felt that whatever pain they went through was not enough.

As soon as the ship was taken, Challa organized the crew, assigning those with the right skills to the cockpit and the engine room. When they were comfortable they knew what they were doing, he ordered the ship pulled out of wormdrive. They lit out again right away, setting course far away from any Corporate territory, but also far away from any known Station, so that they would not draw trouble their way.

We all knew trackers were built into the ship's hull, but none of us had figured out how to deal with that yet. The first step was to get us far away from Nallimar. While Challa dealt with the ship and delegated the problems of feeding everyone and getting them clothed and trying to get us away from Nallimar, I stayed with Renlii.

The doctor came and checked on her and made sure the other wounds were healing, but she slept through it all. It had been a full day and still she slept and I waited.

Challa came into the room when things were settled.

"How is she?"

"The doctor says she will be fine, but she has not woken yet."

"Have you eaten?"

"Yes."

"I sent word on our status, did you receive it?"

"Yes. You have pulled off the impossible."

"All those years raiding Nallimar ships paid in something."

I smiled, but it was a forced smile for his sake.

"What next?"

"We are flying to a safe position where we will wait to see if Nallimar follows. I think they will. If they do, then we run again. We are searching for trackers now."

"You know where they are?" I asked.

He shrugged. "They are built into the hull somewhere and we have no way to get them off without another ship or the specialized trackers, which we do not have. I think the crew knows that, but searching for the trackers gives them something to do while we wait."

"And if they keep after us?"

"We keep running. We keep fighting."

I smiled and this time it was real. He was a true gift, always ready to spit against the Void and tell her to go to hells, and ready to go there with her if he had to.

"Let me know if you need anything," he said. "This ship is yours, if you wish."

"No friend. You led the charge. She is yours. My place is here."

He nodded with pity, smiled and left.

I fell asleep for a short time. I promised myself I would not, but a man can only go so long without it. I heard a voice in my sleep, weak and calling my name. It was Renlii, under a crowd of naked Fillonians, fighting to get at her. She was naked and fighting, but she was weak from the fight and calling my name, but I could not move. I could not help. I was powerless.

Her voice grew louder and I felt a hand on my head and I woke up. I was sitting next to her bed. I had not left her since we came to this room. I looked up and she was awake and saying my name and running her hand through my hair. No sound could compare to the beauty of that voice. She was weak and still showed signs of the fight, but she smiled at me with a radiance brighter than any star.

"Jlaeal."

"Renlii." I took her hand in mine and smiled and tried to be strong for her and not cry.

"You are alive," she said.

"Yes. I am alive. You are alive. We have taken the ship. They are all dead."

She did not say anything, but squeezed my hand and closed her eyes. I did not say any more. I could tell she was relieved, but did not want to talk. We held hands in silence and she opened her eyes again and looked at me and I looked at her.

She would live with the horrors of this thing for the rest of her life, but she was a *puda* tough woman; the toughest I had ever known. She survived many horrific things in life and she would survive this and she would be strong as always.

We slept the rest of the night holding hands, with her in bed and me sitting at her side. We woke when someone brought food and ate together without saying a word. When we finished eating, she spoke.

"How?" was all she said.

I told her about Challa and our escape and our fight and everything we did. I told her that Challa was captain now and explained that we were running and were not sure we could get rid of the trackers.

"How long have you been in here?"

"Since I found you."

"You should help Challa."

"I will not leave you again."

She smiled. It was a brave smile and full of pity for me, but I could see something else there. I thought that maybe she wanted to be alone, to deal with things herself for a while.

"I will be fine," she said.

I did not want to leave her, but she wanted to be alone. I knew she had much to think about and sometimes the battles in the head needed to be fought alone.

I gave her a gentle kiss on the lips. She flinched but smiled at me as I stood up. She was *pada* strong. It would be a long road back, full of pain and frustration and fury, but she would be fine.

I spent the rest of the day trying to help Challa. He was glad to see me back at work and he put me on as Captain. I tried to convince him to put someone else on as Captain, someone more qualified, but he insisted I would do a fine job and wanted someone he trusted. He had done a good job organizing the ship, but now he wanted to focus on finding the trackers. The ship was in anchor in an empty part of the Void. We were there several hours, waiting to see if the Nallimar fleet would arrive. Challa was testing repair drones, to see if we could use them to find trackers on the hull of the ship, but they were designed to do minor repairs on the exterior of the ship, not search the hull for trackers.

Challa stood over a bay of vid screens watching feeds from two different drones. A Drakkaran sat in a chair to his left controlling one drone and a human woman sat to his right controlling another one.

"How does it go?" I asked.

"It does not," Challa answered. "I wish I had some of my own equipment. We would have found it already."

"No one on board knows their design?"

"There are a couple who claim to and they are sitting right here, but neither seem to know what they are doing."

"You can do't yourself if ya like," said the Drakkaran, who turned back to Challa and glared.

"No. Calm yourself, Bechaa. I was merely expressing my frustration. You know as much as I do."

Bechaa turned around and went back to work.

"The real problem," Challa said, "is the software. My drones had very specific software, with thousands of tracker designs built into it, so it knew exactly what to look for. All we can do with these *puda* things is tell them to look for anomalies on the hull, or we use their camera to do a visual scan ourselves, and this —"

"Nallimar fleet just lit in!" came a voice from the scanning section.

"How far?" I asked.

"Maybe five minutes."

"Get this hulk moving. Prepare to light out," I said

"Take those damn drones inside if you can," Challa said. "If not, leave them here."

"I need a few sets," Bechaa said.

"You heard the man! Get it in or do not get it in, we are lighting out."

The pilot increased our speed and prepared to light out. The woman to Challa's right sighed a breath of relief and said, "Drone two is in."

"Bechaa?"

"Ah *puda*, ain' no way."

"Flip it on, Jlaeal."

"Padj, light out."

The hole opened in front of us and we flew in and the giant vidscreen in front of us filled with the swirling gray clouds of the wormhole.

"That settles it," Challa said. "We are bent over if we do not find the tracker soon."

"How many drones do we have?" I asked.

"Five left. We will send out all five next time, but unless we get *puda* lucky, we will never find it. No way these little drones can scan this whole ship in the short time we have at each stop."

"Find more drones, then," I said.

"We took out all the security drones in the fight. These are all the maintenance drones we have."

"What about service drones?"

He looked at me like I had said the dumbest thing he had ever hear me say. "Evac scrubbers?"

"They can fly. Just suit them with enviro shields, attach some sensors and send them out. Worst case, we have some dirty evacs or have to clean them by hand."

He looked at me as if I was crazy and then shrugged.

"Hear that, Bechaa? Find scrubbers, see what you can do."

Bechaa stood up and left, giving me a nod on the way out. There was a strong comradery on the ship. We were all brothers and sisters who fought for our freedom together and were running for our lives. But, there was also a growing sense of desperation, an increasing awareness that we might not get out of it.

I had spent the entire day away from Renlii and I asked Challa to cover for me while I went to check on her. When I arrived, her eyes were puffy and red and she was quiet.

"You want company?" I asked.

She nodded, but did not smile. I walked over to the side of her bed and sat down and held her hand. She looked up and tried to hold the brave face, but I could tell it was a battle. After a while, she reached up to me, wanting me to hold her. I leaned down and held her tight in my arms and she cried. She cried for a very long time and I held onto her and did not say a thing.

The temptation was to say some *haachee* that we both knew was not true, like "it would be all right" or "it is over now" or some other *haachee* phrase, but in truth she would always have this with her and it was not over, no matter what I said. I had no idea what she was going through, or what to say, or how to make it better and I would not pretend. But she wanted me to hold her, and I could do that and was glad to. We stayed like that until my back ached and my arms went numb but I did not say a thing and would not let her go.

THIRTY-EIGHT

RENLII WAS UP and dressed before I awoke the next morning.

"Feel better?" I asked.

"I need to work," she said. "If I stay in bed, I will continue to think about it. I am tired of thinking about it."

"We will find you work then," I said and got out of bed. I threw my clothes on and strapped on my gun and as I did, she looked at the gun.

"I need a weapon," she said.

"We will get you one. What do you want to do?"

"Prepare for battle."

"I hope it does not come to that."

"It will," she said and I could tell that she wanted it. She wanted to fight and maybe even die, but before she died she wanted to kill Fillonians.

"We will keep running and maybe find a way to escape."

"No," she said. She walked up to me and caressed my cheek and looked into my eyes. "What you and Challa have done was remarkable, but if we do not find the tracker, we are done."

"We will find it," I said.

She smiled and left the room and I followed.

I put Renlii in charge of battle preparations. We had someone else in charge of it, but there were several complaints about how he treated people and we were looking for a replacement. It was a huge task, and maybe it was too soon, but she knew as much as anyone on the ship and I knew she could do it. She was in charge of checking the ship's weapons, armor and shielding, and making sure they were in working order and those in charge of them knew what the hells they were doing. She also made sure the commanders were doing everything they needed to do to win once it got to fighting inside the ship.

The commanders took to her right away and she smoothed out some of the rough edges and got things in order. She was wonderful to watch and I loved her even more as she fought to get back to who she was. I knew she would never forget what happened, but if anyone could get over it, she could.

A week later, we were still on the run from Nallimar and had not found the tracker. Things were different between me and Renlii. We slept in the same bed, but she was withdrawn and I could not touch her. I understood, or thought that I did, and did not press it. The worst part of it was not the touching, but that she did not like to talk. Unless we talked of the coming battle or of defenses, she was quiet and did not want to speak. I was worried that the old Renlii would be gone forever, but I could not give up hope. She was strong and this was her way of protecting herself and if we ever got out of this *haachee*, we would work it out and she would be fine.

During the previous week, we would travel to a secluded section of the Void, send the drones out to look for the tracker and light out when the fleet arrived. The time of their arrival always varied, but they always arrived and we lost more and more of the drones, because we could not get them inside in time.

My idea for using cleansing droids was useless. The droids were not made for working in space and in spite of the shielding, they froze up. The techs in charge of them built increased shielding onto them, but they shorted out with each trial until we lost all of them. We had people on board who said they could build new drones from scrap, but it would take them too long and we knew what they built would not work very well. Challa was right. The real problem was the software.

When the last drone was gone and we had not found the tracker, we knew we had to discuss the next step.

"We have very few options," Challa said.

There were five of us at the meeting. Those of us in charge decided to go over the situation before going to the rest of the crew to make a decision. It was decided, first of all, that everyone would have a say in what we did. The crew was happy for us to be in charge, but we all had just as much to gain or lose in whatever happened, and we had all fought equally to gain our freedoms and we should all make the decision equally on how to move forward. But before we could take a vote with the crew, those of us in charge needed to narrow down our options.

"How much longer will the fuel last?" Renlii asked.

"Three days, maybe four," Padj said. Padj, a Shiltiian, was second in command on deck. She had as much experience pirating as Challa, but she had had a larger crew and was a *pada* good pilot. She was very smart and the crew all respected her and obeyed her commands without hesitation. She should have been captain rather than me, but Challa had set me in charge and everyone listened to Challa.

"That is not much," Challa said.

"No," I agreed.

"Surrender is not an option. I think we can all agree," this was Nuchu, a green-skinned woman from the Xacha system, who had taken charge of domestics in the ship, like organizing food distribution, work distribution and living arrangements.

"No. Fuck surrender," Renlii said.

"Not to Nallimar," I said.

"Fuck surrender," Renlii said. I looked at her and saw the anger in her eyes and realized she would not surrender to anyone, under any conditions.

"What other options?" Challa asked.

"Find a large Station," Nuchu said.

"And what?" I asked. "There is a slight chance a few of us could get rides on a few ships, but odds are they would think we were traitors for drawing Nallimar to them and they would be right. We would get them all killed."

"I think that leaves us with GC or TriKarre," I said.

"Surrender to them?" Nuchu asked.

"No," Renlii said.

"What other options are there?" I asked. "When we run out of fuel, Nallimar will catch up and yes, we will fight, but they will overwhelm us and some of us will be taken again."

"No, we will not," Renlii said.

I loved the woman, but she was not being helpful. I knew she did not want to be captive again, to anyone, but there were all of the others to think about and they had not been through what she had been through and might not choose the same thing.

"We choose between GC or TriKarre?" Challa asked.

"I am open to other ideas," I said. "So far, the options are fly until the fuel runs out and fight it out with the Nallimar fleet, or we can pick a Corporation and fly into their territory and let them fight it out with Nallimar."

The group was quiet, thinking the options over in their heads. Renlii did not look happy. I thought of Trask. I doubted any of them would want to go that route and I also knew the toll he would extract from me. If he could even do anything to help. I shoved the thought into the back of my mind and focused back onto the conversation.

"Regardless of which option we take," I said, looking to Renlii, "we will fight. But, if we fight in GC or TriKarre, those of us who survive will have a better experience than if we fight alone against Nallimar."

I could see I had broken through and she could see the logic of it.

"Let us bring it to the rest of the ship then," Challa said. "We will vote and choose together and then we will fight together, whatever the outcome."

We broke up the meeting, stopped the ship and lit out in another direction. We never traveled in one direction for too long, so that we could keep Nallimar guessing, with hopes that they could not trap us. As soon as the ship entered the wormhole, we met everyone at the loading dock. The dock was foul-smelling and made of dark Sethorian, so that even though it was well lit, it seemed dim and murky. It was fitting that we should meet in such a dark place, considering our options.

Challa, Renlii, Padj, Nuchu and I stood up on one of the loading docks, while the whole crew stood below looking up at us. There were over three thousand of them. We estimated that there were eight thousand prisoners at the beginning, but the fighting was rough and when we began to win, the Fillonians started gassing all of the remaining prison cells to make sure there were no more prisoners to help with the fight.

We had discussed how to present the options to everyone and we agreed that Challa would be the one to speak. I stood next to Renlii as we looked down at our crew. It was overwhelming to see all of them in one place and see the community we were responsible for. There were Humans, Drakkarans, Diviians and Shiltians from every part of the Void. They were pirates, smugglers, fighters, traders, shopkeepers or just travelers caught in the wrong place at the wrong time. They were a ragged group, but we all fought hard together and I was proud to be one of them.

Renlii reached out and took my hand. It was a special moment for me, as she had not held my hand for several days, but today I looked over and her eyes were glistening and she gave me a smile. I loved her more than anything. We had not known each other for long, but I was glad that I had met her and I was glad we decided to love each other and I knew that we would be together from now on or we would die together.

Challa looked down on the crew and I saw him tear up. He cleared his throat, took a deep breath and spoke loud with his booming voice.

"Friends!" he began and the crew quieted down and looked up at Challa, ready to listen. "I call you friends and that is what we are. We have fought together and bled together and too many of us have died in the fighting.

"I have found that you make your best friends when you are fighting for your life, or fighting for something worth fighting for," he said and looked over at me and then to Renlii and back to his crew.

"Through our recent battles, I have learned that every one of you fights brave and hard and will watch my back, and I hope you have learned that I will fight hard and will watch yours. This makes us friends and more. We are brothers and sisters."

The crew erupted into cheers and calls of Challa. This made Challa laugh and he looked over at me and Renlii, happy but a little embarrassed at their excitement for him. He was a natural-born leader and people loved him, but he was not used to a crew this large or this much passion from his crew.

"I also believe that a good friend tells their friends the truth, whether they want to hear it or not. So, let me tell you our truth. I am sure you know already, but since we took this ship, we have looked for the trackers that are attached to the hull. If we had our own ships and our own equipment, this would be easy enough, but we have not had these things. We have had small drones with small scanners without the right software and this is a very large ship. We did not find the trackers and now we have lost the last of the drones."

The bulk of the crew knew these things, but a few did not and they wanted to talk about it, and now a low murmur went through the crowd. Challa did not wait for them and went on.

"We are running out of fuel and running out of places to hide.

We have tried sending messages to Stations asking for a ship to meet us which could find the tracker, but we have received no response and no ship has come to help. My feeling is that they believe our call to be some kind of trick or trap by a Corporation."

Challa took a deep breath before going on.

"So, we have talked about our options and believe them to be few. We could light into a Station and beg their help, but the likely result of this is that we get everyone at that Station killed. Aside from that, we are in a Nallimar ship and very few would believe us. I do not think we can even consider this option."

There were more murmurs and some discussions in the crowd this time. I was not sure why Challa brought this idea up, although I suppose people in the crowd had talked about it already and might bring it up if he did not.

"This leaves us with what we believe to be the only three options available to us. First, we run until we have no fuel and then we fight the fleet until we all die or are captured — by the Fillonians."

The crowd did not like this option and shouts and yells came out from them. There was not a person there who wanted to be taken by the Fillonians again.

"Friends!" Challa shouted. "Friends! This is the first option. The second and third are similar. We could light into Galacti-Corp or TriKarre territory where they have a large fleet presence. If Nallimar chooses to fight, they would be fighting GalactiCorp or TriKarre. We would still fight, but GalactiCorp or TriKarre would capture us, not the Fillonians."

The crew began to argue with Challa and amongst themselves, making the noise unbearable in the dock. They had questions and we tried to answer them and spent an hour going over other options brought up by others in the crew, but they were ideas we had already discussed and knew were not realistic.

In the end, it was agreed that the three options we presented were the choices to consider. I was sure they would all vote to light into TriKarre where they are easy on prisoners, but humans in the crowd outnumbered any other race and I think this swayed them to vote for lighting into GalactiCorp territory. I thought GC would be rougher on us than TriKarre, but we had all agreed to settle on whatever the rest of the crew wanted.

GalactiCorp was fair to their prisoners compared to Nallimar, but we would still be sent to work in mines or factories of some sort of hard labor. Life would be harsh and we would never see the light of day again and would probably never see each other again, but we would be alive.

Renlii was quiet that night and held onto me as we both tried to sleep. It was the first time in days that we held each other and she held me as if we were in a room with no gravity and if she let go she would fly away into eternity. I held her just as tight and neither of us said a word. We had little time left and we knew we would both rather die than be separated again. We knew this and held onto each other and tried to remember the good times and the good days, both knowing that they were over.

THIRTY-NINE

I T WAS A long and restless night thinking of the coming battle. As much as I tried to remember the good times, all I could think of was Renlii and Challa and the rest of those on the ship and how to keep them safe. I had tried to give command back to Challa after the meeting, but he wanted me to stay in the Captain's seat so he could lead the on-board defense forces. He had taken the ship and wanted to be there with the crew when they defended it. I thought he was the better captain, but we both knew the ship would not hold out long against Nallimar and the real fighting would take place in the hallways again, unless they decided to destroy the ship.

I thought long and hard about my responsibility as Captain. I thought of what I could do to save them and to save Challa and to save Renlii. We had done everything we could do but there was no telling if it would be enough.

I kept going back to Trask.

I did not know if he would help. He had influence over CEOs and Generals and entire fleets and could probably arrange it if he wanted. I thought it crazy and narcissistic to think he would extend himself so much for one former agent, especially one who had spit on him for so long, but he seemed intent on having me back.

I hated the man. I feared him and raged against him for what he had done, but if there was any chance he could save Renlii and save the others, I had to take it. It would mean sacrificing my life together with Renlii. It would mean sacrificing everything I believed in, but I loved her enough to sacrifice everything. I loved Challa enough to do it. And, I was responsible for the crew.

I swallowed whatever pride I had left and prepared a message to Trask. I used a com system I had found stashed with our clothes and equipment to write a message to Trask using an old emergency message address we used from years ago. The message was all in old code, but I was sure he still had the address and would find the message.

I fully surrendered to him, saying if he could save the ship and all those aboard and keep them away from prison and slavery, I would work for him, no questions asked. I would trade myself for them.

We could not send messages in the wormhole but it would be sent as soon as we stopped. I had ordered the ship to stop several times before arriving at our final destination. It would not buy us much time, but it would buy us some. It was too little too late and it made my stomach turn to do it, but saving those I loved was more important than my *haachee* pride.

It was *chaf* and the situation was *chaf* but I could think of no other way. The Void was *haachee* and the situation was *haachee* but sometimes the choices you had in life were not what you wanted. I had made too many mistakes in the recent past, and had let my pride and misjudgement get in the way of taking care of my people. I was tired of running, tired of losing, tired of letting my people down. It was time to win, for their sake, and regardless of the cost to myself.

We lit into the Ntall system two days later. We could not reach the central systems of the GC with the amount of fuel we had left, so we had to find a place on the outer edges. Ntall was not as populated as other areas, but according to the ship's system, Galacti-

Corp had a decent-sized fleet Stationed there; a fleet large enough to take on the Nallimar fleet on our tail.

We lit in at the distant edge of the system and started broadcasting a prepared distress message. We told them we were GalactiCorp residents taken captive by Nallimar. The odds of them helping us were slim if they knew who we really were.

The GalactiCorp fleet responded right away.

"Nallimar ship NS-8231, you have entered GalactiCorp territory in breach of the Unsla Peace Agreement and are directed to leave immediately."

I responded, "We are GalactiCorp citizens escaped from a Nallimar fleet. We are out of fuel and we need help."

"You are in breach of the Unsla –"

"Turn on the vid," I told Padj while the GC *benetcho* continued his same message.

"GalactiCorp security, do we look like Fillonians?" I rotated the cam to show all of us in the command center. "We are not Fillonians, we are not Nallimar, we are GalactiCorp residents taken prisoner by Nallimar. We have escaped and are requesting aid."

There was a pause and then they came back on the com, "Nallimar ship NS-8231, maintain your position. Shut down shields and weapons. Prepare to be boarded."

"Do it," I told Padj. "Shut her down. Remain in position." The GC fleet was already heading our direction, but they were near the system's core and it would take a couple of rotations for them to arrive. I looked down to Renlii, who was hovering over the weapons consoles.

"GalactiCorp security forces, be advised, we have a large fleet of Nallimar ships following us."

There was silence on the other end for several sets.

"What are they doing?" asked Padj.

"Piching their pants," Challa said to a few chuckles.

"Nallimar ship NS-8231, prepare to be boarded."

"If they try to board, do we let them? Do we surrender or fight?" Padj asked.

"What are the chances they will believe we are residents?" the navigator asked.

"We are not going to surrender," I said. "All they have to do is scan us and check against their records and they will know we are not residents."

"We fight," Renlii said.

"Yes, we fight," I said.

"We have a bigger problem," Padj said. "Take a look at their fleet."

"Sweet heavenly Trill," Challa said. "We are in deep *chee*."

The fleet was a fraction of what we had hoped for. It was just a standard heavy cruiser contingent; a heavy cruiser, two light cruisers, four small destroyers and eight frigates. The fleet on our tail was twice as large.

"*Chee*," I let out.

This was not going to end well for any of us and the rest of the bridge knew it. Our gamble had not paid out. I looked at the crew and saw their fear and determination. I could not let it end like this.

"Padj, keep sending the distress signal. All channels, through-out the galaxy. Send it everywhere."

"You think that will help?" Challa asked.

"It will not hurt. Padj, get the com back on."

"Copy. It's open."

"Commander of GalactiCorp Security Fleet."

Silence.

"This is a message to the commander of the GalactiCorp Security Fleet. Be advised that we are running from a Nallimar fleet much larger than yours. They will be here within the hour. If you have help nearby, you should call them in. We are sending specs on their fleet now."

I signaled Padj to cut the signal. "Padj, send them what we know. They need all the help they can get."

"Right."

I turned to Renlii. "Get the guns set and ready, but keep them offline until I give the go."

"Copy," she said.

"Padj, prep the shields, but keep them down until the last minute."

"Copy."

The GalactiCorp fleet continued in our direction, but did not send any response regarding the Nallimar fleet. While the crew prepared for Nallimar, I thought of the message I had sent to Trask. I could hardly look at Renlii or Challa all day, feeling I had betrayed them. Chances were, they would never know, but I knew and felt I betrayed them and myself. But sometimes you had to throw all your chips on the table. Sometimes you had to throw out pride. Sometimes you had to risk losing the friendship of those you love to save them.

The GalactiCorp fleet was still far out by the time the Nallimar fleet arrived. Their fleet lit in close, but not close enough to fire on us.

"Padj, engines online. All ahead. Shields up. Focus all power on the rear shields. Renlii, keep the weapons offline for now."

"Nallimar ship NS-8231, maintain your position. Shut down your shields."

We ignored the message and listened in as the GalactiCorp commander sent a message to the Nallimar fleet.

"Nallimar fleet, this is Captain Jmalee of GalactiCorp security ship GS-92132. You are in breach of the Unsla Peace Agreement and are directed to leave immediately."

"GalacctiCcorp seccuritty, this is Admirral Sslisha. We arre herre to retrrieve our prrison ship. I addvise you to bacck ddown."

"Admiral Sslisha, prison ship NS-8231 has fallen under GalactiCorp jurisdiction per the Unsla Peace Agreement, Section fifty-five, paragraph six. You are directed to leave GalactiCorp territory while we investigate the ship, or the contract will be in breach and our Corporations will be at war. We have sent for reinforcements. A full-strength Battleship fleet is moments away."

Nallimar did not respond and their ships did not slow down and they were gaining mylons by the second.

"You think it's a bluff?" one of the crew asked.

"I am sure another fleet is on their way, but we will all be slag before they get here," Padj said.

I did not like her discouraging the crew, but I could not argue with her.

"Get this hulk going, Padj."

"She is at one hundred percent."

"*Chee*. How long until they can fire on us," I asked Padj.

"Five minutes."

"Renlii, ready the weapons. Things are about to get hot."

"Copy."

I tried to look confident for the crew, but things were tight. The GC fleet was much too far away to be of any help and I did not expect us to last long without them. Our ship was not made for battle. It had heavy armor and shielding, but it was light on weaponry.

We had gone through different strategies and agreed that our limited weaponry could not do much damage to larger ships, so our main focus would be fighters and drones, until they sent troop frigates our way and then we would blast those to hells.

Challa slapped me on the shoulder and held his hand there. I looked him in the eyes and saw that they were glistening and he wore one of his big smiles.

"I can think of no better place to fight and die than at the side of my old friend Jlaeal."

I put my hand on his shoulder and returned the smile. I did not think I could love a friend any more than I loved Challa. He was always a good friend and brave. We both knew we would die and we were ready for it.

"You have always been the best of friends," I said. "And if they kill us, it will not be easy for them."

"No. It will cost them."

"Fuck Nallimar and fuck the Fillonians and fuck the Void for sending them to us."

Challa laughed and yelled out, "Fuck Nallimar! Fuck the Void!"

There were a few chuckles and Renlii yelled out, "Fuck Nallimar! Fuck the Void! Fuck her in the face!"

This got a great deal of laughter and then, "Fuck Nallimar!" from Padj. "Fuck the Void."

We all took turns saying this in different and more crude and creative ways and I laughed hard and the rest of the bridge was yelling and howling with laughter. I did not want to die, but if I had to go, these were the people I wanted to go with; people who spat at the Void and told her to fuck herself. We were free and if we had to die, we would do it on our terms, as free peoples.

"Jlaeal!" Bfall said, the Drakkaran at the scanning Station. "Nallimar fleet has fired missiles."

"How many?"

His face was pale as he turned to me and said, "One hundred."

All laughter stopped and everyone on the bridge looked from Bfall to me. I did not need to say anything. We were ready as we could be and everything had already been said. I looked to Renlii, tried to give her a brave smile and nodded to her. She turned to her crew and they went to work.

FORTY

NALLIMAR REPROGRAMMED THEIR missiles to use an evasive pattern the auto systems could not handle, but this was not Renlii's first time dealing with this problem and she adjusted the coding on the weapon bays and the guns, so they were still effective. She did a hells of a job, but there were just too many missiles and we had too few guns to fight them.

Nine of the missiles got through. They all hit the ass of the ship. The shielding held against the first five, but each missile wore it down more and more and the last four tore through the shields and into the engines. The ship lurched and shuddered and the power shut off and with it the lights and the life support and gravity compensators. We were sitting pictis.

"Padj, how are we?"

It was dark for several mils and those who were not locked in grasped onto whatever they could to stay in place and not float around. The emergency lights flicked on and Padj was holding onto the main monitoring Station and looking through the readouts. Lights came back on and the systems began to reboot and the gravity system kicked back on.

"Life support back on. Gravity systems back on. Systems rebooting. This will take a couple of sets."

"Weapons?" I asked.

"Offline. Systems rebooting."

"Hells. We are in a tight spot."

The vid screen came back on, but it was rebooting with everything else and we were still blind.

"I had better get ready for them," Challa said.

I grabbed his shoulders and looked him in the eye and he grabbed my shoulders. We did not need to say anything. It had all been said. He patted my shoulder one last time and left the command center.

"Systems up and running," Padj said.

"Weapons online," Renlii said.

"Renlii, you know what to do."

She was already at work, guiding her crew on where to fire, concentrating on approaching drones and fighters.

"How are we, Padj?"

"Rear shields gone. Engines gone."

"Gone?"

"Gone. We float with no control. They did not reach energy core, so all but rear shields are back up. Weapons up. All systems back up. Except for engines. No engines."

The lights and the vidscreen came back and I did not like what I saw. A meteor storm of fighters and drones were coming in from the Nallimar fleet.

"That is a hells of a lot of firepower," I said.

No one said anything. Renlii had put up a good fight and drone after drone went down, but Nallimar was knocking our guns out fast.

"How far is the GC fleet?"

"Ten sets," Padj said.

"We will not last half that," I said.

"Troop frigates!" yelled the scanner.

"Renlii," I said.

"There are ten of them."

"Do what you can." I called Challa on the com, "Troop frigates incoming. You ready?"

"As ready as we can be."

Challa had an impossible task. There were thousands of us on board ready to fight, but the frigates could break through at any point on the hull, making it impossible to know where to set up the defenses, and we were outnumbered and outgunned.

"Nallimar's first frigate group is in firing range. They're trying to take out the shields."

Renlii was a master at weapons, but she did not have much to work with. She took out the ten frigates before they drew close enough to board, but another group of frigates was right behind them and by then all our weapons were gone.

"That's it then," I said. "Renlii, and the rest of you on weapons, brilliant shooting. You did more than any of us could have expected."

None of them reacted much, but nodded their thanks.

"Padj, keep us informed on troop landings and troop movements. The rest of us will go help Challa."

Renlii and her people stood up from their weapons bays. Padj stood at the scanning bays and watched us move toward the hatch.

"Jlaeal," she said.

I turned to look at her. She pointed at the vid screen and we all looked. The GC fleet was closing in and had fired off hundreds of missiles at the Nallimar fleet, followed by a swarm of fighters and drones. I could not help but smile.

"That is nice to see," I said. "It is too late and not enough, but it is good to see."

A giant explosion rocked the ship, knocking us to the ground. All lights and equipment shut off, leaving us in pitch black. The emergency lights flickered on here and there. Gravity control stayed intact, at least in the control room.

"Down to life support and basic systems now," Padj said.

"Come on then," I said. "Let's go help Challa."

They all followed me out of the hatch. It was silent in the lift down to the landing bay deck. I took Renlii's hand. She was intense and looked at me with anger when I grabbed her hand and tried to tear it away, but I held it firmly and she dropped her shields and gave me a little smile and held onto my hand.

The doors slid open, hitting us with a wall of sound from explosions and blaster fire and we tore our hands away from each other and clutched our guns and ran toward the fight.

281

FORTY-ONE

WHEN THE FIRST troop frigates landed, Challa was prepared for them. Nallimar only kept a small supply of explosives on the ship, but Challa set every bit of it in the docks. He waited for the right time to get the best use possible out of them, but Nallimar was smart and landed two frigates at a time and never more. He took the first two frigates out with the explosives, along with all of the troops on board, but two more frigates came in right behind them and the fight was on.

We found Challa ducked back into a hallway, away from the main fighting, so he could direct the battle. I had to yell over the sounds of energy blasts and explosions and shouting and screaming. In spite of the loss of their two transports, Nallimar was giving a good account for themselves. Our crew were *pada* good fighters and brave, but they were not Nallimar Invasion troops.

"GC fleet is here," I told him.

"They are welcome to the party," he said, "for what good they will do."

"How does it go?"

Challa held a system pad with a holo diagram of the ship. It received constant updates from crew as the rest of the ship called in with news of troop arrivals.

"We are doing as good as can be expected. Troop frigates blasted holes in our hull here and here," he said as he pointed at the spots on the holo. "Their troops are trying to send in gas to knock us out, but it has not cut through to us yet."

"Good," I said and turned to Renlii to ask her what she thought, but she was gone.

I grabbed Padj, who was standing next to me. "Where did Renlii go?"

"To the front," she said.

"*Chee.*"

I ran around the corner and dove for the floor, under the continuous barrage of blaster and projectile fire. The hallway was full of smoke and haze and weapons fire and chunks of plasteel and synthsteel flying everywhere. It smelled of piss and *chee* and death. I could not find Renlii.

I crawled through blood and debris and over bodies until I saw her at the front shield barricade, pushing the crew back into battle and directing their efforts. She was fierce and beautiful and without fear. Someone handed her a helmet and she hesitated, but then put it on and went back to work.

Someone handed me a helmet and I put it on. I switched the com system on and heard Challa speaking, "Two more frigates just landed in the dock. Get out of there! Plan Deya five. Deya five."

Under plan Deya five, everyone split into pre-designated squads, to scatter and hide throughout the ship and try to get behind them and create as much damage and havoc as possible. It was a suicide mission, not designed for victory, but to take out as many of them with us as possible.

"Deya five!" I yelled out at the crew at the front. They began a retreat, but Renlii was not listening. I crawled up behind her and pulled her down. She tried to hit me, but I blocked it.

"Deya five," I said.

Her eyes were full of fury and madness and I was not getting through to her. I took her face in my hands and looked her in the eyes.

"Renlii," I said calm but loud enough for her to hear. "Deya five. Come with me."

Some of the madness disappeared and she followed me away

from the barricade. We crawled backwards with the rest of the crew, firing back down the hallway in retreat. Challa was waiting for us around the corner.

"We are all going to die here," he said, "but there is no need to rush it." He directed this to Renlii, but I had shown a bit of madness myself in going out after her.

"From now on we stick together," I said to both of them. "We fight together and we die together."

They both nodded and I gave Renlii a hard kiss. She kissed me back, but it was short and full of anger.

"Come," Challa yelled and we followed him down a hallway. All of the crew had split up into their squads already. There were ten in our squad, including me and Challa and Renlii. Nallimar troops entered the ship by the hundreds.

We fought hallway to hallway again and room to room for what seemed like rotations upon rotations. We were exhausted and covered in cuts and bruises and blaster burns, but we were alive. We had lost the rest of our original squad, but had met up with another one and joined forces.

I fought with Challa and Renlii and five others in the hatchway of a small room. There was another hatchway at the other end of the room leading to a back service area. One of our team was on guard there for our escape if things got bad, but we were running out of places to run. We had lost communication with the rest of the crew. Nallimar controlled most of the ship.

Renlii, Challa and I fired down the hallway, while the others rested. The room was full of smoke and smelled of charred flesh and melted synthsteel. I shot a trooper in the eye and he went down, but then blaster fire hit the hatchway above us and glowing hot synthsteel showered down on us.

"Fuck!" I yelled and the three of us ducked back inside. I

popped back out and returned the fire, staying as close to the floor as possible. Renlii fired in the other direction. We fired and then ducked back into the room, but we always adjusted our position so they could not get a good bead on us and sometimes we would just fire the guns without looking.

"Challa!" I heard and spun around. One of our squad had run up to Challa who was bleeding out of the neck.

"Take my place," I told the fighter and rushed to Challa. A piece of the wall had pierced his neck and was burning its way through. He was losing a lot of blood.

"Hold on, Challa," I said and took my shirt off to staunch the bleeding. Our squad had run out of med supplies a while back and I had nothing to help him. I pressed the shirt against his neck, but felt the warm blood ooze through the shirt and onto my fingers. It was a deep wound in the worst place and I knew he would not last long. My knees were wet and I saw that I was kneeling in a pool of his blood.

Challa smiled up at me as best he could. He tried to speak, but he was weak already from the loss of blood.

"Jlaeal," he whispered. "Jlaeal."

His voice was faint so I crouched down close.

"I am here, friend," I said.

I put my ear to his mouth so I could hear what he was saying over the blasts and explosions.

"Jlaeal," he said and I felt his hand on my shoulder and looked at him again and he smiled. Then I felt his hand drop and saw the light leave his eyes and I knew he was dead.

I closed his eyes and stared at him for a while, blocking out all the chaos around me. My old friend was dead.

The blasts and explosions grew in intensity and I turned back to the hatchway where Renlii and the rest of the squad were fighting. It had grown so intense there was no way to even stick their weapons out to fire. After a while it died down and the squad edged back out to fire and spun back in.

"They leave," one of the fighters said.

"What?" I asked.

"They leave! They go!"

I rushed to the doorway to get a look, but just as I did Renlii stuck out too far and took a shot from a fractal bullet to the chest near the shoulder. I pulled her inside and laid her on the floor next to Challa. The hole in her chest was small, but fractals can tear through anything and it had gone all the way through, leaving a hole from her chest to her back that oozed blood from both sides all over the floor.

"Give me a rag! A shirt!" I yelled. One of the squad ripped his shirt off and tossed it over to me, but the others were busy fighting at the hatchway.

"The Nallimar troops are leaving," one of them said.

"Go find out why," another said. "Follow them."

I could not speak. I was pressing hard against the wound to stop the bleeding, but she was bleeding from both sides and it was too much. Renlii put her hand on my hand. She should have been in shock, but she was calm and smiled up at me. It was warm and filled with love, the kind of look that liquified my insides and made me fall in love with her again, but this time it was terrifying.

"I love you," she said, "I —"

"Do not do that," I said. "You will make it."

I knew it was *haachee* and she knew it was *haachee*, but I did not want to believe anything else.

She smiled at me again with love and pity. "Always truth," she said. "I am done. We know this."

I knew she was right and began to cry so that it was hard to see her through the tears.

"I love you, Jlaeal. It was worth it."

I tried to answer her, to tell her that she was right but I could not. I tried to say yes, but it would not come. The tears filled my eyes and my throat would not work and I could not say anything. I would not trade anything in the Void for the time with her, not freedom or peace or life or anything.

I kissed her hard, as if trying to compress every kiss I would never get from her into that one kiss. She returned the kiss with the love and passion I had craved for the past week. After a long time, I released her so that she could breathe.

The crew around me ran in and out of the doorway and I could tell something was going on. People asked me things, but I ignored them. I just kept looking down at Renlii and holding her as tight as I could without hurting her. I held onto her hand and we stared at each other and she struggled to breathe. I cried, with nothing to do but watch her last battle. She was ferocious, as she always was, and struggled to win in spite of the odds, but finally, she took one last breath and looked at me and smiled and let it out again and she was gone.

I picked her up in my arms and held her close and cried.

GC troops entered and took the rest of the crew away, but I held on to Renlii. My eyes were swollen from crying and filled with tears. I knew nothing outside of Renlii and Challa. It was too much and I wanted to die with them.

I did not fight when they pulled my gun away, but then one of them tried to pull me away from Renlii, and I knocked him on his ass and was ready to take them all on, ready to die, but the others jumped in and forced me away from her and out of the room. I was out of my mind with fury and fought them every inch down the hallway, until one of them hit me in the head with their gun and everything went to black.

FORTY-TWO

I WOKE UP alone, in a dark room, surrounded by dark-gray Sethorian synthsteel. The walls and ceiling were bare. The floor was bare, except for a drain in the middle. As my head cleared I realized the floor and portions of the walls were stained with dried blood. I sat in a cold synthsteel chair in the middle of the room, naked again. I was not bound at all with anything that I could see, but I could not move anything below the neck.

A man entered the room and asked me questions, but I did not look at him. He asked who we were and what happened and who was in charge. He asked about Trask. He asked a lot about Trask. But I did not answer.

I thought of Renlii and I thought of Challa. This man did not matter. He hit me when I did not answer, but I did not care and then he hit me some more. The hits to the face were nothing. The hits to the stomach and the chest were nothing. He even hit me in my soft areas and I almost blacked out from the pain, but it was nothing. Renlii was dead and Challa was dead. Everything else was *haachee*.

I hoped that he would kill me. With every punch I hoped that a blood vessel would explode and I would hemorrhage out until I died, but he was good at his job and knew how to hurt me without doing real damage.

Another man came in and was nice to me and ordered the men to give me clothes and water and feed me. I took the water, but I did not care about the food and I did not talk to this man either. He gave the appearance of being fine, but he was no different than the first man. He tried to convince me that he was on my side and that we were friends so that I would talk to him, but I was not trying to be brave and I was not trying to protect anyone. I just did not care.

He explained that we had restarted the war with Nallimar and they wanted to know who was in charge and who to blame. I looked at him this time and laughed. What a question. Nallimar was to blame. Blame them. If you want to blame us, then we were all to blame. Challa was to blame, Renlii was to blame, Padj, Nuchu and the rest of the crew. We were all equally to blame. But then I decided that maybe some of them were alive and wanted to live, but I was tired of the fight, tired of the Void.

"Blame me," I told him.

"That is what all of you say."

I laughed. They were *pada* good people, all of them.

"Yes, we were all to blame," I said. "But check the vids we sent you. You will see that I was their captain."

"You were their captain?"

"Check the files. It was me. Always me." Then I passed out.

I woke up again, but this time I was clean and lying on a comfortable bed in a comfortable room. The worst of the wounds and bruises were healed and I was in a room designed for an officer. It looked like an apartment on a GC core planet, with carpeted floors, a cleanser with real water and a vidscreen on the wall presenting a view outside of the ship.

I thought that I was dreaming or dead, but I knew I would not be in a place like this if I died. I was not sure if I believed in life after death, but if there was one, I figured I would end up in one of the harsher places.

I stood up and looked around the room and looked at the vidscreen showing the outside of the ship. All I saw was the milky purple gray of a wormhole. I thought about Renlii and Challa and wondered what they did with their bodies, but I guess it did not matter. I would never see them again.

The Void was darker than any of us had ever imagined. She let us win our freedom from Nallimar. She let us take the ship. She let us fight Nallimar together. We were prepared to die and knew that we would die, and were all right with that, knowing that we would die together. But then Challa died and Renlii died and I was still alive. They died moments before GalactiCorp lit in with a larger fleet and obliterated Nallimar.

If they arrived any sooner, Renlii might be alive and Challa might be alive. If they arrived any later I would be dead with them. It was a cruel twist by the Void and one I would never forgive her for.

FORTY-THREE

THEY DID NOT speak to me again. An ensign brought me food and left without saying a word. I ate, but did not leave the bed. The next day, I went into the cleanser. I stayed in there for a long time with hot steamy water running over me. It helped to ease the aching muscles and burn away the stiffness, but it did not help with anything else.

I went back to the rack and could not stop thinking of Renlii and Challa and the Void. Then I felt a change in the ship. I looked at the vidscreen and saw that we were back in normal space. I got out of the rack and walked to the vidscreen and looked outside. It looked like we were far out in the Void. From the angle of the screen, I could see nothing to indicate life. I tried to change views, but it was a single-view screen.

Then I saw a wormhole open and a TriKarre Heavy Cruiser lit in. I thought there would be a battle, but our ship turned and ran parallel with the TriKarre ship toward a massive star base. It looked like an old Galactic Federation model, but newer, with upgrades and a sleeker design.

There were dozens of large cruisers from every Corporation parked near the base or even attached to the Station. None of it made any sense. Smaller independent ships came and went, lighting in and lighting out and docking with the Star Base. None of the ships fought at all. I found the whole thing confusing until it hit me. A lump formed in my throat and my stomach felt as if I swallowed half a ton of alidnum.

Trask's base.

I watched the activity in awe. I never could have believed that all of the Corporations would operate so close without a battle. There was even a Nallimar Battle Cruiser docked at the base. It was unbelievable.

I thought of my message to him and tensed, but then got angry. Fuck Trask. The offer was to save my friends and my friends were dead. If he did send the larger fleet to save us, he was too late. I owed him nothing.

We headed closer and closer to the base and docked with her and then an officer entered the room.

"Captain Jlaeal," he said. "Please follow me."

"Where?" I said.

"We are taking you to The Center."

"The Center?"

"The headquarters for Universal Intelligence."

"He calls it the Center?"

"Yes," he said. "Please, follow me."

The man stood waiting at the hatchway and did not respond. Two troopers stood outside the hatch with guns ready. I thought of attacking the officer, and drawing their fire, but I knew it would be no use. If Trask wanted me alive, he would get me alive.

I followed the officer out of my quarters into a broad hallway. The troopers stepped into line behind me. Everything was white and clean and perfect, as if the ship just came off the line and flew into service. We walked past a long line of hatchways until we came to a lift and the doors opened.

"Please," he said and indicated that I should go in first. I stepped in and the officer followed and then the troopers.

"Entry dock five W," the officer said and the lift doors closed and the lift moved.

He treated me more as a guest than a prisoner. Considering the vast change in how they were treating me, it grew apparent that Trask made some kind of deal for me. It was hard not to be impressed at the sway Trask held over these people.

My head scrambled through plans of what to do to Trask

when I saw him. The lift stopped and the officer led the way out, with the troopers marching behind me again. We strode into a large hallway, past crowds of people scurrying in all directions on urgent missions. The ship seemed to be one of the big Command Cruisers or maybe even one of the larger Battleships. She was a big cretch, whatever she was.

We arrived at a hatch connected to a long tunnel and walked down into the Center. It was all white Sethorian, polished and clean, like it had just come off the GF factory docks. How Trask found this star base and kept it operating in secret all these years, I could not fathom. It was a colossal task, even for him.

The officer led me over to a Shiltian standing near the main entry hatch, dressed as if she just left a corporate meeting. A single guard stood by her, with his blaster holstered.

"Thank you, officer Kehn. Your assistance is appreciated."

The officer saluted the Shiltian and turned back toward his ship without a word. The two troopers followed him, leaving me alone with Trask's tool. The Shiltian turned to me with a broad smile, her arm extended, hand pointed in showing that she wanted to greet me and was at my service.

"Jlaeal, welcome to the Center. I am Shnoli. I will escort you to your quarters."

"My quarters?"

"You are Trask's guest. I have been instructed to take you to your quarters and provide you with whatever food or refreshments you care for."

"How about you just take me to the *benetcho*. I have words for him."

Shnoli flinched, as if she had never heard an insult against the man.

"He is in a crucial meeting with Corporate officers at the moment, but he will see you as soon as the meeting is complete."

"Fine," I said.

I was too tired to fight. I was too tired for anything. I followed Shnoli down a maze of hallways to a hatch. She keyed a command

and it opened. I followed her into the room while the guard stayed outside.

The quarters were luxurious by any standards of the Void, with thick plush carpets, soft comfortable furniture, a separate room to sleep in and a giant vidscreen on the wall displaying the outside of the base.

"What is all this?" I asked Shnoli. "What does the *mata* want with me?"

"I do not know. He gave orders to provide you with officer's quarters and to make sure you had everything you needed. There is a refresher unit on that wall. There is also food here. If you would like something specific, just order on the com system and the kitchen will provide it."

She handed over a new com unit.

"This is yours while you are on the base. You can reach me at any time."

I took the com but said nothing. She did not seem to mind. She gave me a slight bow and walked out the door. I tested the door, but it was locked from the outside.

"Fuck you, Trask," I said to no one in the room, although I had suspicions he could see and hear me.

"Fuck you! Fuck you and your fucking Center and your fucking UI and your fucking plan!"

I looked around again at the luxurious surroundings with a bitter taste in my mouth. Memories of Challa and Renlii came to mind and I began to tear up again, but I had cried enough. I was done with crying. I stepped over to the refresher.

"Gru," I said, and it poured me a shot of gru. I slammed it down and dropped into darkness and was at peace for the first time in a long while. I came out of it too quick and ordered another one.

"Gru," I said and it poured another shot and I drank it down as soon as it was ready. This time it lasted longer and it was the best I had felt in a very long time. I came out of it and ordered again.

"Gru," I said and shot it down. The blackness lasted still longer.

I was disappointed to come out of it. I kept shooting gru until I lived longer in darkness than reality. I drank one last gru and it took me under longer than I had ever been before. When I woke up, I was lying on the floor with Trask standing over me.

I stood up and tried to hit him, but I was too far gone and fell to the ground without getting close.

"You have been through much, Jlaeal."

I tried to say he did not know *chee* but it came out in a garble. I tried to get up again. I wanted to hit him and throttle him and kill him.

"I tried to warn you. I tried to get you out."

"Fuck you," I managed to get that out so that he could understand.

"I wish I could have done more."

"Fu —" I had started to say, but I was also trying to stand and I fell down in a heap and tears began to come. I hated myself for crying in front of him. I hated myself for getting too drunk to hit him. I hated myself for being alive when everyone else was dead.

"You are my guest here. I know you do not understand anything at the moment. I will explain it when you have recovered. Please send word if you need anything."

As he turned to leave, I tried to get up one last time, but there was no point.

Just before he reached the hatch, he turned back and said, "I did send help, Jlaeal. I am sorry it arrived late."

It could have been the gru, but he looked sincere.

As I watched the hatch doors close behind him I passed out.

FORTY-FOUR

I WOKE UP in a pool of vomit. Every breath I took felt as if it started a chain of eruptions in my head. I crawled to the refresher and ordered glephash. It was hard to even speak the word. The thought of drinking it made me feel sicker than what I was, but I forced a small sip into my mouth and swirled it around and then eased it down my throat. Then I took another small sip and then another.

I sat on the floor sipping the glephash, trying to remember what happened after Trask left, but I could not remember anything and realized I had passed out. I finished the glephash, forced myself to stand and stumbled over to the sleeper room, where I stripped down and walked into the cleanser. It was a large and luxurious one. I turned it on and tried the different options and chose the shower mode where a gentle spray of real water hit you from every direction. I sat on the floor and let the hot water and steam wash away the vomit and filth.

By the time I came out of the cleanser, my clothes had been hauled off and clean clothes were waiting for me on the bed. The main room had been cleaned with no sign of the mess I left the night before.

I found something to eat. Once I had something in my stomach other than gru I felt much better, but then I started thinking of Renlii again and of Challa and went for another gru. I took things slower this time and enjoyed the numbness for longer and waited longer between shots, but it did not take long for me to get bad again and I ended up passing out and waking up soaked in vomit and piss.

It was like this for several days. No one bothered me at all. I did not see Trask or anyone else. When I came out of the cleanser, everything was cleaned and fresh clothes were set out.

On the fourth day, I cleansed and ate and found a system holo on the desk. It might have been there the entire time, but I had not noticed it. I ordered a krem from the refresher, sat at the desk and placed my palm on the security pad. It was set for my genetics and opened up as soon as I touched it. The holo came up over the desk and the opening message told me that I had access to everything on the Center's system. I did not believe that at all, but was curious to see what I could find.

I ran a search on myself and was surprised at the vastness of information available. Every file from every Station in the Void was on there and every file from every Corporation, with every pseudonym I had ever used and every experience they ever had with me. There were images and vids and reports of every kind, including reports on movement, known trades and known associations. There were files listing associates, friends, enemies and everyone I had ever met and all the trades they knew about and every trip and every battle. My entire life was there.

I ran a search on Renlii and found the same thing, infinite files on every experience known by Stations, Corporations and even files from the Valliati. I could not believe Trask had files from the Valliati. Everyone knew about the Companions and that the organization existed to protect Diviian society, but it was so secretive that no one ever had any actual information on them. But Trask had entire files from their organization and on Renlii's entire life before the Liquidation. Tears streamed down my face as I opened image after image and watched every vid available. It was too much and I found myself drinking gru again until I passed out.

When I awoke the next day, I cleaned up and continued searching the system. I did not look up Renlii again, knowing it would just lead to tears and gru. I looked up Challa, which was just emotional as Renlii, but it was hard to pass on opportunities to learn about your friends when everything you could want to know was all right there.

Seeing images and vids of Challa was just as difficult as seeing Renlii and I cancelled the search and ran a search on Trask instead. There were far fewer files on him. The few I did find were Corporate reports, and held nothing of any specific interest, other than speculation and written plans or attempts at getting some kind of leverage on the man.

I gave up on the search on Trask and researched Stations I had lived on, such as Nathara. I was able to access every file and report ever made on the Station. I was surprised to see a report saying that Corporations had found out about Nathara, but held off on attacking it. But then Trask met with Nathara and the meeting did not go well and that is when Nallimar attacked.

I had always imagined that Trask met with the Station and if they did not comply he turned them into the Corporations, but according to the files, the Corporations infiltrated the network long ago and had found every Station in the Void. I was not too surprised by this. All of us in the Void felt the Corporations knew where we were. It would not have taken much to find where the Stations were. But I could not figure out why they would not attack before they did or what it had to do with Trask.

I looked up Station after Station and found that they were all gone. All remaining Stations were those protected by UI. If the reports were true, then Trask did what he could to save them, but then I remembered where I was and whose report I was reading and knew it was all *haachee*. I was sure some of the report was truth, but I was also true that they were written to make him sound like the hero, rather than the conqueror.

I ran a search on my old friend Qodja. He was my closest friend in the Void before the Liquidation. We were friends before I worked for Trask and then I convinced Trask to recruit him. Trask partnered us up and we worked together for years. We went on missions together. We fought together. We had great times together. He was loyal and true and knew how to have a good time just as well as he knew how to fight.

Then Trask ordered a mass extermination of agents within his organization. Many of my friends were killed, including Qodja. That was when I found the truth of Trask, when the curtain was pulled back and I saw him pulling the strings over the galaxy.

Trask was convinced that Qodja was part of the group trying to take over his organization. He sent a Syndicate group after Qodja and had him killed. I was with him at the time and barely made it out alive. I left Trask and took the *Sun* with me after that. Not long after, Trask sent his man to kill me and get the ship back.

He denied it later, but I did not buy any of his *haachee*. He was power-hungry and paranoid and full of *chee* and murder. And now Renlii and Challa were dead.

I went through the files on Qodja and the early ones were what I expected. I knew Qodja and knew his past and I knew what he was about. Then things got confusing. There were vids of meetings with people I did not know. They talked of Trask's power and they thought they could do more with the organization. The other man was very convincing and he swayed Qodja to join him. There were other vids of Qodja recruiting and forming alliances.

The vids could have been fake. They could have been created for my benefit, but that was a lot of work and creds to try to get me on their side. It did not make sense. But as I watched the vids, I knew they were real. I knew that Trask was right and that people in his organization were trying to take over and Qodja was part of it.

I thought I was already broken, but the news of Qodja broke me further and I thought again of Renlii and Challa and my friends who died during Trask's exterminations, or on Stations or that died in Corporate raids or who were slaves to the Corporations. I slammed my palm down onto the system and shut it down and walked over to the refresher for a gru.

It was another long night of darkness and gru. They were the darkest of times and I grew to hate the Void and where she had left me; safe in a plush apartment in the Center, far from any harm, while the rest of my friends were dead. I hated her for that. She is cruel and heartless.

I thought these things through a dark cloud of hatred as I drank myself to oblivion again.

FORTY-FIVE

IT WAS HARD to believe the things I saw and read about Qodja. I woke up the next morning feeling worse than any other morning. It was a long fight to force myself across the floor to the refresher and order the glephash. It took me several sets to force it all down, but I still felt like walking *chee* and had to drink another one.

I took a cleanse and came out to a clean apartment and went back to reading the files over krem and a full breakfast of menas and ochols. I reread everything I could find on Qodja and then I read everything I could find on his associates. They were not good people. Qodja was. Like other good people, Qodja was fooled into following someone under false pretenses.

I looked up Ctok. I did not know Ctok as well and was surprised to find out about his past. He was always quiet about his childhood and anything before working with Trask and I could see why. It was the worst of childhoods and he was abused and mistreated and abandoned. I imagined he found a home with Trask's organization, as I did, which made it even more surprising that he would betray him. There were vids of him being swayed. His contacts showed him vids of Trask talking of plans to take over the GF. I watched the vid myself and it was compelling. Then I watched another vid, which claimed to show how they faked the vid.

It was hard to know what to believe with all of the information available. I looked up Rej and Klush and all the files pointed to their betrayal of Trask. It was heart breaking. I did not want to believe it, but it was all in the files.

I tried to convince myself that Trask created all these files to sway me over, but then I thought it through. There were thousands and thousands of vids available on all of them. To create one or two vids was one thing, to create all them would take a team of people years to complete. Even I was not so arrogant as to believe Trask would go through all of that to get me on his side.

I was a good smuggler, a good fighter, I was a good spy for Trask, but I was nowhere near his best and I was not his most loyal and I was not worth spending the time on one vid, much less thousands. But it was still hard for me to believe.

I remembered that I had mentioned all of those names to Trask when I talked to him earlier, so I looked up other names, people who were killed during the elimination, but with whom I was not very close. The vids all pointed to the same thing. It was the same man showing the same vid, or another man showing the vid of Trask. It was all the same pattern. The pattern showed that Trask was not paranoid, that his organization was being attacked from within.

It was a lot to think about. But none of it mattered. Even if everything was not the way I thought it was, he was still to blame for the purge of the Stations, which made him responsible for Renlii and made him responsible for Challa.

The vids proved that he was less a son of a cretch than I thought, but he was still a son of a cretch and I still wanted him to die.

But then I considered my pride and where it brought me since I met Renlii. Maybe it was my pride that killed them as much as Trask's guile. I pushed that aside. It was too much to think about. I was hurt enough.

It was a long day of searching through the files and I got sick of it. By the end I was already drunk from krem and decided to finish the job with gru. There was no better drink for forgetting things and fooling yourself that things are not as bad as you think.

I drank many grus that night, but it was not as bad as the other nights and I was able to crawl into bed.

303

FORTY-SIX

THE NEXT MORNING, I was hungover, but it was a normal hangover and I did not have to crawl over to get my glephash. I drank it down and took a cleanse, got dressed and felt better than I had felt in days. When I stepped into the main room, Trask was sitting on one of the chairs waiting for me.

"Jlaeal," he said and did not move.

I stood in the doorway, my hand reaching for the gun that was not there. I thought about rushing him, but attacking him without a gun was no good. The man was all biocybertronics and although he looked old, I knew he was quicker and stronger than most men in the galaxy. That was true when I knew him before and I was sure he kept his systems and hardware updated.

Instead of attacking him, I walked to the refresher and ordered a gru. I would need one if I was going to speak to him.

"Gru," I ordered and slammed it down. The black numbness disappeared quick and I turned to Trask. "Gru?" I asked.

"No," he said. "Thank you."

The refresher had heard my voice and poured another gru, so I drank them both down. When I came out of it, I felt better and it was enough for the moment.

"Krem," I said and the refresher poured a cup of krem. It looked good and I took a sip. It was Drakkaran and it was *pada* good. I raised the cup to Trask to see if he wanted some and was surprised to see hear him say yes.

"Krem," I said to the refresher and brought the krem over to Trask. I was tempted to throw it in his face, but there was no point. He had me. He had won. And all the files and the research had taken much of the light out of the wormhole and I found myself confused and in the dark and it tempered my anger.

Trask took a sip of the krem and set it down on the table next to him. I sat across from him and took a long pull from mine and held onto it.

"So?" I asked.

"You have been reading some of the files."

"Some," I agreed.

"I hope you see that I did what I had to do back then. Killing them was a defensive maneuver."

I stared into the krem and wanted to take another drink. I did not want to admit that he was right, but if all of the files and vids were real, I could not blame him for what he did. Not really. I still resented the man for killing my friends, but they had gone against Trask, and they had lost. He was cold and calculating and manipulated the hells out of the entire galaxy, but I could see why he did what he did.

"And I hope you can see that I did what I could for the Stations."

I smiled and let out a bitter laugh.

"I realize the reports will say what you want them to say, to make you look the hero."

Trask sighed, picked up his krem up and took another sip.

"You have made me out to be the villain in all circumstances."

"How could I think anything else?"

He took another sip and stared off into space. He did this often and it was always disconcerting. I could never tell if he was thinking about what to say or if he was reading reports in that damned cybertronic brain of his.

"Jlaeal, let me tell you the real sequence of events and I will let you decide their merit."

"Your krem, your Station. You can tell whatever stories you like."

He nodded. "When the Federation fell apart, you knew of my plans to bring it back."

"Sure. You told us all. Some bought it. Some left. Some you killed."

"I did not tell all. I told those I trusted the most. A large portion of them left, and I understood and did not argue with them, as long as they did not try to damage the organization."

"And those who did…" I let it trail off and took another drink.

"I did what I had to do. You know this."

I shrugged, not ready to agree with the man.

"Over time, the chaotic madness of the galaxy settled into some type of structure. The Corporations battled for territory and power, but none of them had any real power, not in the beginning."

"I remember."

"Yes, well, I still had a good network. It was not what it was before, but I had planned for the worst and had a plan to rebuild. Some people worked directly for me. Others were willing to sell information about the Corporation they worked for. In this way, I collected large amounts of information. It did not take long to figure out that one Corporation would pay large amounts for information about another Corporation. I knew the information could hold great sway over them and I realized the potential of the information to change the galaxy."

"I expanded the network, focusing efforts on technological advances, private affairs, information that could be used against individuals as much as the Corporations themselves. If you control the board members, you control the Corporation."

He did not say any of this to gloat. Trask never gloated. He was stating simple facts and presenting them to me as an advocate would present his case to a judge. If I was to judge Trask, it would have been guilty. Yes, he was a genius, and had accomplished much, but he was like a giant spider, sitting in his Center, building his webs of power throughout the galaxy, with no regard for how his actions affected individual lives.

"Up to this point," Trask continued, "I have maintained a certain level of power while preserving my anonymity in 'the Void,' as you call it. At first, I focused all my efforts on the Corporations and gaining a foothold there. I was not interested in the Void or the Stations so much."

"What about the syndicates?" I asked.

"I already had them in hand. It did not take much effort to keep the relationships going and use them whenever necessary. The scales of power were shifting and they were less important than the Corporations. But as things began to solidify and control of the galaxy rested with just three Corporations, I realized that those who lived and operated out of the Stations could be useful tools to provide valuable information about the Corporations. At the same time, the Corporations made peace with each other and began looking beyond their territory, changing their attention to the smugglers and pirates who were picking away at their profits."

"Right," I said.

He took a sip of his krem and continued, "It was not very difficult to break into the Stations' networks and find out whatever you wanted about the Stations."

I frowned.

Trask smiled. "You are smart, Jlaeal. You know this. They capture a smuggler on one of their planets and what do they find on her ship? All of the records of travel and trade and a connection to the network. Yes, you all have them set to auto destruct, but all it takes is one failure, one intact system and the entire network is done."

I finished off my krem. He was right. We all knew this. Regardless of safeguards we all put in, the Corporations were bound to find out the whole system. We should have been surprised things did not fall apart sooner.

"The Stations and their network of smugglers were far too important to my plans. I could not allow the Corporations to destroy them all or my job would be much more difficult."

"Your job?"

"I will get to that. I decided I needed to protect the Stations, but I did not have enough leverage to negotiate all of their safety. Additionally, it would have been suspicious if I asked the Corporations to let them stay. They would wonder what reasons I could have for wanting to keep them out there. This would turn to suspicion and end in my destruction. I have leverage enough to stay alive, but my leverage does have limits. They all have their own network of spies now and I am in constant danger of obsolescence."

Trask continued talking while I stood up and walked over to the refresher. "Krem," I said and it refilled the cup. I took a sip and went back over to sit across from him. His glass was still near full.

"I came up with a solution that would ensure the safety of the Stations and help with my long-term goals — I would create a partnership with each of the Stations, putting them under my jurisdiction and protection."

"How does that protect them from the Corporations? Why would the Corporations stop just because you have a deal with them? I thought your leverage was not that good."

"I have a treaty agreement with all of the Corporations. I have near unlimited information on each of the Corporations and each of the board members. If any of my assets are attacked by one of them, I release all information on that Corporation and its Board Members to the galaxy."

"So, you blackmailed them."

"Of course."

I smiled. The man was a *benetcho* and Helo fucker, but he was brilliant. I hated the Corporations more than I hated him and it made me feel good to think of the board members losing sleep at night knowing that at any moment vids of them in some embarrassing situation could be launched throughout the galaxy.

"My attorneys reviewed all the agreements I had with the Corporations and they determined that if I came to an agreement with a Station, wherein the Station was a part of my organization, then the Station thereafter was protected under the blanket of the Corporate understandings."

And there it was. If this was true, then he was right. He would not need to blackmail the Corporations to attack any Stations not under his protection, the system was already in place.

"Unbelievable," I said.

"I did not seek to destroy any of the Stations, Jlaeal. I tried to save them, as I tried to save you and your friends."

I did not respond. My whole world was spinning. Everything I believed since the Liquidation was unraveling. I still did not understand the why of any of it. I knew who he was and who he claimed to be and none of it seemed to fit.

"Why?" I asked.

"You know why," he said. "My goals have not changed."

"The GF?"

"Yes."

"*Haachee*," I said.

"The galaxy lived in peace under the Galactic Federation for over five hundred years. Were things not better?"

"Sure," I said, "but that was then. You cannot go back. The galaxy changes. So does the Void. *You* cannot change her."

"I can and I will."

"Arrogant *haachee* dreaming."

Trask shrugged.

"You would lose much of your power," I said.

"My power has always been in the interest of the Galactic Federation. Of the galaxy."

"*Haachee*."

"I want you to join me."

I laughed again. He was such an arrogant *mata*.

"You said it yourself. The ships did not arrive in time. You did not save my friends. I owe you nothing."

He grinned. "I am not trying to leverage our deal. I am making you an offer aside from that."

"You show me some vids and spin my world upside down and

I am supposed to forget everything that happened and sign up to fight with you?"

"What do the vids show?"

I shrugged and took another drink.

Trask smiled, the *mata*.

"You are such a stubborn man, Jlaeal. Once you set your head on your version of the truth of things, nothing can deter you. It is one of your most endearing qualities. You are loyal to an absolute fault, and once you set your sights on things, it is impossible to veer you away from it."

I shrugged again and stared down at the krem.

"That is why I could not go to you when I was clearing out the organization."

I looked up. What did he mean?

"You were one of my favorites, Jlaeal. Always were. What made you my favorite was your boundless loyalty. Once you were attached to someone, nothing could break you away. But your loyalty had attached itself to your friends more than me or the organization. I could not risk approaching you about their betrayals for fear that you would confront them about it, and by confronting them you would ruin the element of surprise and they would all have escaped."

The logic held up. I hated him for it, but he was right. If he showed me those vids years ago, I would have confronted them, would have asked them about it.

"I do not know what you want from me. Everything I thought I knew is in question. Everything I loved is gone. I do not know whether you deserve my hate, but I still want you dead. Rational? Irrational? Who the hells knows, but do not expect me to watch some vids and look at you as some Jtarran savior."

Trask took a sip of krem and looked at me. *Puda.* He had that look that could burn straight through to your soul. *Puda benetcho.*

"I do not expect anything right away," he said. "I will give you time. But I do want you to work for me again."

I did not have the strength to fight or argue with him. I did not say anything. I just stared down into the empty cup.

"You know the offer. Your own ship, unlimited access to information, and reasonable creds. You would work as my agent in the Stations and the Void, and on occasion, in Corporate territory."

"Doing what?" I had no intention of taking his offer, but the conversation was taking my mind off things I did not want to think about.

"Smuggling, gathering information, very similar to what you did before. No one would know that you work for me."

"I am burned. I am no good now."

"That can be remedied."

I laughed. "Is that why you saved me?"

It was all too much. I knew he had sent the GF fleet to save us and that he had told them to bring me to him. Well, that is what the files said. I had no idea what to believe anymore.

"Yes and more," he said and took another sip of krem. "I know we saw things different, but you were always my favorite. You have your flaws, but you had all the attributes I required of my agents; you were intelligent, resourceful, reliable and above all, you were honest and loyal. Of all the agents in my organization, you were one of the few whose loyalty I never questioned. You would always obey orders, but you were never afraid to tell me if I was full of *haachee*." He said this with a smile, as if it were an inside joke.

I stood up and drank the rest of the krem. It was too much. It was too soon. "Speaking of *haachee*, that is enough for today," I said.

Trask laughed and drank the rest of his krem and stood up. He set the cup down and offered his hand to me to lock wrists. I looked at it and at him but did not move. It was too soon. The hatred still ran too deep. It might not have been rational to hate him, but it was still there.

Trask pulled his arm down and walked toward the hatchway, "There is no rush. I will come back to talk more tomorrow."

He reached the hatch and it opened without him setting his palm on it.

"You know," I said, "if I find that you did have anything to do with Renlii's death or Challa's death, and I mean anything, I will kill you."

He stood at the hatchway and returned my stare.

"One of the oldest manuscripts of Trill says, 'Truth hath no fear in the investigation of facts.'" He turned and walked out of the hatchway and it shut behind him.

FORTY-SEVEN

I GLARED AT the hatchway a long time after Trask left, thinking about the conversation. I ordered up another krem and sat on a seat facing the vidscreen and looked out into the Void. I thought back to the days of GF and working for Trask. They were good times. Working for him was not easy, but I always had the best ship and plenty of creds and the right connections.

Was he the cause of the Stations' downfall and the deaths of all my friends? It did not seem like it. He was right. Once I set my mind to something, I did not change it. I was like a stubborn helo, resisting change and raging against the Void. I had convinced myself that he was the devil and the cause of all the ills in the Void and took what little evidence I had against him and built a full case.

Did he try to help us? He helped me out of GalactiCorp territory and warned me to get to a safe Station. I saw files and vids showing he tried to get us off of Tarvil. I saw files where he tried to free us from Nallimar, but they claimed we were dead. I saw the files where he requested that GalactiCorp send a fleet to help us, at no small cost to him or his organization.

Was he the hero or the devil? He could have faked any number of files and vids. I was on his Star Base, using his files and his system and I could not verify anything. But it all seemed to make sense and I felt more and more the fool and the *mata*. As much as we all think we see the galaxy for what it is, we are often wrong and are often the last to know.

I thought of Challa, and I thought of our conversation on Nathara, before he took me to Tarvil for the surgery.

I smiled at the memory of him saying, "You sit and feel sorry for yourself and say foolish things like, 'I am without an engine, lost in the Void,' like some panty-wearing artist or a dreamy boy at a GC University. Fuck that Jlaeal! I want no part of that Jlaeal. The Jlaeal I know and love would say fuck him too. And fuck the leg and fuck the hand and fuck anything that would try to stop him!

"'Yes, that is the Void," he had said. "She is harsh and unrelenting and if you sit sulking, feeling sorry for yourself, she will eat you alive and smile as she spits out the dust of your bones. Stop this *haachee*. So, you lost your leg and arm — in a few days, you will have new ones. So, you lost a ship — you will get another one. Maybe not right away, but it will happen.

"You are alive and nothing has changed but you."

The rest of what he said was about Renlii, and I did not want to think about it. But he had been right then, about me and about her and about the Void. I thought of what he would say to me after everything that happened, feeling sorry for myself and sulking in my gru and waking every morning lying in piss and vomit.

What would he say to this Jlaeal?

"Fuck that Jlaeal," he would say. "Stop this *haachee* sulking." That is what he would say.

He would say that I was alive and to stop sulking, that I should bend with the Void rather than fight her. The trick to the Void and the lesson from my old friend was that sometimes you bent with the Void and sometimes you fought against her. The real trick was fighting until you knew she was going to break you and then find a way to bend and not break.

Puda, I missed him.

I missed Renlii. Almost more than I could bear.

But they were gone now and I was here.

Fuck Trask and fuck the Void, but maybe it was time to bend.

I thought of the other prisoners on that ship. I thought of

them fighting by my side and wondered who made it out alive. They were not in a soft apartment on the Center. If they were alive, they were prisoners. I thought about Trask's offer and I thought back to them. If I took Trask's offer, I could help them. Make a deal for them.

My thoughts drifted back to Challa. Back to Renlii. I felt a deep pain, but I did not cry. I did not think I could cry anymore. It was as if the tears had dried out, leaving an emptiness inside filled with a deep and unfathomable ache.

I stared out the viewscreen into the Void.

That heartless cold space.

The *cretch*. The fucking cold *cretch*.

My friends were gone and I was alive. What would they want of me? What would they say?

I thought again of the prisoners and I felt as if I had abandoned them and that brought another pain in my stomach. I could save them. I could make a deal.

I heard the words in my head as if Challa himself were there.

"Keep living, Jlaeal."

"Keep fighting."

"Bend and do not break."

Puda right.

Fuck the Void. I will live.

www.ingramcontent.com/pod-product-compliance
Lightning Source LLC
Chambersburg PA
CBHW071533110726
47908CB00007B/1866